The Half-Torn Page

a tale of the Valley of Witches in 17th century Germany

David Palin lives in Berkshire and is a writer of dark tales. His first book containing two short novels, *For Art's Sake* and *In The Laptops Of The Gods,* was published in 2006 and he has caught the attention of, amongst others, BBC Radio and Waterstones. David has collaborated as editor and co-writer for various authors, as well as producing screen treatments and screenplays for writers whose novels have sparked potential interest from film producers. His own screenplay of *For Art's Sake* attracted the interest of Raindance, who were only too happy to offer editorial assistance, and is currently under consideration for production. David lived in Germany for a few years and feels "no country better understands the impact, for good and evil, of our actions on those around us." His love of travelling, with visits to places such as pre-Glasnost Berlin, Dachau and Auschwitz, have shown him we can never imagine anything that the shadowy corners of our minds haven't imagined first! This latest novel, *The Half-Torn Page,* wanders into those corners and the mystical past of a Germany that inspired the Brothers Grimm, where a town hiding dark secrets and unwelcoming to strangers seals for itself an eternal fate; a curse that only an outsider can lift.

The Half-Torn Page

a tale of the Valley of Witches in 17th century Germany

David Palin

Arena Books

First published in 2019 by Arena Books

Arena Books
6 Southgate Green
Bury St. Edmunds
IP33 2BL

www.arenabooks.co.uk

*Distributed in America by Ingram International, One Ingram Blvd., P.O.
Box 3006, La Vergne, TN 37086-1985, USA.*

David Palin
The Half-Torn Page *a tale of the Valley of Witches in 17th century Germany*

British Library cataloguing in Publication Data. A Catalogue record
for this book is available from the British Library.

ISBN-13   978-1-911593-49-2

BIC classifications:- FA, FFH, FHP, FV, FJH, FK.

Cover design
by Sharon Akers

Typeset in
Times New Roman

PART ONE

Back in the days of this story, mankind had not yet taken to the skies, but if it had, only the most intrepid would have headed for the Hexental - the Valley of the Witches - despite the soaring majesty of its mountains. Its steep, tree-clad slopes and fearsome forests afforded no safe landing-place, and there were other dangers besides the rugged landscape. Let's just say; the wolves had not yet learnt to fear man. In fact they liked him a lot - found him a rather tasty treat.

But let's imagine an aviator; a brave soul, who circles above that dramatic scene. He can't help but be moved by the sight below him. Reimersberg; last and most beautiful stop on the so-called Adventurer's Road – a name that speaks for itself – that runs all the way from the Alps to that remote outpost in Bavaria. It nestles in the valley, almost glowing in the slanting rays of evening sunlight; a walled town, with gas-lamps shimmering above the narrow, cobbled ways, which tumble down towards the River Regen running through its centre. Pennants flutter from red-tiled turrets of white stone in the light winds that cascade from the mountains. Ancient, half-timbered houses lean in conspiracy towards each other across picturesque lanes, which look as if once they might have echoed with the secretive, scurrying feet of revolutionaries or lovers, but comprise now the little shops and dwellings of ordinary, proud townsfolk.

There are larger, grander buildings surrounding the perfectly-proportioned main square and nearby, the clock on the town hall, which sends forth a procession of marching figures when it strikes the hour. Long ago, it was a source of pleasure to the inhabitants of the town. Yet no-one looks at it any more, even though, or perhaps because, it is one of the few signs in Reimersberg that actually, time and the universe have not stood still; that, and the woodworm and the spiders.

As our imaginary aviator sweeps lower, it is clear that distance has lent false enchantment to the scene. This is not a taste of the past, it *is* the past. On closer inspection, the gas-lamps are revealed to contain crude candles, or wicks made of wool soaked in heaven-knows-what oil and emitting brown smoke. The cobbled ways beneath them no longer seem quaint and mysterious, but rather shadowy and sinister. The timbers of the houses are dry and cracking through lack of protection and care. There are tiles missing from the turrets and the steeple of the main church, more than one thousand years old, has gone for use as firewood. The fluttering flags have been blown ragged by a chilly wind, which does not quite disguise the faint, but unpleasant odour rising from the river.

Flying lower still, our adventurer can see the upturned faces of the townsfolk, and this is the worst part of all. They are looking at him with a peculiar mixture of amazement and despair, as if someone has shown some children the presents of their dreams behind a shop window before leading them away.

They, and the once beautiful town of Reimersberg, bear the look of the cursed. And while our aviator is imaginary, that curse is very real.

CHAPTER 1

It was a fateful day for both Ilsa Wlich and Reimersberg when she walked through the town gates that evening, just as the dipping sun was turning the mountains to fire.

She'd heard of the place, of course, but was wary, knowing how unwelcoming townsfolk in that region could be. Famed for its unspoilt architecture and dramatic surroundings, the town expected visitors, but the inhabitants always viewed them as interlopers. The saying went; you had to be strange to take the road to Reimersberg, but even stranger to live there.

Then there were the rumours; the whispers of dangers, which were not quite as old as the mountains, but just as likely to claim a life. Those whispers were as faint as the gentlest ripple that reaches the shore of a lake; no obvious sign of the cause, but no denying it was once there.

Nevertheless it was Ilsa's plan to stay in Reimersberg for a little while, being weary both in limb and heart after wandering for longer than she cared to remember. She knew, in such a place, keeping a low profile to begin with was probably her best plan.

But as we've said, Fate took a hand that day.

Firstly, in the way Ilsa fell in love with the town as she walked through the gates; all the pretty, half-timbered houses painted in their earthy colours; the grand civic buildings with their whitewashed walls and noble turrets, above which the bold colours of the city flags, bearing the symbol of an eagle, unfurled against the backdrop of deep blue evening sky, sweeping green forests and looming mountains. It seemed to be a little touch of heaven on earth.

Secondly, because someone was dying.

Her arrival went almost unnoticed by the crowd of people, which had gathered outside the bakery. At first she assumed there must have been some favourite local delicacy on sale, but she dismissed the thought immediately; bakeries – good ones at least – rarely had anything left to sell at that time of evening. She couldn't help it; curiosity got the better of her and she sidled up to the back of the throng.

"What's happening?" she asked those nearest to her. Though she spoke in the common language, her accent caused a few heads to turn. Luckily, events in the bakery seemed of more immediate interest, so at least she received an answer before the usual scrutiny.

"The baker's wife has died," said an old lady in a bonnet, who crossed herself. She looked Ilsa up and down quickly, noting many things, including her hair and the unusual coat she wore, before continuing. "And their son looks set to follow her."

"What is it?"

The old woman crossed herself once again. "Es sieht aus wie der Schwarze Tod."

The Black Death! This was when Ilsa noticed that everyone was looking towards the shop, but nobody dared to venture too close, and that appeared to include the doctor - recognisable by his distinctive hat and his complete helplessness - since his only instructions were being given at a safe distance from the bakery to a distraught man, whom he held by the arms.

"It's no good, Mr Baecker, it is the work of God or the devil, but either way there is nothing we can do."

Ilsa felt irritation stretching her insides bowstring-tight. She pushed past the people and a murmur followed in her wake. As she walked towards the window she felt the doctor's restraining hand on her shoulder. "Where are you going?" There was the contempt in his voice of someone used to being obeyed.

"To help."

"You cannot."

She looked at the hand on her shoulder, then along the arm towards the face with its weasel-like eyes. "I can try."

He, too, looked into the piercing green of *her* eyes; took in her copper red hair; and the strength of his immediate dislike for her shocked them both. He released his grip. "If you go in there, I cannot help you."

She looked in through the window, and then back at him. "Evidently."

With that she opened the door, to the accompaniment of a communal gasp from the onlookers.

"So much for my low-key arrival," she whispered to herself as she stepped inside.

No more bread or pastries had been baked. Instead, on trestle tables, lay two forms; one completely covered with a sheet, the other lying almost deathly still, barely breathing, his adolescent body glistening with sweat.

Ilsa sensed a presence at the window and turned to see Mr Baecker's face pressed against the glass, desperation and hope playing by turns across his features. She gave him a faint smile of encouragement and then walked over to where the figures lay. Lifting the sheet from the woman's face, she placed two fingers on the neck, then straightened up and replaced the sheet. At least the bumbling fool had got that one right – unfortunately for the husband; the poor woman was definitely dead. Now she looked at the young man, felt his forehead and examined the marks that had come up on his body.

What she saw caused a sharp intake of breath and she grabbed his limp arm, looking intently at the wrist. Now she returned, almost feverish herself, to the body of his mother and looked in the same place. And there it was; exactly what she had feared to find.

Ilsa exhaled shakily and wandered back to the door, which she threw wide open. Everyone backed away three paces, and not just because of the fear of infection. She'd seen that look before in people's faces, born usually of ignorance. She spoke: "Does ragwort grow in these forests? And milk thistle?"

"Yes," said several voices.

"Fetch some immediately." Nobody moved. "Now, please – before the wolf-hour."

Two men spun on their heels and set off towards the town gates.

Now Ilsa removed her rucksack, fumbled in it, produced a tiny vial containing a white powder and another containing red flakes. She handed these to Mr Baecker. "When they return with the plants, boil them, add this," she gestured towards the vial, "and make the lad drink the tea every hour." Folding the baker's fingers around the vial as if moulding one of his cakes, she said: "He will be fine." She gave his hand a squeeze. "I am sorry for your wife." Then she started to walk away.

"Tea?" said the doctor, the first letter emphasised with pompous indignity. "Tea?!" he spluttered again. "Tea to cure the plague?!"

Ilsa halted for a moment, but didn't turn. "You're right," she said. "Tea, tea and tea again." She continued on her way and spoke over her shoulder as she went. "To cure the food poisoning. I suggest, Mr Baecker, that you check your stock of yeast." Now she stopped and looked up at the sky, while still facing away from the crowd. "This can be a bad time of year for such things."

She moved on, and heard several pairs of feet doing the same, hurrying home to throw away any recent purchases of bread.

"Do snowballs contain yeast?" she heard someone ask.

"No," replied another.

Despite the circumstances, Ilsa smiled. Snowballs were a sweet speciality for which the town was famous throughout the region. Doubtless this would give some folk a good excuse now to eat a few more of them - provided they were prepared to trust the stranger. It was a smoke screen, of course, but she hadn't wanted to start a panic. Not yet; she was nowhere near ready and she was tired.

As Ilsa Wlich headed along the street a tall, slim, but powerful figure caught her eye as it strutted from the town hall, resplendent in robes and chains of office even on this humid evening. Clearly the mayor had taken time over his appearance before coming to check out the crisis. He couldn't know yet what Ilsa had done, but still he slowed for a moment and eyed her with suspicion. She saw so much in that look; could imagine his thoughts: *What was this? A woman, who dared to look at him with such openness, even disdain. And wearing trousers?! A stranger, what's more.* Even now, Ilsa knew she would be the only pale-skinned, copper-haired person in this town. She saw the man's mistrust; and that other element, which was always there in the faces of men, wherever she went; never quite dissolving away, like salt in water – their fear of her; suppressed, and all the more dangerous for it.

As they passed each other, as one more glance from his dark eyes flicked across her, something else happened, and it took all Ilsa's self-will to keep walking until she knew he had gone, at which point she stopped, looked round and shuddered. So strong! How could she have been so wrong about this town, when such ancient power was abroad within its walls? She would have to tread very carefully indeed.

As if on cue, she noticed the top of the mountain range, or rather, she could no longer see it because of some clouds that had gathered. The twist of her mouth was almost a smile. "There you are," she said, "I knew you'd come".

··

Once out of sight, the mayor stopped in his self-important tracks and put out a hand against the nearest wall for support. When you had lived so long, it was sometimes possible to forget the very essence of yourself; to be confused by the memories awoken suddenly by a particular smell or sound. Of course certain things, by their very nature, evoked a universal response. The call of a wolf from the depths of a forest would never lose its power to chill – unless it was the last of that noble kind crying a last farewell, when the sound would doubtless induce melancholy.

But what was this turmoil in his guts? As he had walked past that woman, something long-dormant had turned in its sleep, and this time he knew it was a prelude to an awakening. There had been a scent, for sure; one that only he would notice, even in this torpid city. It had given him a thirst such as he'd not known in centuries, which could only be slaked by drinking at a forbidden pool, not from the stale, stagnant rivers of the last years.

But it had been much more than that. His head was still reeling at the sense of having encountered something as ancient as him. There had been wisdom in those green eyes – the wisdom of the snake. There had been danger.

****

With all chance of anonymity gone, Ilsa thought this would be a good time to check the lay of the land; see for herself what drew intrepid travellers to the town. News of her arrival had not yet spread to all corners, but still she drew the customary stares; some wondering, some accusing in advance, and some pleasant neighbourly smiles – or what passed for them in Reimersberg. It was the same everywhere in this region – this suspicion of outsiders – and had been so for as long as she could remember … which was a long time.

Still, despite the shadow that had fallen across her soul already, Ilsa could not deny there was a magical feel to this town, with its higgledy-piggledy houses, many of which leaned over so far, they seemed about to head off for a stroll, but were clearly solid enough to have withstood the passing of the centuries. A variety of enticing aromas assailed her nostrils and caused a rumbling in her stomach. Knowing how to live off the land as she did was a precious gift, but nothing could ever replace the smell of fresh baking.

She wandered through into Clock Square and spotted the famous Reimersberg Uhr; a magnificent and gaily-decorated clock from which, every hour, a procession of figures emerged. It was showing one minute to seven. Checking she was alone, Ilsa reached into her pocket and produced a tiny timepiece. The town clock was one of the wonders of the Adventurer's Road, but she doubted the people of Reimersberg, with their conservative ways, were ready yet for this miniature version. It was, after all, only the year 1695, and she didn't want to arouse any more suspicion among the locals. Her watch seemed correct by the big clock, which was famed for its accuracy, so she put it back in her pocket.

Just then, there was a whirring of springs and the clunking movement of large cogs; and out they came, beautifully carved and varnished. Two knights on horseback, with jousting lances raised, advanced on each other from opposite directions, each followed by a squire and a fair maiden, with a wolfhound bringing up the rear. Ilsa watched the spectacle with a smile, waited for the hours to chime, which they did in a complex sequence of bells, and then moved on.

She noticed that the town walls also enclosed some grazing land and pens full with sheep and cattle, which she presumed were brought in at night to avoid becoming a banquet for the wolves from the surrounding forests. There were pastures outside the walls for flocks and herds to graze during the day, and Ilsa observed a handful of men with muskets on the battlements, who she guessed watched over the animals during the day, since there was little fear of invasion from anyone at that time as far as she knew. She raised her hand in greeting to one of them, but he didn't respond. It seemed men with weapons always liked to be taken seriously, even when they were just well-armed shepherds.

She passed through a number of narrow, shady alleyways and lanes, over which the eaves of the houses reached so far, it would be impossible to tell if, indeed, people were eavesdropping above, and now she found herself entering what seemed to be an older part of the town. One of the lanes emerged into a square, which surprised her both by its scale and the fact that it was almost empty. Through this ran the River Regen, babbling beneath three stone-balustraded bridges. One side of the square was dominated by a striking, pink-fronted church, with a wooden spire that had twisted and warped over the centuries under its own weight before settling in its chosen shape. Ilsa stood here for a moment, hands on hips, looked around - then nodded. Yes, there was something charming about this town, even with storm clouds gathering. She would stay awhile; find out whether the townsfolk knew what was living in their midst – and whether they were worth saving from it. The hard years and miles travelled had rendered parts of Ilsa's heart tougher than the ancient leather of her boots. Some folks reaped what they had sown; some terrible fates were merely hard justice. Her help was not always given.

All of which begged another question. She had felt such strength in that restless spirit and seen, as only her kind could, how the mayor's body had struggled to contain it, even though he and it were now one. If she were inclined to fight it, would she be powerful enough to withstand it?

But still; as she looked around at the living history that was the town of Reimersberg, she realised she had already decided to try. Who knew; perhaps, like the twisted church steeple, she was ready to settle.

****

The tea took quick effect. The marks of sickness on the young man's body were soon gone. Likewise the onlookers had also dispersed once the immediate danger had passed. Only then did the heroic doctor dare to enter the shop and place a bold hand on the forehead of the cured patient before pronouncing: "The fever has passed".

The shop was filled with an unusual aroma; ragwort, milk thistle and arsenic tea. Of course nobody knew that arsenic was one of the ingredients, and Ilsa had been careful to give only enough for a palliative effect and to attack the poisons. In the hands of an expert the powder was most effective. Dr Arzt, still recovering from his belittling at the hands of the eerie woman, had another term for the tea; witch's brew. Of course he smiled as he said it, but the smile didn't reach his eyes; just like the smile he'd given on finding the lad had recovered.

However, Hans Baecker couldn't keep the smile from *his* eyes. "We must find her," he said to the doctor, and then looked across to the other corner of the room, where the mayor now sat. "We must thank her."

"Are we sure that she's done anything?" asked the mayor in response, in that peculiar nasal drawl of his. "After all, it was only food poisoning."

Only respect for the ancient mayoral position stopped the normally passive Hans Baecker from striding across and driving his fist into the mayor's smug face. Instead he pointed towards the draped and silent figure of his wife on the other table. "Only food poisoning?"

And suddenly it hit him. He crumpled to his knees and started to sob. So wrapped up had he been in the saving of his son Karl's life, that he'd almost forgotten what he had actually lost. He looked at both men with tears streaming down his cheeks, said: "Find her" – and then buried his face in his hands again.

The other two men looked at each other. The mayor would never have admitted it of course, but he knew his last comment might seem thoughtless and he would need everyone on his side. He rose, came and put a hand on the baker's shoulder. "Of course we'll find her. And then I'll call a meeting of the Elders to discuss the best way to thank her. I'll send some men now to look for her. What did she look like?" But even as he asked the question he believed he knew the answer.

Baecker realised he'd been so busy following the woman's instructions and saving his son's life, that he'd not really questioned her arrival. *'An angel'* was what he wanted to say.

"Strange," interjected Dr Arzt.

The light went on in the mayor's eyes: "Then I have seen her." Under his breath he said to the doctor: "I think we may have a problem here."

CHAPTER 2

Tillman Meister, mayor, vessel of an ancient vampiric spirit, treated the word as if it were a mouthful of dead blood that he couldn't wait to spit out.

"Stay!?"

The glass of Pils stopped halfway to his lips and returned to the table with a bang that sent froth spilling onto his fingers.

"Yes," said Captain Ordner, head of the City Guard. "When we finally tracked her down…"

"Hmm, that must have been difficult," said Mr Droger, the apothecary, with a humorous glint in his eye. "*Excuse me; have you seen the only flame-haired, pale-skinned gypsy in town?*"

"When we finally tracked her down," continued Captain Ordner doggedly, ignoring Droger's jibe, "she was enjoying a bowl of goulash soup at the Three Barrels Inn, where she is staying tonight."

"So, where is she?" asked Dr Arzt, looking around.

"Well…" The captain was still standing, having just arrived, and shifted awkwardly on his feet. "She hasn't come with us."

"Hasn't come with you?" spluttered the mayor. "And who is she - a mere woman and a stranger - to act this way?"

"Well, she's done nothing wrong; far from it," said Mr Droger.

"Yes, but she's now disobeyed an order from a representative of the mayor." Meister produced a handkerchief from his pocket with a flourish and wiped the beer froth from his fingers before lifting the glass again and taking a satisfied swig. The sound of the last sentence had pleased him.

"With respect, sir," said the captain, standing a bit taller, "you only asked us to find her, not bring her here to the Stammtisch, so we didn't actually ask her to come."

"But…but…" The mayor groped for something to say next. "One day this will be the downfall of the Germanic people, this need for specific orders." He looked at the captain in frustration and as his lips narrowed his moustache bristled, while tenacious beer froth clung to it. "Why do you think I asked you to go and find her; so you could ask her how she was, or whether the soup was to her liking?" He slapped the table with his palm. "Of course I wanted you to bring her here!" He looked at the other Elders. "The moment I saw her, I knew this would happen."

"Knew what would happen?" asked Mr Metzger, the butcher, whose meat pies were probably the most important feature of any council meeting.

"Trouble."

"You mean the trouble she caused by saving my son's life," said another voice from the darkness near the entrance. No-one had heard Hans Baecker arrive.

The mayor managed to look embarrassed and tried to gather his tattered dignity. "Karl is fully recovered?"

"Yes, thanks be to God, and to…damn, I didn't even ask her name. What sort of man am I?"

"That is wonderful news." Meister called out to the innkeeper in his best politician's voice. "Mr Wirt, another round of beers to celebrate."

Hans hesitated for a moment, but then stepped forward and sat at the gnarled wooden table - the Stammtisch - which had been the regular meeting point for the Council of Elders for centuries. Everyone insisted it was the most central and convenient point for all of them to gather and there was no denying that the alcohol usually helped the decision-making process.

"So," said Baecker with barely-concealed irritation, "how far had this discussion got? Something about the trouble this mystery lady has caused us."

The mayor flushed and looked down into his beer-glass. "Perhaps I was hasty." He looked at Captain Ordner and gestured for him to sit. "So she would like to stay. Well, she seems to have found herself a room at the inn."

"That was good enough for Our Saviour," said another voice, silent till now; that of Mr Pfarrer, the town priest.

"And our town has a deserved reputation as a wonderful place to spend a few days, so…"

Ordner cleared his throat nervously. "You misunderstand me, sir. When I said to her that the town leaders wished to thank her in some appropriate way, she said it

18

would be thanks enough if she were allowed to settle here. She has travelled far and feels the time has come to put down some roots – her exact words, I believe." He removed his cap and placed it wearily on the table, as if this was all too much for a simple Captain of the City Guard.

There was a pause of several seconds, until the mayor realised that all eyes were on him. "Impossible." He remembered then to glance in apology at Hans Baecker. "Of course we're all very grateful for what she has done for Karl, but we have no houses to spare here, and those we have empty are needed for the next generation."

"What generation is that?" asked Droger with obvious irony. "The Palatinate War took many of our younger men. Birth rate has dropped. Infant mortality is high...that cursed anaemia. I would say more than half of our inhabitants are older than forty years. Then, of course, we have the return of the Plague." Here he looked at the doctor with a crooked grin. When his comment finally registered with Dr Arzt, the latter glared at him, while everyone else except the mayor stifled a smile. Beyond the window, out in darkness, the town clock struck ten.

"I have a spare room above the bakery," said Hans. "She could stay there."

"Also impossible," said Pfarrer, the priest. "Your wife - God rest her soul - has not yet returned to the soil and you would have another woman under your roof?"

Suddenly Meister slapped the table. "The Kriegerstrasse."

They all exchanged dark, uneasy looks.

"Nobody would want to live there," said Dr Arzt. "And nobody has; not since…"

"The real plague," said Hans Baecker.

"Oh this is ridiculous," said the mayor. "People have to earn the right to be citizens here."

"And saving a life on your first day doesn't earn you that right?" asked Baecker rhetorically. He stared at the mayor; fear helping him to conquer his usual timidity as he held Meister's gaze, daring him to contradict.

"And let's face it," said Droger, "if she's prepared to live in that sad corner of our town, she's more than earned her right."

****

The next day, Maria Baecker was laid to rest. That evening, finding solace in activity and not wanting to be alone, Hans took Ilsa for a walk through the town, a move that caused much glancing and whispering amongst the townsfolk. No-one outside the Council of Elders knew that Hans had volunteered to show Ilsa the site of one of the darkest passages, in all senses, of Reimersberg's history – and then explain to her that she would be living there or nowhere.

Ilsa looked across in amazement at Hans as they moved through the church square, not quite believing what she'd heard. "Walled them up?"

"Yes. They felt it was the only way to contain the plague."

"Or the food poisoning," she said, but immediately regretted her cheap, ironic jibe as they walked on in silence. This man had lost his wife, and because he had faced it with bravery, it was easy to forget his loss. She would have to put her anger at the doctor's cowardice and incompetence to one side.

Except...was it purely incompetence, and not collusion? She had seen the marks of poisoning on the bodies of Baecker's wife and child. Who better to administer that poison than the doctor? All the ancient demons had used human accomplices to infiltrate the world of man. And there was double cunning at play here. By allowing the poison and anaemia to finish off Frau Baecker, and not draining her to the point of death, the vampire – for Ilsa had little doubt that this was the horror they were facing – prevented her becoming a *strigoi,* wandering the night, alerting everyone to the presence of evil. Instead, she would rest easy in her grave. Unbeknown to Hans Baecker, in a strange way he had something to be grateful for.

"Those were dark times." Hans' words were more appropriate than he knew, as they interrupted Ilsa's thoughts. "Perhaps the people back then did the wrong thing, but it seemed to be a choice between that and the death of this entire community. Kriegerstrasse is a particularly narrow, dark and damp place. For whatever reason, the sickness started there and raged through the street. The Elders decided to try to contain it. The far end of the lane finishes at the town wall, so they bricked up the near end and left the people to..." He hesitated. "They continued to throw them food and water over the wall. Of course there are all sorts of tales about the place now; you know, ghosts, that sort of thing. Even back then, those living in there used to speak of a presence that came in the night – many said it was Death himself - and in the morning some of the healthy would be sick."

"Sounds charming," said Ilsa. Hans flushed with a mixture of guilt and embarrassment as he realised what he was doing. This place he was describing was where Ilsa was being asked to live. But she put a hand on his arm and they stopped walking. "Stories of ghosts and spirits – indeed the real thing – don't bother me."

"Then you've seen them?"

"They're everywhere. Where do you think our life-force goes when we die?"

Hans looked at the floor. "Then you think it's possible that Maria…" His eyes started to glisten and his voice caught.

"Of course, Hans. Your dear wife is probably looking at you right now."

They stood for a moment in a silence that signified many things, but not awkwardness.

"But back to your story," said Ilsa, and they continued towards the northern end of town.

"When it was thought to be…" - he paused - "…safe, they knocked down the wall." He stopped and considered. "It was the strangest thing; there was no-one there."

"What?!"

"Yes, no-one. Neither living nor dead. No-one knows why; what happened? All I can say is it all added to the legend of the Kriegerstrasse. I remember, as children, we used to take dares about who would be brave enough to walk down the length of Kriegerstrasse, go into the house at the far end, wait one minute and walk back."

"And did you manage it?"

"Once."

"And is that house now to be mine?" Hans looked shamefaced again. "No-one lives there now?"

"No, nor in any of the other houses. Nobody wanted to. You can take your pick. But I'm sure it's fine." Enthusiasm was notable by its absence from his voice.

"So am I. It will suit me anyway to have my privacy. There are *things* I like to do, which I think the good burghers of Reimersberg would not yet understand or be ready for."

"I can come and help repair any parts that look in need of it."

She smiled. "That's kind of you. You're welcome any time, with or without tools." Now she gave him a knowing look. "Though I can imagine what the townsfolk would say if you came visiting. This evening's stroll has caused enough of a stir already. Perhaps you might want to leave it for a time."

He laughed. "You may be right, but I wouldn't let them stop me."

But now he did stop. They had halted by an opening that two suckling pigs might have struggled to enter side by side.

"This is a street?" she asked, with a smile hovering somewhere between amused and bemused.

"This is one of the oldest parts of the town. You should see what the alleyways look like."

They laughed.

"Given the history," said Ilsa, "why didn't they just knock this down."

"People here are superstitious. They probably didn't want to anger the ghosts. Or perhaps it stayed as a memorial to the victims; and a reminder to us all."

Ilsa nodded. "Quite right."

With that she stepped forward into the opening. The cold struck her immediately. She doubted much sunlight ever found its way in there, even at the peak of the day. There were of course other reasons for the chill. She looked up at the narrow ribbon of evening sky above and her eyes darkened. "Perfect," she whispered.

CHAPTER 3

He had now fully recovered, but found that his friendships with the other young people had not. It was as if the finger of the plague had touched him after all. When Karl got time off from working in the bakery, he found the others had usually started some activity or other without him. He had no way of knowing what the other parents had been saying about the strange sickness that had been serious enough to carry off his mother, but from which he had been saved by the arrival of a mysterious woman, who had cured him with one touch of her hand to his forehead. Worse, he had no memory of it, or even of getting ill.

Of course, there was the usual embarrassment; people never knew what to say or how to behave towards the bereaved, but, perhaps because he was at that age – sixteen - when it seems the world is against you, when you know that neither boyhood nor manhood is yours, he felt that, somehow, he was being excluded. And it meant that Karl took more and more to wandering alone. He didn't know what had become of his saviour, except that she was living somewhere in the town, and it became his mission to find her. His father warned him not to, saying that she wanted to be left alone, though Karl sensed there was more behind those words.

That was why, one evening, he followed his father when he went out for a walk.

The twisting, turning, narrow streets made is easy to stay out of sight, but soon they were in a part of the town he'd never dared to enter before, and he was caught between keeping his distance from his father and not wanting to be alone in these shadowy, spooky lanes between run-down houses. He knew the stories of course; the sadness that meant visitors were always kept away from this area of Reimersberg, which stood more or less empty.

Those stories were given added impact when he peeped around the next corner to find that his father had disappeared.

His first reaction was panic; alone – hopefully – in this creepy place. This turned to dismay when he realised the only place his father could have gone, if he hadn't entered one of the houses, was a narrow opening, blacker than the surrounding evening gloom. Still there was a strange thrill to this; a little adventure; a mystery on his own doorstep. The other kids could keep their childish version of hide-and-seek.

He tip-toed cautiously down the street towards the alleyway, then craned his neck to peer around the corner. He saw nothing, but someone could have been standing a few feet away and he wouldn't have seen them in that blackness. The whole length of his body trembled; an uncontrollable spasm. He squinted at the wall of the house on the corner. There was a little rectangle of rusting metal and he could just about make out some letters: 'KRIEGERSTRASSE'. Now he shuddered again. From tiny, every child in this town knew the significance of that name. So this was the actual place; where boys told each other they had reached manhood if they could wander down to the end and back.

He looked again into the nothingness and decided manhood could wait. Besides, was there anywhere in the rules that said he couldn't do the task in daylight?

So Karl turned and headed for home. He was a little bit lost, but luckily, in Reimersberg most roads eventually led to the middle.

He guessed he had just found the hiding place - well, how else could he describe it? – of the woman who had saved his life. There was also plenty he didn't understand, particularly regarding his father's actions, but things moved slowly in Reimersberg and he had patience.

Not that much patience was needed. The following day he picked up the inflated pig's bladder which, in keeping with many of the lads in the town he had taken to kicking about, and headed out. His father didn't expect him to work in the bakery that day, seeming in a mood to be alone and to indulge his son's need to be out in the fresh air.

With that almost touching, simple cruelty that is the way of youth, Karl had indeed been shut out by the others, so it wasn't long till he was able to allow his ball to roll down one of the streets away from and unnoticed by the main group, and set off in pursuit.

He was accompanied from time to time by the indulgent looks and questions of citizens; asking after his and his father's health; still expressing their sympathy for the loss of his mother. But at last the passers-by and the voices dwindled, and then disappeared altogether.

And here he was - surprise surprise - at the entrance to Kriegerstrasse. It wasn't as fearsome, or as dark, as the night before, but it wasn't welcoming either, despite the flawless blue sky of that August morning. Karl stood transfixed for a moment. He'd been hot in the summer sun as he ran with his ball, but his sweat was cooling now in the air that came from the narrow opening, replaced by a more nervous perspiration.

But then an alien thought came to him, as if put there by an adult; Death was nothing to fear. He had made its acquaintance, shaken its hand and moved on.

With that, he stepped forward into the Kriegerstrasse, leaving his ball in the shadows. As he moved down that confined passageway, the cobbles were slick with slime beneath his feet, and as his eyes adjusted to the dim light he saw, in the mildew, cracks and flaking plaster around him, what it meant to be forgotten. He discovered that a house does have a soul that can depart. A few nights before, his father had said that his mother's spirit now looked over them. But these houses were not so lucky; their guardian spirits had vanished, never to return.

He was no longer scared, just sad. That sorrow deepened with the realisation that, if his suspicions were correct, the people of this town had allowed the woman who saved his life to end up here. He felt some of his sadness turn to anger, like bread that has caught slightly in the oven.

All of this meant that the thin frame of light he could see around a pair of shutters at the end of the street provided a welcoming beacon in that melancholy place. It took a few seconds for Karl to question why the shutters were closed, but when he did, the fear returned; for what type of person would want to close out whatever meagre daylight there was?

He stopped, nearly turned back, and then came to his senses. If it *was* her, from what his father had said she'd not hesitated to come to him in his hour of need and he had not yet said thank you. Whatever it took, that was the least he could do.

As he drew nearer he could hear a strange rushing, hissing sound and a rhythmic whirring. He'd heard nothing like it before. Curiosity got the better of any fear. Karl noticed that one of the shutters had a knot-hole. Approaching with caution, he placed his eye against it to look in. Then he recoiled as he found an eye staring back, astonishingly green, as if another world, were contained within it. Then the shutters flew open and he fell in fearful love with the face he saw there, both frightening and kind, wise and generous.

"Karl!" she said with a big smile, and his name on her lips enslaved him forever. He couldn't speak. "How wonderful to see you looking so well."

She left the window and moved round to the door. He could have run, he supposed, but didn't want to. She opened the door and he saw her smile change to a frown as she looked down the narrow street. "How did you find me?"

"It doesn't matter," he answered.

She gave a knowing nod. "You followed your father when he came to check if I was alright."

"Only to the end of the street."

She narrowed her eyes. "Mmm." But then the dark cloud was gone as she smiled again. "Come in." She looked out again. "Are you sure *you* weren't followed?" She peered through the shadows. "Better go and collect that ball of yours, just in case."

"How did…?" He couldn't see it himself and *he* knew where he'd left it, but he didn't complete the question. Suddenly all things were possible. He set off quickly, checked no-one was around – but why would they be? – and hurried back.

As she went to the window and closed the shutters again he saw that her flaming hair lost little of its colour when the murky daylight was closed out. In fact it grew more like the firelight that played on it.

Then he started to notice other things and his mouth opened wide, as did her smile as she observed him.

For example, there was a cauldron – well, there had to be one, didn't there? Ilsa shrugged when she saw him looking at it and said in a playful tone:

"I guess that makes me a witch."

"Are you?" he asked innocently, almost wanting her to say yes.

"In the eyes of the ignorant perhaps. It's like a convenient label on a jar when you don't know the ingredients." For a moment there was a faraway look in her eyes. Then she turned back to Karl and the look was replaced by something that, just for a moment, could have been mistaken for fear. "Will you tell anyone?"

He gave her a very frank gaze; one older than his years. "I've heard some of the tales from travellers and tinkers who've passed through this town, about what people have done to witches." He shuddered. "I think there are a lot of things I want to see in life, but plenty that I don't. So no, I won't be telling anyone." Then he smiled. "But as you're not a witch it doesn't matter anyway."

She put a hand on his shoulder and as it rested there he experienced a wonderful feeling; the happiness of seeing a million different things in a thousand different places. She saw him look at her hand; felt him tremble. "It's this place," she said, looking around her.

"What is?"

"The power you feel."

"I…I don't understand."

She crouched in front of him, pushing back the long, grey-green coat she wore with a rather unfeminine movement. Their eyes met and her gaze was almost too intense to bear; not cruel, but fierce. "These things are not easy to explain." She touched his face. "But I think you're special, Karl. I feel that about you already. And please believe, not every child..." she hesitated as she saw him frown, "...sorry, young man would have survived your illness, even with my medication. You are strong - so one day I know you'll understand."

Only now did Karl realise that the whirring sound he'd heard when approaching the house must have stopped in the meantime, because it started again, and he looked to his right to see something like a small spinning-wheel, apparently turning on its own. His attention was drawn to the new wonders of mechanics and physics for the moment, rather than those of the universe.

He saw how the wheel was being cranked by the movement of a series of delicate, complex levers, the last of which disappeared into a thin tube of metal. This in turn slotted into a slightly larger one, that one into another, and so on in a telescoping arrangement that led finally to a funnel fixed in the lid of the cooking pot, or cauldron as he had taken it to be. He knew all the tubes would slide into each other, like some little dolls he'd seen on the cart of a tinker who had come from the east.

"What's moving the wheel?" he asked.

"The steam from the pot," said Ilsa. She stood up and ran her finger above the length of the tubes. "As it passes through the smaller tubes it gets thicker and hotter." Karl frowned. "Right; imagine a foggy day here by the mountains. If you took all that fog and tried to put it inside one of these houses, it would be so thick you wouldn't be able to see anything. Now imagine that fog is hot; just think how hot it would be if it was all in one house. You've felt the steam coming from your father's oven. That amount of power can push things around; and that is the heat and pressure, which, through some little tricks inside these tubes, make the wheel go round."

"Wow!" exclaimed Karl. "Where did you learn this?"

"Oh, I've travelled a long way in my life, and seen many things that people in towns like this are not ready to know."

"Is that why you keep your shutters closed?"

"Yes. That and other reasons." There was that peculiar look in her eye again and he knew not to ask – for the moment. She smiled and waved towards the pipes. "But this is just...a hobby; something that interests me. I was given this gift by a man who knew I wouldn't yet pass it on to an unprepared world. Quite when the world will be ready…" She sighed. "Perhaps it won't be in my lifetime."

"So what *do* you do?"

"Do?"

"Yes; my father is a baker, Mr Metzger is a butcher, Mr Droger is an ath…apoc…apothecary." He spat the last word in frustration and Ilsa laughed, which annoyed him slightly. "What do you do?"

"I'm a traveller."

He frowned. "You can't live by travelling."

She lifted one finger. "Correction; it is the only way to live." As she stood before him she seemed to grow taller in the firelight, her shadow deeper, and he decided he had better drop his sulky tone. "I gather things. I gather knowledge; and every now and then I find a place where I may rest, grow strong and perhaps put my…" she searched for a word, "…harvest to use. When I have to move on, the Earth Goddess provides. But if I am needed, there is always a sign."

Karl nodded, wisdom suddenly his. "A boy who is dying, for example." She smiled at him, their bond needing no words. "What is it that strengthens you?"

She crouched again, and the light from the fire blazed in her eyes. "There are lines of power in the earth and at certain places they conjoin. Then inexplicable things happen. The feeling is particularly strong in this valley; this town; this house. The mountains, the forests and the river exert their own influences. I imagine it is no coincidence that this is known as the Valley of the Witches. A combination of all the things I mentioned creates forces very few people would understand. Sometimes those forces channel through women whose sensitive souls make them perfect vessels. In other times, as now, people have feared those forces and the women themselves, and called them witches. And Karl, add to all of this the history of this street; the extremes of emotion experienced, both by people left to die and by those forced to abandon them. Is it any wonder there is so much energy here?"

"Doesn't it scare you?" said Karl, looking around as a chill crept over him.

"Strangely, I feel also much happiness here, as if those people pulled closer together in their time of shared need, and also found their peace with their God."

Then Ilsa leaned back, as if exhausted all of a sudden, before continuing: "That's the most I've talked to anyone about that topic in a long time – other than myself."

She put a hand on his arm. "But now, young man, I think you should be going, before you are missed."

He felt the pain of parting, though it was better than not being able to say goodbye at all; a chance that had been denied him when his mother had died while he was still in his fever. "May I come again?"

She smiled. "Of course." But just as swiftly her features darkened; some storm cloud covered the light in her eyes and she raised one finger, prodding the air for emphasis. "But be careful. We wouldn't want you being mistaken for a witch's familiar."

"But you're not a witch."

"Know this, Karl; for every witch, there are a thousand women accused of being one, and a hundred thousand people only too ready to accuse. And usually, at the head of those people you will find one man; one dangerous being." Ilsa leaned forward and gave Karl a look that made him shiver. "I believe I saw him the very day I arrived here. It scared me; not because of what might happen to me, but what might happen *because* of me."

CHAPTER 4

Five weeks had passed; more than enough time for Dr Arzt's resentment at his new nickname of Dr Plague to fester into something dangerous. He blamed Ilsa Wlich for that and found die-hard support from Meister the mayor and Pfarrer the priest. They were only three men, of course, though Meister was so much more than that – it was as well Pfarrer didn't know the half of it, for that really would have been a clash of two beliefs. But because of their standing in the town and the number of ears into which they poured the oil of comforting words, it wasn't long before there was a grumbling groundswell of opinions and views about the woman, with her strange looks, her strange name and her even stranger ways. Had anyone actually seen her arrive on the day of Maria Baecker's death? When questioned, the look-outs on the battlements said no, and that was taken as gospel; as if these bored men, who hadn't shot at a marauding wolf in anger for months, were always on their sharpest guard. It was as though Ilsa had materialised from thin air.

"And we all know what that would mean," said Arzt with a significant nod and a knowing look at his fellow Elders, who had gathered for one of their Council meetings.

"I thought we prided ourselves on being a welcoming and enlightened town," said Droger. "I remember the…" he paused, "…bad days better than I care to; they were not so long ago and even though I am a man, so wasn't the target of his persecution, I still recall the feeling of relief the day the witch-finder was found dead – though it shames me to say so. I don't know what illness carried him off so suddenly – more importantly our good doctor here likewise had no idea – but I do remember the putrefaction of his body as it lay in the street. It was as if all his sins had found him out." Droger crossed himself and was offended to find the mayor turning away from him. "Given your disdain for matters spiritual," he said to Meister, "I'm even more amazed that you allowed a witch-finder to hold such sway here. After all, why should someone like you, who doesn't believe in God, believe in Satan, never mind his sisters?"

Now it was Pfarrer's turn to look uncomfortable; his angry eyes may have been turned on Droger, but that was because his own hypocrisy was on show. By staying close, the mayor, the doctor and the priest were able to drive much of the Council's decision making because of their respected positions. If ever there was a marriage of convenience and self-preservation, it was between the mayor with no time for God, the doctor who couldn't cure and the priest who was hungry for earthly reward.

Droger continued: "Anyway I will need better proof than the word of some half-asleep guard before I venture down that path again; the one where every signpost bears the word *witch*."

"Very well," said Arzt with resentment. "But she *is* practising medicine without the proper training. I did not spend years in Tübingen studying in an ill-lit garret to stand by and see some quack dispensing potions to my patients."

"He did not spend years in Tübingen *at all*," whispered Droger ironically to Baecker.

"Some people, notably the younger inhabitants of this town – those with less regard to its proud traditions – are running to her for her so-called treatments, all on the basis of the lucky recovery of one boy."

Now Baecker bristled; wanted to say something, but held himself back. This was heading a dangerous way. He needed to watch and wait.

"Not just medicine is she dispensing," said Pfarrer, aggrieved. "She also bestows advice – wisdom some say. But *"the fear of the Lord is the beginning of wisdom"* says the Bible. She does not attend church; how then can she be wise? People should be seeking counsel from God through me. What say you, Mr Meister?"

Now there was a very embarrassed silence. Pfarrer hadn't so much stepped down from his soapbox as fallen off it. Everyone knew the mayor never entered the church. Every function that required him to do so seemed to generate an excuse, or found him sending someone as his representative. Now the priest had said, in so many words, that those who failed to attend church could not be wise. Pfarrer seemed to shrink in his chair and Droger watched the fear burning in his eyes. The apothecary saw also how Arzt, in particular, had gone deathly pale, his mouth falling open as he waited for the mayor's response.

Now Meister might not have been wise, but even his worst enemies knew that he was clever and cunning. He drew himself up in his chair and made a sweeping gesture towards all present with his arm. "I say the evidence is here before my eyes, that already this woman creates a division within our town. It would be better were she not here." He turned to the butcher, silent to that point, for his support. "Mr Metzger?"

Metzger's florid face grew redder before he replied.

"Well, she's not affecting my business. In fact we've had more council meetings since she came, and that means I've sold more of my large pies." He gave a nervous chuckle.

The mayor raised his eyebrows, and then shook his head slightly. The Metzger business might have been the oldest in Reimersberg, hence the place on the Council, but this lump of a descendant was just a fool. Meister lifted his hand in the direction of the apothecary. "Droger? Surely you can't be happy with her handing out pills and potions."

"On the contrary," said Droger, "some of them – the potions; I know nothing of any pills – really seem to work, and I've asked her for the recipes, which, I may add, she was only too happy to give. All except the tea with which she cured young Karl. She said that was a secret, jealously guarded by her family for centuries, and the ingredients are rare."

Meister shot him a look, and then said in a dismissive tone: "Pah! This is getting us nowhere."

"But where exactly do we need to go?" asked Baecker, speaking for the first time. "What is our aim?"

The mayor looked evasive, and then something dawned on him. "Perhaps you're right." He ignored the intake of breath from Dr Arzt. "Perhaps we need to talk to her. Mr Baecker, she trusts you. Ask her to meet us here, at this inn, tomorrow evening at six o'clock."

"To what purpose?" interjected Arzt. For once, his question was the one on everyone's lips, though he seemed to regret asking it the moment Meister cast his baleful eyes in his direction. The calmness of the response didn't fool the doctor.

"As I said; to talk. To try to understand her, and to make her understand how we feel. Can you bring her, Mr Baecker?"

The baker looked puzzled, like all the others. "I can certainly ask." Then his back straightened. "But I am a man of honour, and if this is some trick then I will have no part of it."

The mayor raised his hands in a placatory gesture. "What trick could it be? Please trust me. This matter needs resolution quickly." He picked up his beer with a self-important motion. "And in my experience, I am the one who can bring it."

****

Karl was lost for words. It was the most amazing thing he had ever seen.

"Here, take it." She handed it to him. He hardly dared to touch it. "Go on, it's for you. Besides, I have another one."

"For me?" The light inside it was almost out-dazzled by the one in his eyes. "How did you capture fire?"

"It seems that wonderful, doesn't it? But all I have done here is harness some of the little pieces of which everything in the universe is made, as a man might catch wild horses and contain or direct their power." She pointed to it. "This is not my invention, but from someone far more learned than me. It was seen and misunderstood by others." She closed her eyes. "You do not want to know what they did to him and his laboratory." Opening her eyes again, she saw Karl's puzzled expression. "A laboratory is a place where people like him work and make such discoveries as this." The joy of this boy's innocence – the opportunity to write so much knowledge on the pages of his open book – made her smile again, and she turned both of their minds back to the object. "When you move this piece here," she pointed to a little lever at the bottom of the glass sphere, "you open the gate for those wild horses to run through, and the glow you see in this thin piece of metal is their joy at running free. Never forget that joy, Karl; always run free."

He held the glass ball in two cupped hands like a rare bird. "It's so small," he said.

"One day it will take flight, and mankind with it," said Ilsa. "But for now keep it a secret."

"It's fading," he said fearfully.

"To make it live again all you need to do is move it. The movement of air through this piece underneath here causes tiny wheels to turn and they give it the power it needs."

"I'll treasure it always," said Karl. "It's just such a pity that other people can't enjoy its beauty."

"One day."

****

On the day that things started to go horribly wrong for Reimersberg, Ilsa gave Karl two more gifts, none of them with the immediate appeal of the prototype light bulb, but both of them valuable; one more so than even Ilsa could have guessed.

As she had walked through the town square that morning she had a sense of something brewing. There was trouble in the air – for her. She looked up at the tops of the mountains, except they weren't there; the huge lumps of rock hidden by something as insubstantial as vapour as the clouds gathered. It smelt like rain. She wished humans could be as easily read as the elements. Just a nuance here and there in the 'Good *morning'* of the people who did speak to her; a particular glint or evasiveness in the glances of others; she knew these things might even be happening at a subconscious level. It wasn't that she felt there was a plot. But even Mr Droger, who struck her as one of the most intelligent people in town, carried a distant air in his friendliness.

So when Karl came by that afternoon, she asked him: "How is your father, Karl?"

"You've not spoken to him?"

"I've not seen him in a couple of days."

"Why do you ask?"

She looked away towards the shutters, though as usual they were closed. "I don't know; a feeling."

She got up from her chair, walked over to a shelf that Hans Baecker had erected for her, on which stood some ancient-looking bottles containing powders and liquids, dried fruits and grains. One of the bottles held what appeared to be a handful of fruit seeds. She took this, hunted down a pouch, from which she emptied some strange reddy-brown flakes and replaced them with the seeds. This she gave to Karl, closing his fingers around it as she had done to Hans when she'd given him the arsenic.

"Take these, Karl. You'll know when the time is right to use them. Something in your life will tell you."

He unfurled his fingers to look at the pouch. "What are they?"

"They are the seeds of a special tree. I gathered them in an oasis far to the east of here."

"An oasis?"

"Yes, a place of water and life in the middle of a desert. There is knowledge in those faraway, seemingly barren lands; things almost forgotten, which the people of the west may never know. These seeds were the result of joining two different types of tree. What grows from these grows quickly, and is strong and hardy. It will take root in the unfriendliest of places. It brings life where there is none; food where it is most needed."

Karl put the pouch into his pocket.

"Take care of those now," warned Ilsa, sensing it wasn't the most exciting present she could have given the boy. "Promise me."

"I will."

She hesitated. Should she tell him more? Oh, she wanted to, but something held her back, including the desire not to terrify this young life. Instead, she said:

"Good – because it will also protect life; perhaps even yours."

Karl laughed. "Dear Ilsa; a tree, or maybe bush, which protects people. This I have to see."

"Save your laughter; it might be a rare thing in the future." She saw the hurt in his eyes and moved to place a hand on his cheek, when suddenly she looked up anxiously towards the window.

"What is it?" asked Karl.

"Someone's coming," she said, and saw doubt now, still tinged by mistrust, in Karl's eyes. "This part of town is so quiet and my ears are attuned to the slightest sounds of nature." She looked nervously at him. "It must be your father."

"Wow!" said Karl, impressed, forgetting that he was supposed to be annoyed, "you can hear that too."

"No, but no-one else would come here on their own. Cowards believe in safety in numbers." She put her hands on Karl's shoulders. "Look, I don't think it would be good for your father to find you here. You should go."

"But it's the Kriegerstrasse. There's no way I can avoid him."

She led him towards the back wall of the house. "I'll show you something. But we must hurry. He's not yet in the Kriegerstrasse, but he will be soon."

With such a gift of hearing, Karl understood why Ilsa's green eye had been looking out for him the first time he'd come here.

Ilsa probed with her fingers at the mortar between two of the huge blocks of stone and a large chunk of it dropped away. She pointed into the hole and Karl could see that carved there was a recess big enough for four fingers to slide in. Now Ilsa probed again, four blocks of stone to the left, with the same result.

"Quickly," she said, "two pairs of hands will make this easier than one."

Karl put his fingers into the left-hand gap – his hands had grown strong from helping his father to knead bread – and Ilsa put hers into the other one. They pulled, and a block of stones, about shoulder-high to a man, came away, rolling with surprising ease. Karl looked at the base of the block and saw now that it was raised ever so slightly off the ground; something that wouldn't be visible to the casual observer.

Despite the urgency of the situation, Ilsa couldn't help but smile. "Incredible, isn't it. I was standing by the wall and felt a draught on my feet. Amazing! There were tradesmen in this street. I have wandered in the ruins of the other houses and found artefacts belonging to a cobbler and a goldsmith. A stonemason must have lived here. Such ingenuity! From what I can see there are tiny spheres of stone in recesses under the block. They roll, and act like wheels."

Now Karl looked behind the block of stones and his mouth hung open in amazement. There was a tunnel, at the far end of which was the outline of a similar block.

Ilsa picked up a lantern and led Karl into the tunnel. "I'm not sure why this was built, or when," she said, "but the owner of the house must have had his reasons. Maybe he just wanted to know that there was always a way out other than the narrow entrance to the street. Perhaps he was involved in some secret activity that he wanted no-one to know about. Whatever the reasons, this bit at the end is even cleverer."

Ilsa used the light to find a handle, pulled, and a door opened inwards, to reveal the outside world. Karl looked at the door. It was wood, but the outer side was clad in stones, so that from a distance no-one would know it was there.

"What craftsmanship," said Ilsa. "I can imagine the stonemason insisting this part of the wall needed repair, so he could work openly, but still create this secret route." She lifted the lantern. "Look at the roof of the tunnel; very solidly made. This would have been the work of several men."

"I wonder why," said Karl.

"I guess we'll never know, but sometimes that's just not important." Now Ilsa looked around her. "This must be part of the reason for the positive energy and happiness I have been feeling in here; people pulling together against a common enemy; knowing they could escape from the plague prison; taking pleasure in defeating the odds. Of course some people would have been too ill to save. But for the others; if they were going to die, it wasn't going to be walled up in the darkness, but out in the freedom of the valley. There would have been no guards on the walls here; they'd have been too terrified of becoming infected by the plague. For me, this explains why the people disappeared. Better to die in the jaws of a wolf than... " She looked over her shoulder. "But now you must go – hurry!"

Karl was able to walk through the gap - he was still shorter than Ilsa - but before he did he turned. "Goodbye Ilsa; see you soon."

Suddenly she leaned forward and planted a kiss on his cheek. She'd never done that before and it sent a shock through his entire body. Hours later he would lift his fingers to that part of his face as if in remembrance of that moment. For now he headed back around the town wall, clinging to its base as much as possible so as not to be seen, and sneaked, with all the ability and cunning a mischievous boy could muster, back through the gates.

Now Ilsa pushed the stones and mortar back into place, and stepped out of the house just as Hans Baecker approached.

****

"Why do they want to talk to me now?" They were walking past the clock, heading towards the main town square and the Eagle Inn. The joyful babbling of the River Regen contrasted with their anxiety. "It's been what, five weeks or so, and all I've sensed is resentment from the three wise men – and something else from the mayor as well."

Hans looked at her. "What do you mean?"

"Oh, nothing."

How she wanted to tell someone! She'd been working her stealthy magic where she could - though actually it was science, not some black art - but years of prejudice and discrimination against her kind had taught her to tread carefully and she would only help where first some trust was shown. Those townsfolk who had come to her, displaying faith in her, had, unbeknown to them, received something more than the medication they sought. Those who had not – the majority, who still avoided her whenever they could – had not yet earned redemption. Of course, she could have simply treated the town's water supply, but for two reasons she did not.

Firstly, she could still remember – it was too ghastly ever to forget – standing helpless in the crowd, watching one of her sisters burning at the stake; her alleged crime – witchcraft; the evidence - the curing of an old man's gout; the real crime – being a flaxen-haired stranger. That had been in another country, many years before, when a self-styled witch-finder called Matthew Hopkins had terrorised the east of the country. Ilsa had forced herself to watch as the girl was brought hobbling to the stake, her feet deformed from wearing the Spanish Boots they'd used to torture her. It had been so hard to stand and witness, but she needed to try to send her spirit through the flames to calm the girl; bring her peace at the end.

So Ilsa had indeed taken a huge risk in curing Karl, hence her lie about the food-poisoning. But there had been something about the wretched sight of dead mother and dying son lying on those tables, or more truthfully, about a desperate father and husband peering through the window, which had moved her. Then she had seen the signs of a far greater evil on Karl's arm and knew she couldn't just turn the other way. It was against the code of her people.

Still, that mercy wasn't for everyone. The townsfolk had to earn it; reap what they sowed. Ilsa sensed a trial was fast approaching. In this summons to see the mayor, she smelt a rat; a great big corrupt one.

Her second reason for not helping the whole town was that he would have known, from the moment he smelt the aura in everyone's blood. Meister might have been a weakened spirit, hiding in this remote town where the insularity of the people kept him safe, but he was still ancient and powerful.

Hans was speaking and as Ilsa looked at him, she realised that, on reflection, there was a third reason for her hesitation; her reluctance to take on the mayor. Her guard was down slightly. Love had weakened her. She wasn't ready or strong enough for the showdown yet, though she knew the time must be approaching.

Hans had stopped. "No, tell me."

Though this was her chance, she would have to let it go for now; spin a tale. Yet for a moment she was a vulnerable woman like any other. "Well," she hesitated, "from the others I sense professional jealousy - in the case of Arzt and Pfarrer – or just distrust. Though it's wrong of them, to some extent I understand. The doctor believes I am taking his patients, and the priest believes that only his version of the laws of the universe can be expounded. They're wrong because they're..." she shrugged, "...wrong. But with the mayor; what threat am I to him?" She looked intently at Hans. "Let me guess; there *has* always been and *will* always be a man in the position of mayor here."

"Yes," said Hans, "of course."

His blind acceptance of that fact stung her, but she let it pass. "So what is his problem with me?"

Hans lifted his hands, palms outwards, in a questioning gesture. "I don't know. Perhaps that you're wiser than him."

That redeemed Hans in Ilsa's eyes.

"I see something else in his eyes, too. I am a strong woman, and that is something he can't deal with."

Now they could hear the beginnings of a whirring from the clock. The ancient figures were preparing to advance. Ilsa saw the concern in his Hans' eyes - he was going to be late if he wasn't careful. Besides, she could tell this discussion was heading in a direction he couldn't understand. "Ok," he said, "but we need to get moving."

She put a hand on his arm and became aware, all of a sudden, that several pairs of eyes were watching her, from the street, from doorways and from behind windows. She dropped her hand. "Why are you all so scared of him? Does the mayoral chain hold that much authority in Reimersberg? He's so pompous and ill-bred"

He's a vampire.

Hans sighed and nodded. "Unfortunately, yes. That's the way it's always been." He leaned forward and whispered anxiously. "He could close down any business in this town. He has the authority. It is best to stay on his good side."

"So your Council of Elders is just a front; a farce."

He looked afraid. "It hadn't seemed so till you arrived." He knew that response was double-edged, but lacked the skill, or the will, to make his words clear. He turned to go, and despite the passers-by watching, she put a restraining hand on him.

"There's something else, Hans." He was panicking, not wanting to be late, but did her the courtesy of listening. "I've touched on one 'W' word, but there is a more dangerous one. I lied when I said I saw only professional jealousy from Arzt and Pfarrer." She lowered her voice. "Tell me, Hans, is a witch dangerous because she is a woman, or a woman dangerous because she might be a witch?" She took one look at his expression and felt pity for him. "It's not a question that has an answer – or rather, it would take longer than the one minute we have."

They entered the Eagle Inn just as the last wolfhound was retreating into the town clock; about five minutes past six.

"Now look what's happened," said Hans in frustration. "They've gone. We've missed our chance for you to talk. Mr Meister might be many things, but he is never late for a meeting of the Elders."

"He is indeed many things..." Ilsa paused with sudden concern, "...never, you say?"

"No, not in my living memory."

"And if some Elders were missing at six o'clock, would those who were here have all disappeared again by five minutes past?"

Her deepening frown was matched by Hans's. "That's unlikely. Some at least would stay to wash away the dust of the day with a beer."

"And is there not also a chance, my dear Hans, that even if they did leave straight away, we might have passed some of them on our way here?"

39

"Yes." Hans removed his hat and scratched his head. "Unless we're in the wrong place."

Ilsa's head snapped around towards the door. "Or they are?" Her eyes flashed in anger and she was gone, trailing Hans Baecker in her wake.

****

As Ilsa and Hans had left the Kriegerstrasse at quarter to six, a group of men had emerged from a neighbouring alley.

It had rained that afternoon. As that group turned, with much hesitation, into the Kriegerstrasse, they trod with care through puddles of mucky water and across slick cobbles. From the corners of ancient, moss-tiled roofs water still dripped like blood from the proverbial stone, and the unseasonal September heat left a mist hanging in the air. This group – comprising all of the Council of Elders except Hans Baecker, and a knot of thickset, small-eyed men, whom the mayor used for any dirty work – moved where none of the townsfolk had dared to venture for a very long time.

Soon they were outside the house which, in their ignorant pride, they had considered a suitable place for Ilsa Wlich to stay.

"I don't remember the door having a lock," said the mayor, looking at one of the thickset men, who swung a boot, splintering it from its hinges.

"And now it doesn't," said Dr Arzt. "That is magic indeed." He emitted a high-pitched, but unconvincing giggle.

"I'm not happy about this," said Droger. "It's an abuse of trust; of hers, and Hans'".

"I'm just looking after the interests of this town," said Meister. "If we find nothing, no harm done."

Smirking, the mayor motioned for the others to step forward, pretending politeness, though actually, through long tradition, it was a habit of his never to be the first to enter a place.

Though the world outside was old, dark and dripping, the one they entered filled them with equal foreboding; even Droger and Metzger.

It was nothing that would have bothered the reader of this story, but they all exchanged glances and even the mayor said nothing for a time. In the absence of a broom, a pointed hat or a black cat, probably the most damning thing was the cauldron. The fact that it was just a small pot of vegetable broth warming over a banked fire meant nothing. The long series of thin tubes leading to a wheel was intriguing and almost certainly incriminating. Then there was the shelf full of bottles and mysterious vials. If any of those men had been brave enough to open one of them, in most cases they would have recognised the smell of rosemary and basil, thyme and sage, and a number of other herbs and spices; some of them familiar, others less so. Instead, they just stared at what they assumed to be the ingredients of some more witch's brew.

That was, until Meister took an interest in some reddish-brown flakes lying on a table, where Ilsa had emptied them only minutes before. Meister leant in close; sniffed. The other saw his eyes narrow, heard him hiss and then, almost without warning, he swung his walking cane at the shelf, scattering and shattering the bottles.

Then one of the thickset men, gaining confidence from having smashed the door, spotted a small glass sphere and picked it up. Out of curiosity he moved a tiny lever. Nothing happened, but when he lifted the sphere to look at it more closely he let out a cry and released it. The others saw the glow too, growing stronger as the sphere fell to the floor where it smashed.

"Witchcraft!" cried the man, who looked at his hands in panic to see whether the marks of devilry were upon him.

"She creates false light!" exclaimed Pfarrer the priest. "God created light, and only he."

But worse was to come, for Metzger's unerring nose for the smell of meat drew him to the far end of the room, where he found the sliced-open body of a frog. Not wishing to touch it with his hands he picked up a long metal stick that lay next to it. The others had moved nearer to see what drew his attention. He placed the stick in the large incision in the frogs' stomach, prodding at it in curiosity. That stick still carried static electric charge – a phenomenon unknown to any man or woman in that town. Ilsa had been preparing to show Karl this latest wonder of science; the effect of electricity on the nerves and muscles of a dead animal. Unfortunately for her, the experiment worked perfectly. The frog's remains leapt and twitched, as did the men several feet backwards. The metal stick fell with a clang from Metzger's fingers.

"Witchery indeed!" he cried.

"And we have found her familiar," said Arzt.

"Worse, it is dead."

"Yet it lives still," said the mayor. "I have seen all I need to see in this foul pit. And you, gentlemen?"

They were too stunned to speak.

At that moment they heard the town clock strike six.

"Come, let us leave," said Meister. "She will know soon that she has been tricked."

"And if she doesn't," said Arzt, "she will know when she returns here." He looked at the others. "And a tricked witch is a dangerous witch."

"You're right," said Pfarrer. "Even though God is on our side, we will need the support of each other."

"And Baecker?" said Arzt.

"He may be a problem; he likes her," said Meister. "But that will change when he hears of her witchery. For the sake of his son he will agree with what we do."

"What will we do?" said Droger. "I could not bear to see us return to the old ways."

"You are a good man," said Meister, even though he would have liked nothing better than some old-fashioned justice, "and your sentiments do you credit. But I think I have a solution. We will put it to the men of this town. If I have my way the stones of Reimersberg will protect us. Come."

As they stepped out of the house, Dr Arzt slipped on a wet cobblestone and landed on his backside in a puddle. That sealed the fate of Ilsa Wlich as far as he was concerned. The others were now too scared to laugh at his undignified state; too keen to be away. So they just helped him up and made their way out of the Kriegerstrasse, but not before the mayor had given them instructions to gather a hundred men each and meet in the town square at ten o'clock that night.

CHAPTER 5

"**I** swear I didn't know," protested Hans. "They tricked me like they tricked you – if what you say proves to be true."

They hurried back through the town until they reached Ilsa's house.

"If they are still there," said Hans, "I will kill every one of them for this; well, Meister and Arzt anyway."

"No you won't," said Ilsa. "You don't have the devil in you. If you had, then they wouldn't have tricked you."

The open shutters were enough of a sign, but the door told the full story. It seemed there was no longer any pretence. They ran in full of fear.

First Ilsa saw the smashed bottles and vials on the floor, then the shattered glass sphere. She picked up the remains, looked at the position of the lever and sighed. Then she saw the metal stick on the floor, saw that the frog had moved, and her blood ran cold. She knew what must be coming now.

She realised she couldn't hide her news from Hans any longer; time was running out.

"Hans, I would understand if you want nothing to do with me now." She saw him looking at the frog and thought that he might misunderstand her statement. After all, she'd not shown him half the things she'd shown Karl. "I don't mean I'm a witch. I am not, and you know it. What I am is far too complicated to explain now, where time is of the essence. Normally, I would have hidden certain things away from ignorant eyes, but you were hurrying me out earlier and I forgot. There; if ever you needed proof that I am but human, it is in that simple act of forgetfulness. But the things these men have seen here today will be taken wrongly."

"Such as?"

"Let's just say, it doesn't look good for me."

"Then you must leave here." He looked down. "I'm so sorry; so ashamed that my people have done this; so sorry that you must go."

"It's not as simple as that."

"Why not? You told me you had been made unwelcome in places before."

She looked at him with pleading eyes. "Yes, but this time I was hoping I could stay."

He didn't know what to say. Then she put a hand on his arm. "Hans, before I tell you something, I want you to know that I release you from any obligation, for your sake and Karl's. Anything you do from now will be down to your own free will, and will mean all the more for it if you choose correctly. If you choose wrongly, on the other hand, I cannot answer for the consequences. You will have to decide what you hold dear."

"You're worrying me."

"Let's just say, I may not be a witch, but something magical did happen in here between you and me. And now I carry a child." She heard the hollow click in his throat. "It is a child of Reimersberg; a half-sibling to Karl, conceived that night when you were in despair, I was lonely, and we clung to each other for comfort." He opened his mouth, but couldn't speak, and she put a finger on his lips. "I expect no answer now, only when the time comes, which will be soon I think. But please go now. There is nothing you can do and for the time being the Elders will expect your support. You must look as if you give it. Just remember me when the time comes. Go now." He hesitated at the door, dazed by the news and the events of the last few minutes. "There *is* something you can do for me though,"

"Ilsa?"

"Send Karl to me."

"Why?" He looked concerned and she couldn't deny the hurt that caused her. "If you have something for him I can take it to him."

"Just send him." Already she felt his weakness.

"Won't it be dangerous for him, coming here?"

"There is nothing to fear in this part of town except superstition. Believe me, there are much worse things than the dead." How she wanted to tell him, but no, not yet. She had to be strong and wait.

"I meant because the Elders have been here. Who knows what they are planning."

"Not if you send him straight away. Even the all-important Mayor Meister needs time to organise things." She looked at him and felt the pain of parting for the second time. Soon it would be three times in an hour. "Please," she said, "for the sake of the moments we had and the child that is in my belly."

With that Hans turned and headed down the Kriegerstrasse."

"Remember me!" she called after him, and then turned her attention to salvaging whatever she could from the destruction of her property

44

"Poor fool." She spun round to find Meister standing in the doorway. "Surprised? Oh, I can be quiet on my feet when I have to. Surely you know that. Those who were free of the plague discovered it too – to their cost." He reflected. "But that was another time; another incarnation."

So, he had escaped even her keen sense of hearing. He was much more dangerous than she had thought. Had he overheard her asking Hans Baecker to send his son? Was Karl now in danger? She thanked the universe that he had drunk her tea; it would offer him some protection.

"What did you mean, *"poor fool"*?"

"Any man in love is a fool. Women are so full of deceit?"

"And a vampire is not? Karl Baecker has no memory of what you did to him and I'm sure his mother never knew why she felt weak, nor that she had drunk poison."

He stepped through the door before continuing.

"So, you have been making blood-bane." He pointed with his cane to the smashed vials and the reddish brown flakes.

She said nothing. A third party had slipped in through the door; fear. It was a rare visitor in her house. She wasn't scared for herself, but for Karl and Hans; for all who trusted her. Not the whole town, of course, but some good people.

"How long have you known about me?" she asked.

"From the moment we passed in the street."

"A shared experience then."

"So you're saying you haven't come to this town in search of me?" His surprise seemed genuine.

"No, but now that I'm aware of your presence..."

He stepped towards her. "My presence?"

He knew what he was doing. The words were mocking and his aura made her feel giddy. She hid it as best she could, trying to keep the quiver from her voice. "Oh, you are strong and ancient - perhaps one of the oldest – but not as powerful as you were. Why else would you hide in this place, content with your limited kingdom?"

He gave a nod of acknowledgement. "It is true. As your kind drove us out of the east, as we were hunted, and slain, and driven from our resting places, so we grew ever fewer in number. Eventually our bodies died. For a time some of us settled in the Slavic lands, empowered by their inbred superstition. Still your people insisted on driving us away, not content that many of us were inhabiting the bodies of half-wits in our bid to stay alive." His eyes grew as dark as the memories.

"Alive; hah!" Ilsa barked a laugh. "It is the very fact that you are not alive – an abomination – that caused those of us who encountered you to try to drive your pestilence from the face of the earth - " she paused, " - though I have never knowingly hunted you down, or your kind. We could have co-existed, if that was not dependent on you taking lives."

Suddenly, Meister thrashed his walking cane against the floor and his eyes blazed, causing Ilsa to be grateful for the centuries of blood-bane flowing in her veins. He wouldn't dare – would he?

"Taking lives! I arrived in this pitiful little town carried in a rat! That is what you reduced me to. And yet thanks to you, hundreds of lives were lost by the plague that I spread. But needs must when the devil drives, and I did grow stronger."

"Would you, by chance, have been the dark shape, which they said sometimes haunted this very street?" Her question was rhetorical.

He nodded again and humour twitched at one corner of his mouth. "There were victims aplenty. They would have died eventually. As you know, I cannot drink the blood of the dead or dying. It was not my decision to entomb the healthy here, with their sick relatives. No, that was glorious, noble humanity's handiwork."

"And the witchfinder?"

"He was indeed a perfect vessel; at last somebody I could inhabit without suspicion. A thoroughly nasty piece of work. I thrive best in such circumstances."

"Yes, blood is just the sugar-coating on the snowball for your kind, isn't it? Wherever there is malice or blackness of heart, you can survive well enough."

"Indeed, his dark soul and malevolence were ideal." He nodded. "Besides, like you, I had grown tired of wandering."

"So everything was perfect for your other agenda," snapped Ilsa, "the subjugation of women."

He came closer still. "Ah yes, women."

He was close enough that she could feel his breath on her face; smell it – surprisingly sweet. He reached out a hand and touched her neck, tracing a line down its smooth curve with his fingertips.

"You have remarkable beauty for one so old," he said. "In that, you are as much of a lie as me." She felt herself swaying slightly, tilting her head to one side, exposing her neck further. He leaned in closer still; tilted his own head. Till now she'd not noticed the soft brilliance of his dark green eyes. His lips tickled the fine hairs on her neck as he spoke:

"So tempting. Surely it would be the very way to die."

She closed her eyes, felt him withdraw and stumbled back. When she opened her eyes again it was in expectation of seeing a triumphant leer on his face. Instead he looked distressed and that was when she knew; neither of them had power over the other, yet both did.

His next words confirmed his fear. "I'm surprised you haven't poured blood-bane into the water supply." Then he seemed to recover. "But no; you and I do know better. They - " he made a sweeping gesture with his cane intended for the citizens of Reimersberg, " – haven't earned it yet, have they?"

She said nothing. Now the walking stick pointed at her and its owner grinned in irony.

" Ah ha! Ilsa Wlich is not feeling loved."

"It's not a case of not feeling loved," she retorted, wincing at the slight whine in her voice. "People must earn redemption. The mistrust of these..." She stopped and swept an arm, mimicking the movement of the cane moments before, "...sticks and stones, as they say. But I will not just give them something they have not earned."

Meister turned and paced away, as if deep in thought, but Ilsa knew he had a plan. She took in again the destruction around her and spoke:

"So I am to be burned as a witch."

Meister turned and laughed. "Again we both know, if you truly believed that, you would not be here. It would be difficult to convince the burghers with long memories to allow the stench of burning flesh to fill the town once more. But still; mmm. We both know something must be done. We can't both live here." He tapped the floor with his cane, pretending to consider something, and then looked up at her, watching with the steady eyes of a snake. "I tell you what; we'll let the people decide. Faith against faith." He gestured around the room. "The evidence of your witchery and my power as mayor against...well, against what? A few of your potions and emetics? Let us see what tonight brings."

He backed towards the door, giving a mock bow.

But Ilsa was not of a mind to be mocked, or bow down before evil.

"Tell me, vampire, King Leech of Reimersberg; just how bad a man was Meister before you abandoned the witch-finder's body in favour of him? Was it a move of necessity, of desperation, before they drove you from the town walls with their flames? Or was he already truly corrupt?"

"Oh, I had earmarked him," said Meister. "He showed great potential. But more importantly, with the witch-finder gone he was the most powerful man in the town."

"So really you will have nowhere left to go if the people turn against you; no greater vessel to fly to."

Meister cocked his head. "An interesting thought," - he gave a wolfish grin, "but a dead one, one way or the other, Wlich the witch."

He turned and left, and though she called after him it felt like empty defiance. "We will see who is dead. I have one more weapon; one you have not reckoned with."

She thought of the child inside her. Then she thought of Karl and was afraid – not for herself, but for what she had to do.

****

Karl arrived an hour later.

"Father said you wanted to see me. Does he know I've been..."

"He knows nothing of your visits," she interrupted. "Now listen carefully, Karl. Keep hidden those things I have given you – from everyone; even your father."

Only now did the boy's eyes register the state of the room. "They came here, didn't they?"

"Yes, and I may have to leave for a while, and very soon, although I don't want to."

She saw his eyes fill with tears. *Save those,* she thought, *you may have need of them for yourself later.*

Suddenly she drew him to her and held him. "Listen; we have no time. I fear the worst, Karl, for now I am sure they believe I am a witch."

He held her tight. "I'll protect you. I'll tell them you're not."

She smiled at his innocence, but couldn't play along. "And why would they believe you? I cured you when they could not; showed you things none of them have seen." She looked at the frog. "Unfortunately they have seen something *you* have not."

He leaned back to look at her. "You must escape," he said urgently.

"All in good time," said Ilsa.

"But you just said you had no time."

"I was wrong. There is always time," she said, "nothing but time. What we sometimes lack is hope, and I want to see if there *is* hope; for the people, not for me. I want to hear what they have to say."

"I don't understand."

"You will."

She released him from her embrace and both of them wiped their damp cheeks.

"Anyway," continued Ilsa, gathering herself together, "I wanted to give you this." She crossed to one of her shelves and picked up a book. "I know you're a good scholar, so reading this won't be a problem, except you won't have heard of many things in here."

She handed him the tome and he looked at the cover. *The Travels* by someone with the strange name of *Marco Polo*. The thickened pages looked and smelt old and he could see that it was hand-written.

"What is it about?" he asked.

She smiled. "The travels of Marco Polo." She waited for the impatience to register on his face, and enjoyed her little joke. "More than four hundred years ago he went to places far from here, many of the paths never trodden by men of the west, and saw wonderful things. And then he was sent to prison. While he was there he wrote this – dictated it, actually, to a fellow prisoner. Ignore some of the spelling; the other prisoner almost certainly made some mistakes."

She saw the realisation dawn on Karl's face; in its own way an easily-read book. "But that would mean this is…"

"Let's just say it is a very early edition. Very early. Treat it like the precious thing it is. And take your time. Read it well, whenever you need to. Who knows, perhaps during those two years in prison, telling these stories helped Marco Polo to run free. I hope they will do the same for you during your life."

"But this book must mean so much to you. Why give it to me?"

"Because you also mean a lot to me; and because it is your turn."

"My turn? And Marco Polo doesn't sound very Germanic. How will I be able to read it?"

"You'll learn."

"How did you get this?"

She smiled. "So many questions!"

He smiled back. "So many riddles."

"A woman must have some secrets. Maybe I'll tell you one day." With that she stood. "Now you must go, Karl. It is probably not good to be around me right now."

His eyes were wide and frank – almost too much for her. "You're going, aren't you?"

"I don't know."

"Let me come with you."

"For the sake of your father you must not."

"He would come too; I know he would if you just asked him."

"I'm not so sure, Karl. There are things a man needs that you, as a boy, cannot understand yet."

****

If Mayor Meister did know something, it was the minds of men. Women he had given up on long ago, except as prey, which was why they were barred from that night's gathering; those you expected to be soft were as hard as iron, but where you least expected it in a woman you found weakness. With the men he knew that if only a hundred were selected by each of his council, others would come anyway, for fear of being excluded, and they would not disagree with anything he said; mob rule, it was

50

called. Meister made sure that, despite his dislike of fire, there were plenty of flaming torches to create an atmosphere of brotherhood and theatre, now that the sun had disappeared from an unusually balmy September sky.

When they were all gathered he waited and waited for silence. When it came at last – when the last twitterings had subsided and the stage was his before an expectant audience - he said:

"Good townsmen of Reimersberg, thank you for meeting at such short notice. And I will indeed keep the meeting short. I see more people here than expected." He smiled and raised his eyebrows in mock-despair to his new-found comrades: "What am I to do with you? When there are no orders you wait for them and when there are orders you disobey them. Truly the men of this town are unique." There was a general laugh. "But seeing you all here reminds me that I must be quick, for the sake of your unprotected women and children at home. Who knows what fearful things might befall them."

Unease rippled through the crowd like a breeze through corn.

"We have no guards on our walls," continued the mayor. "Of course, *usually* our town does not need them except to scare away the wolves. But our walls are strong and they should keep us safe from the new danger."

People began to agree, until the meaning of the words sank in.

"What danger?" shouted a few voices.

He ignored them, playing on their fear. "But of course, walls are only safe if the danger remains outside. Here, in Reimersberg, we have not been careful; not been diligent. We have allowed danger to enter and live amongst us."

A cry of enquiry went up from many throats. Some people looked behind them, as if expecting slavering demons to emerge from the darkness of the adjoining streets, which now appeared to have been thrown into deep shadow by the torchlight.

"There is one newly amongst us who could wreak havoc and destruction if we do not act. I speak, of course, of Ilsa Wlich." There was a peculiar rumble in the crowd; sea-currents converging from different directions, causing an ominous swell. "Now I know some of you will say that she does good; that she means no harm. But today, I, and six other good men, have seen evidence of her witchery." There was a communal gasp. "All of these men standing here beside me," - the sweep of his arm took in Baecker as well, who remained silent, clearly intimidated by the situation - "saw devices, which could have no earthly or godly purpose. Yes, in the house that we gave her in the bosom of our town," – there were a few uncomfortable glances as people thought of the Kriegerstrasse, but the next words salved any bad consciences – "near a cauldron brewing some recipe for evil," *knowing nods and grunts from the crowd*

"we saw the devil's light trapped in a sphere of glass,"

gasps and cries of outrage

"and the dead body of a witch's familiar,"

a horrified communal intake of breath followed by outraged jeers

"that came to life at the touch of a satanic wand."

The uproar, which had grown as each item of treachery was listed, was now a fully-formed monster. From the chaos of those voices, a chant took shape, its dark shadow rising with remarkable ease above the crowd, and though it signalled his triumph, even Meister shivered. The same chill passed down the spines of the Elders, and of many in the crowd even as they chanted:

"Burn her! Burn her! Burn her!"

But this was Meister's chance; his moment to seal forever his reputation as a wise and merciful man. He stood with his arms raised, palms downwards, and motioned for silence.

"Of course, my friends, we live in more enlightened times, and I am sure none of us wants our women or children to see a smouldering corpse, albeit that of a witch, in the town square. Some might even say it is not witchcraft; it is science." Cries of *'no'* and *'shame'* rose in unison. "But what evil science would seek to raise the dead?" Clamour. Silence. "Here is my pronouncement, though as we are a community I will ask your final judgement.

"I say that, this night, we should once more wall up death in the Kriegerstrasse; wall up Ilsa Wlich and her devilish instruments in a fitting tomb, and let God and fate judge her."

There were general cries of agreement, but then a worried voice from the crowd shouted: "If she is a witch, surely she can escape and curse us in anger."

There were cries of support for this new concern.

"My friends," said Meister when things had calmed down, "I told you the stones of our town would protect us and so they shall. What we do is right, and God is on our side. Our good priest here, Mr Pfarrer, will sprinkle holy water when the work is done. By the grace of the Lord, good men of Reimersberg, there will be no burning for us to witness this night, just the certainty of God's punishment for this wife of Satan. Indeed, most of you can go back now to your homes, hold and treasure your loved ones, knowing that, if your answer to my next question is good and true, you will have protected them. That question is: do you approve this, my judgement? All those in favour?"

There was a roar of approval.

"All those against?"

Silence followed. Meister looked at each of his fellow Elders, almost daring them to disagree. None did, but at least three of them couldn't hold his gaze

"In that case, I need twenty good men with strong arms to assist the bricklayers. There is work ahead tonight defying this evil; work with good earthly mortar and bricks from the very clay of which we are made. I leave it in the hands of all of you. This has been an onerous duty and I need to rest. Those not detailed to help, go home knowing Reimersberg is safe. And I recommend that you spare your families the details of what happened this night. That burden is ours."

As he headed towards his residence, where he was tended by a single manservant and the occasional whore who fed the various appetites of this body he'd chosen - until he tired of their inbred blood and they went the way of all female flesh – the night air could not cool the heat in Meister's body. Not only was the town safe; more important was that he had made it so. That strengthened further his position as mayor, and the way ahead was clear. He thought the people had long ago ceased to believe in witches, tired and horrified by the burnings, but clearly the flames had left a deeper taint on Reimersberg than just the smell.

It had been important to put this woman in her place, just as the witch-finder had done. This little episode had served as a good reminder, to all the people, about the natural order of things; mayor, then Elders, then townsmen, then townswomen. But most important of all had been to dispel the shadow of blood-bane from his world. He didn't pretend to understand everything the Wlich woman was up to in her darkened house, but it had all served his purpose in the end.

The heat continued to suffuse his entire body as he went on his way and he wondered whether she had indeed put a curse on him, for certain desires had reawakened.

He cursed her and all her gender as the shadow that was his soul continued to rage, and turned his attention instead to the fine piece of steak waiting for him. It was late, but his body was hungry.

****

For Ilsa Wlich it was a night devoid of sleep. First she'd had to prepare for what she was convinced was her imminent departure; there were things she'd had to do. When they were done, she lay listening to the sounds - the scraping of trowels and the thudding of stones - knowing their significance and guessing the sentence that had been passed on her. If she hadn't discovered her escape route, the noise might have driven her mad, which had been the sad fate of other women she had known across the so-called civilised world. She was almost tempted to take a lantern and walk down to have a look at the work in progress. It would have been amusing to see the faces of the people entombing her as she stood like a curious passer-by, watching them. But she decided to provoke no further reaction. And besides, she was sad. There was much to reflect upon; how ironic that she'd been so bewitched by her first sight of this town, yet the happiest moments she'd known had been here, in this damp, abandoned house in a lonely street in the unhappiest part of Reimersberg. The rest, with its quaint beauty, had proved to be a sugar-coating masking something unpleasant.

When it seemed she might fall asleep, other sounds kept her awake as the past came to visit her. She lit a candle for them; the silent screams of a street full sick people. Then those screams became whispers; prayers for the dying and for the living as they found their own peace. Another sound came; hopeful voices. And these faded as if they had passed through the city wall and off into the forest to whatever the future held for them. The sad history of Kriegerstrasse passed by Ilsa's door that night and she would become a part of it when, like those last survivors, she went through the wall. The difference was, she was about to influence the fate of this town in a way its people couldn't possibly imagine.

CHAPTER 6

A strange atmosphere hung over Reimersberg the next morning; it could be felt, but not seen, as if there had been a storm, which had caused no damage. It was market day and stalls were being set up early, but conversations seemed muted; laughter stifled.

Only if someone had ventured into the old, dark part of town would they have noticed anything tangible; a couple of guards posted at the newly bricked-up entrance to the Kriegerstrasse and the filled-in windows of the houses on either side. The labourers had done a fine job, if walling up an innocent woman was something to be admired.

As the sun had not long risen, the town gates weren't yet open. No armed look-outs broke the profile of the battlements. The rains of the previous day were long gone, but the sky was still a pastel shade.

It was a timeless scene.

Then the town was awakened by a voice; familiar, yet almost otherworldly in its power. Filling the void, it came from beyond the walls.

"PEOPLE OF REIMERSBERG HEAR ME!"

The guards at the Kriegerstrasse shuddered and looked behind them, but the sound didn't seem to be coming from there. It was everywhere, fracturing even the dreamless sleep of Mayor Meister.

Reimersberg was a town of early starters, so most of the bewildered people who gathered now in the two main squares were already dressed. Still, one or two, including Meister, stumbled onto the streets with robes covering their nightshirts, though Meister's was the robe of office; nothing, it seemed, ever threw him enough that he forgot his status.

"PEOPLE OF REIMERSBERG HEAR ME!"

The townsfolk looked around as the sound echoed between the buildings. Dr Arzt and Mayor Meister bumped into each other in the clock square.

"It's her, isn't it?" said Arzt

"Nonsense," said Meister, but without conviction. "Her voice cannot carry from the Kriegerstrasse."

"That's not coming from the Kriegerstrasse."

"PEOPLE OF REIMERSBERG HEAR ME!"

The sound sent goosebumps across everyone's skin. And now, perhaps too late, it occurred to the mayor that he might just have made a mistake.

"It's coming from over there," said Arzt pointing towards the main town gates. "You were right," he said, unwittingly rubbing salt into the mayor's wound; "such witchcraft."

"*I* was right? Don't try passing the buck now. You said she was a witch from the start."

"PEOPLE OF REIMERSBERG, I HEAR YOU GATHERING IN THERE. I DEMAND THAT YOUR BRAVE, APPOINTED LEADERS, THE COUNCIL OF ELDERS, SHOW THEMSELVES."

"I'm not showing myself," said Meister, "she's not ordering me around."

"Me neither," said Arzt.

But the decision was taken out of their hands, because a space had opened around them, lined by reproachful faces and wide eyes. With rank went responsibility, not just the chance to claim the best cuts of meat from Metzger's shop. The people paid for their mayor, and now they expected him to deal with this unseen threat. They looked for leadership. What they seemed to have found was a man in slippers, a nightshirt and an ermine-lined robe stealing away in the opposite direction; except his way was barred by the throng. He looked up and thought on his slippered feet.

"Is the voice not coming from this direction?" he asked, pointing the way he'd been heading. There was a general shaking of heads, and fingers pointed back over his shoulders towards the gate. Meister gathered himself together in as dignified a manner as he could and swallowed hard. "In that case, I, the other Elders and subsidiary council members will do our duty, but I suggest we go up to the battlements rather than open the gates to heaven-knows what danger."

With that, the merry band of Meister, Arzt, Droger, Metzger, Baecker and Pfarrer, plus a couple of farmers who'd been trying for some years to gain admittance as Elders and looked none too pleased to be signalled forward now when it suited the mayor, headed towards a set of steps alongside the town gates. They climbed, while most of the rest of the population of Reimersberg pressed forward. Reaching the top, they looked down and got a surprise that fell into the 'unwelcome' category.

Far below them was the figure of a woman; slight, but with a presence that belied her size. Her blazing red hair, falling across her shoulders like a cloak, left no doubt as to her identity.

"How did she escape?" whispered Arzt, his stomach cold and knotting.

"By force of will," she responded; it seemed her hearing was as powerful as her voice. The Elders cast nervous glances at each other, but all eyes then locked onto Meister. It was expected of him that he took the lead.

"We are here to listen," he said, "as you requested." He tried to sound composed, but only succeeded in sounding asthmatic.

"And I am here despite your expectations," said Ilsa. "Indeed, I offer you the unexpected; a chance of redemption."

"And who are you to offer redemption?" said Meister, knowing he had to be seen to stand up to her. There must have been a rational reason for her escape. Had those foolish bricklayers checked she was in her house before they started? This wasn't witchcraft at play here, just trickery.

"I am the person you sought to entomb – and still I offer you forgiveness for your wickedness."

Ordinarily, nothing would have scared him so much as losing face in front of the townsfolk. Yet Meister knew she had the power at this moment. She would unmask him. He had to brazen this out; deny everything she said. If not...

He didn't want to think of the consequences for any of them. He was the cornered spirit of a vampire from the very beginning of time. He would not go without a fight.

There was a murmur from below; for the women in the crowd the revelation about Ilsa's entombment was news. Wives stared at their husbands; mothers at sons. For the old amongst them it brought forth shadows from a dark episode in their history. The collective feet of the menfolk shuffled in discomfort, but the mayor knew he would have to stamp his.

"We require no forgiveness. We found proof of witchcraft in your house. Is that how you repay our hospitality?"

"Oh you have a mighty opinion of yourself and your so-called hospitality. The dead were better hosts. Would any of your other citizens have been asked to dwell in that place; to live alongside such sadness?"

"You are not a citizen of this town, nor will you ever be."

"Now that, my dear mayor, is where you are wrong. A part of me will always be a citizen of Reimersberg."

"That cannot be," said Meister. "For an outsider to be granted citizenship of this town, it has always required a unanimous vote of the Elders or a blood tie, and you have neither, as far as I am aware." He turned and surveyed the crowd. "No; not a single carrot-top out there." There was laughter, some of it mocking; from others it sounded uncomfortable. Meister turned back to Ilsa, his smile and his confidence growing. "That would appear to be that, then."

Ilsa looked up at the smug figure and fought hard to control the hatred growing inside her; the loathing she felt for this cruel being. He stood forward of the other Elders, whose faces were mostly hidden by the crenellations. She couldn't make out Hans's face at all, but was grateful for that, fearing what she might see. At least this way she could cling to hope. "What about a marriage tie?"

She heard the tumult her question caused behind the high walls and firmly-closed oak gates; the amused braying of the men, trying to convince their wives that they had never looked at another woman. But Ilsa had felt the eyes of many of them wandering over her body during her time in the town.

When the hubbub had died down and all was silent, Meister said: "Are you proposing to me, Mistress Wlich?

Now great waves of laughter rose into the air. She watched the mayor preening; he was enjoying his moment of triumph. *Well enjoy it while you can*, she thought. Meister turned back to the crowd, which fell quiet again, out of sight of Ilsa.

"Indeed, are there any takers for this…" he paused for effect, "…once-in-a-lifetime offer?"

There was more laughter, and then a silence so profound one might have heard the petals falling from a rose. It pulled at Ilsa's heart, even though she knew there was no way that Hans Baecker could speak up for her now; not with his wife so recently deceased.

As he turned back to Ilsa, any pretence of humour disappeared from Meister's face, replaced by a contempt that only she could see as he looked down on her isolated figure. "You've tried your best, or worst, Mistress Wlich, but now I suggest you pick up that moth-eaten pack by your feet and disappear; whether by witchcraft or on your legs, I care not. If you do not, I shall turn out the City Guard to hunt you down." He put his hands on the stones of the battlements and leaned forward. "And then there will be no mercy." Even at this distance his eyes danced with a preternatural blaze.

Again Ilsa wondered at the strength of that ancient spirit; most vampires struggled to imbue the bodies they occupied with any sense of the remarkable during the daylight hours. But she didn't move. "Well, if you will not show mercy to me, show it to the child I carry." She avoided looking at Hans Baecker as she made this revelation.

"She is with child!" said Droger. Behind him, there was an intake of breath from hundreds of mouths.

"The spawn of the devil," said Pfarrer.

"No," said Ilsa, "the child of one of your citizens."

"You expect me to believe this?" asked Meister rhetorically, though she could see he was shaken.

"But if it's true," said Droger, "we cannot banish her."

"*If* it's true," countered Meister. "On the other hand, the father of this child should perhaps be banished too, for consorting with this wife of Satan. But let us put this to the test." He turned once more towards the gathered crowd, which had fallen into an appropriately pregnant silence. "Is there any man here who wishes to claim paternity?"

Silence; and still silence.

Now Ilsa tried to catch Hans Baecker's reaction. Partly her heart went out to him. He was in an impossible situation; facing banishment from the town of his birth, the only place he'd ever known. He would be aware that the mayor's sly eyes were on him. But another part of her heart grew angry as Hans held his awful – and cowardly – silence. She so wanted him to be brave; knew she was more than able to take him out into the wider world, care for him, love him, help him to become the man he could be; care also for his fine boy Karl; be a mother and a wife; stop her wandering; if only he showed that he was prepared to make a stand. After all, she was a woman; a strong one, but still one who might need a good man. Still, she recognised the mayor's cunning. He allowed the silence to drag on, as if to emphasise the void where words might have been. At last he turned to her and said:

"I think you have your answer, and know your fate."

Now Ilsa spoke again, her voice still full of power despite her sorrow: "Is there no man or woman in there who will take pity on a homeless mother-to-be who has done no wrong; indeed has always sought to help?"

There was some murmuring, mainly, it seemed, in the pitch of female voices, but this died down to nothing again. Meister looked down at her with utter disdain and took an almighty chance as he said:

"Be gone now, Ilsa Wlich, and take the bastard inside with you."

And then something happened.

Ilsa stared with her piercing green eyes into the dark soul of Meister and beyond. When she spoke, her voice carried effortlessly to the furthest reaches of the town.

"Reimersberg, you have become a place of black hearts and blacker souls. You have lost your way; sheep misled by a wicked shepherd, till you are unwilling even to grant a home to one of your own; an innocent as yet unborn." Her words came over the battlements like stones raining down on the townsfolk. They would learn soon enough that stones might have been preferable. "You have refused to take this last chance to shake off the parasite clinging to your walls," here she pointed a strong, accusing hand at Meister, even though the people couldn't see her, "and your failure to show mercy was your last chance to receive it." Meister opened his mouth to speak, but now Ilsa threw open her arms and suddenly a wind sprang up. Her hair danced in it like fire. By a peculiar trick of the air currents, her coat barely moved, as if it was the calmness at the heart of the tempest, so that she resembled nothing so much as a flaming cross. The trees on the edge of the surrounding forest started to sway in the growing storm. Ilsa spoke again, her voice filling everyone with dread. "When I arrived I thought this town had been touched by heaven, but beauty is truly only skin deep and before me I see a grim hell, doomed by false pride. Well then, like hell let it be yours forever."

The winds grew stronger still and the whole forest swirled in a dance of tattered robes. The Elders pulled back in terror, except for the mayor, who seemed unable to move, held transfixed by green eyes in which destiny gathered force. The crowd in the main square appeared to shrink as the people pulled together, clinging to one another as the dreadful words came– all the worse for flying disembodied over the walls.

Ilsa's outspread arms seemed to encircle the town as she spoke: "Hear my judgement, cursed town. As Reimersberg is now, so shall it always be. Neither progress nor change will be yours. The world now within your walls will be trapped there forever, while the one beyond them will move on. Should any person seek to leave, the guardian powers of nature that I harness here will not allow it – for two worlds will be colliding – and you will be walking to your doom. You will learn during your long, endless crawl through time – slower than a snail or a worm – what it is to be excluded from the universe. When sickness takes you, how you will cry for the medicines that science could bring you. When the darkness comes, how you will seek the light. When those passing through with fresh knowledge exit the gates of your crumbling town, how you will long to go with them. When travellers drawn to the fabled beauty of your home stare in dismay at its dismal streets, how you will hate the look in their eye, though not as much as you will hate yourselves. When one of you dies at the hands of your hapless doctor, how you will envy that escape from the eternal, ageless lives to which you are here condemned.

"May the storm end and the curse begin."

Now Ilsa's arms fell limp by her sides, her head slumped forward as if her strength was spent, and as it did so, the wind, which had started to swoop and rage, stopped with a suddenness that might have signalled the end of the world.

All was silence.

If it had felt earlier that morning as if a storm had passed leaving no visible damage, that was a literal truth now, and the same sense of latency and change was in the air. People who had closed their eyes and held each other while the winds howled opened them again and looked around them. The stillness was unnatural.

Up on the battlements, the council members had been grovelling on the floor for fear of being swept away. Now they rose and, as one, looked at the mayor. He stood exactly as he had when they'd last seen him, his hands clutching the stonework and his eyes staring straight down over the edge, wide open in a face paler than a cold moon.

Then the voice of a child could be heard from the back of the main square below.

****

Karl had read into the night, till his eyes felt full of sand from the deserts his mind had wandered. Though he didn't understand every single word, he'd been held enthralled by the stories of Marco Polo and the descriptions of distant places so different from his home. As he'd looked at the book and flicked backwards and forwards between the pages, new delights and wonders had flitted before his eyes like exotic birds. Not stopping to question why he could read the language in which this ancient book had been written, he was just grateful he could share in the fascinating world it described. He knew that Reimersberg was on something called the Adventurer's Road and had always looked forward to the day when he might travel it, but here was something called the Silk Road that seemed altogether more exciting, infinitely longer, more dangerous perhaps. There and then he had promised himself that he would one day risk the perils in pursuit of adventure. Also something told him that Ilsa had travelled that road. She'd spoken of the East as if it was a place where someone could find whatever there was to know. Perhaps she would return there and take him with her. Indeed, she'd written a message for Karl on the inside cover of the book that suggested it was her plan: *'Karl, may the end of this Road be the beginning of your journey.'*

It was while he was reading about a place called Kamul, where all visitors were given a warm welcome, that he'd fallen asleep. The last time he'd looked at his candle clock it was about two in the morning. He'd dreamed that he was far in the East, in a market in one of the magical cities along the Silk Road. There were strange people with sallow complexions and a peculiar slant to their eyes. The market was full of colourful stalls containing fabrics of every shade and hue, food that looked unlike anything he would ever consider eating, some of it still moving. The size of the market made the one in Reimersberg look like a tinker's cart. There was noise and bustle, and the cries of the vendors filled the air. But the cries turned to warnings and the stall-holders started to cling to their canopies in the brunt of a strong wind that sprang up all of a sudden; a wind that grew ever stormier, till at last it woke Karl from his sleep.

The candle clock had burned out and daylight filtered through the shutters – as did something else. The cries and the wind hadn't stopped.

Suddenly Karl knew something was horribly wrong, and a word sprang to his lips: "Ilsa".

He jumped from his bed, sending Marco Polo's book, which had lain open on his chest, tumbling to the floor. Running out into the street he heard a confusion of noises from the main square and headed there.

A voice, both familiar yet unlike the one he knew and loved, could be heard above the storm.

"Ilsa! Ilsa!" he called, but the wind snatched his breath away greedily and threw it in pieces behind him.

Her words filled him with horror, but as they stopped so did the terrible wind; instantly. All was quiet.

Despite the circumstances, hearing her voice had, in its own way, filled him with joy, but now he was terrified of never hearing it again, and he called till he thought his chest would burst "Ilsa, don't leave me! Don't let them drive you away!"

Ahead of him a field of faces turned and he started to push his way through the people, while they parted like corn before him. All the time, he repeated his plea, till finally he reached the massive barrier of the gates of Reimersberg, towering above his insignificant figure. Strong youth he might have been, but he was unable to move them; the huge bolts that required the strength of two men didn't budge. Karl slapped his feeble hands against the wood in frustration.

"Let her in again! Let her in!"

****

The spell had exhausted her and she stood almost unconscious, but then the voice that she both loved and dreaded hearing reached her ears, making her burn with frustration that only some thick pieces of wood stood between them. But it was too late. She was not some witch who could wave a wand and lift the curse. She'd invoked both earthly and universal forces to cast the spell and it was not within her powers to lift it again so easily, if at all. A chill of dismay passed through her, but she had tried – how she'd tried – to avoid this.

Did you Ilsa? Could you not simply have walked away?

"Ilsa, take me with you!"

"For your father's sake I would not. I wouldn't part you from each other and leave him alone in this world."

"Then take us both. Why don't you take us both?"

"It's too late. I cannot undo what has been done."

"I don't understand." She could hear his heart breaking and her own was tearing.

She thought of Hans's silence again and knew that it had destroyed something, which could never have been made whole again. But she had another concern. That the townsfolk would now believe her to be a witch was beyond doubt; she didn't want them to damn Karl as well, for having befriended her. She would have to choose her next words carefully; show kindness through cruelty and hope that he picked up her message of love.

"What is there to understand, boy?" she said, hating herself for the harshness of the last word. "Around my heart is a wall of stone. Only those who can walk through stone walls could ever touch it."

There was silence. Ilsa hoped that into the dark despair of that young heart beyond the gate a little ray of light now shone. She continued, her voice carrying once again to all the citizens. To those who knew no better, which was all bar the powerful few, she had to offer some hope, even though it hung by the slenderest of threads:

"Hear me all of you. The laws that govern my universe are not lightly broken, and do not allow me to leave you without some chance of redemption. And because you did not try to burn me for a witch, I grant you some mercy. Listen well; *the stranger who is no stranger stays, and at the ending of the days, with a broken verse might lift this curse and drive the darkness away.*"

Without further ado she picked up her pack, and as she hoisted it onto her shoulders glanced up at the battlements. The mayor stood in the same pose as before, uglier in her eyes than a gargoyle. Indeed, she wished she could turn him to stone, but her soul was white. Perhaps such tricks lay within the powers of others who travelled the darker regions of the earth, but not within hers. So she had done the next best thing. He would find out, trapped here till such time as her curse lifted or a wise head forced Fate's hand. Her hope was that such a head would have wisdom enough to deal with this monster.

She hadn't been looking for *him*. She glanced to the left and saw the face of Hans Baecker staring out between the crenellations. She saw him put his hands together as if in prayer, but knew that it was a gesture combining apology and thanks. She raised a hand in acknowledgement, but under her breath, this time heard by no-one but herself, said: "No, it is I who am sorry." Then to the boy she added: "Look after your father, Karl."

The boy's reply might have been the word "No". It wasn't meant as a refusal to do what she'd asked, more a refusal to believe that the world could be so cruel. Whatever the word, it issued from Karl as a long, keening cry of pain.

Ilsa turned and headed towards the forest. The Elders watched her go as she disappeared into the darkness at the edge of the trees.

"I thought you said the stones would protect us," shouted a voice from below, and hundreds of others supported the sentiment.

"Mayor Meister," said Droger, "the people of the town need you."

"Mmm…what?" It was as if he'd been slapped out of a dream.

"I said you need to turn to the people; reassure them."

The mayor's fingers seemed to have become as one with the stone, and while Meister struggled to loosen his grip the hubbub below got through to him.

"What are they saying?" he asked.

"That you promised the stones of Reimersberg would protect them."

Meister was clearly shaken, but as a politician of many years and a hunter of immeasurable time, he was used to twisting and turning; to gathering his wits as quickly as a housewife might snatch in her washing from out of the rain.

"And so they shall," he said. "Look at us; the witch has gone; none of us is harmed. Nothing has changed."

"Umm, that won't really do it," said Droger. "After all, that was the whole point of her curse. The people will need proof."

"Yes." The mayor chewed his lip. "You may be right." He turned to the people below. "Open the gates."

Hans Baecker had been in a state of shocked dismay till then, but the sound of the massive bolts on the town gates sliding back helped him regain his senses, and he cried out: "Don't let my boy go out!" while he raced down the steps. But a lot of people were in the same stupor and didn't react, so Hans reached the gates just in time to grab Karl by his collar and stop him from racing through the widening gap. Once he had him, he hesitated, staring at the forest, and to many it seemed as if he wished the two of them could have run out together.

Meanwhile, up on the battlements, Meister was recovering fast, even though his mind was still struggling to come to terms with his mistakes. He'd been wrong. Ilsa Wlich had indeed been a witch, or at least possessed of some eldritch powers. And he was not the fool who was going to rush in, to satisfy the townsfolk's need for a scapegoat. What he *could* do was satisfy their need for action. If the worst came to the worst, he'd show them he was right to banish her. And if her curse proved to be nothing but empty words, well then everyone would be very relieved, he was sure. But Droger was right – they needed him to do something.

He took Andreas Hof to one side - one of the two farmers who hoped to become Elders - and said in a soft voice: "Hey, Andreas, how foolish are these people? All this superstition and hocus-pocus."

Andreas frowned. "I thought you said she was a witch."

"I banished her because the Council forced me to. I had to put on a show for them. They saw things in the woman's house they didn't understand. But here's the chance to show them that you are more worthy than them to be an Elder." He put an arm around the burly farmer's shoulder. "To show everyone here that you are courageous enough to be – who knows – the next mayor?"

Andreas couldn't help the surge of pride he felt, nor pass up this chance to step ahead of the other Elders and, more importantly, ahead of Michael Bauer, the other farmer and would-be Elder. Gone soon might be the days of him and his family having to drive their herd of temperamental cows out into the surrounding pasture every morning. Although he wasn't the brightest man, he possessed enough cunning to see that Meister hadn't handled the situation very well; that people might be calling for him to resign; looking for a bold man to lead them. Who better than the man who had the courage to step out and disprove all the fears? From would-be Elder to mayor in a few easy paces.

All of them made their way down to the gate and before Andreas even realised that he had agreed, the mayor had turned to the expectant crowd and spoken:

"Our fine citizen here, Andreas," he slapped the farmer on the back, "wants to demonstrate that life in Reimersberg can go on as usual." Meister turned and gestured towards the open gates, beyond which stood the bare patch of land that led to the forest. Only he could see the light sweat, which had broken out on the farmer's top lip, and that Hof was hesitating. He stepped forward and, putting an arm on Hof's shoulder again, turned him gently, leading him towards the gate and whispering so that only the farmer heard him. "Believe me, there is nothing to fear. And the sooner this is done the sooner we can all continue our lives; some of us in a better position than others, hey?" He winked.

Hof was suddenly not feeling all that brave any more, faced by the outside world and the brooding forest where possibly the Wlich woman still lurked. "But what if...I mean...we walled her up. And...and then there's the storm."

"Really, Mr Hof." The use of the less familiar surname brought the farmer up with a jolt as he realised he might be losing his precious finger-holds on his ambitions. "I'm surprised that a down-to-earth man like you would believe that woman had such powers. I told you these stones would protect us. Do you really think she could curse a whole town? And if we are cursed, what do you hope to gain by just waiting around? What use would a farmer be, who cannot take his herd outside the walls?" Behind them the crowd was getting restless. "On with you, man, and I will be as good as my word." Then he clapped the farmer on his broad back and said out loud for the benefit of the townsfolk: "As you wish." It was a strange remark that many heard but few understood.

With that, Andreas Hof, almost despite himself, stepped through the gates. Everyone saw him leave, with his distinctive red cap standing out against the backdrop of the forest, but no-one really saw him go. To the accompaniment of a thousand gasps, he had disappeared.

****

Andreas Hof felt his legs shaking as he took his bold steps towards immortality. He walked a few paces to make sure that he was clear of the thick walls, all the time looking at his hands and his feet. Nothing changed. They didn't start to wizen up, or disappear, or turn hairy. He was alright! Joy of joys, there was no curse. Ahead of him a light breeze whispered through the trees. Strange that it didn't touch his face and cool the sweat on his brow, but that didn't yet fully register. With a broad grin he turned to tell the people of the town - of which he, one day, might be mayor - that there was nothing to fear.

Except the town had gone; vanished. And in one of those moments when a thousand things become clear without the questions ever having been asked, he knew that he was doomed, but didn't understand why.

Andreas let out a horrible cry of fear. Though they couldn't see him, the people of the town heard it; just the one cry, not the others that followed as the big farmer wandered into the forest; a wandering that would last forever.

****

Back within the walls of Reimersberg, loved ones were holding each other for comfort. Mistress Hof, Andreas' wife, fainted and was immediately surrounded by concerned family and friends. Karl Baecker moved a little closer to Hans. The boy had been surrendering to the anger he felt towards his father for preventing him from running after Ilsa, but now he saw the reason and looked up at him.

"Why did she do this to us, father?"

"I'm not exactly sure what she *has* done, but if it was done in vengeance I understand why, and I will explain to you; just not here."

In other parts of the crowd the mood had turned ugly, particularly near the mayor.

"You said our walls would protect us," – fingers pointed – "poor Andreas...doomed...witch...should have burned her..." The snatches of accusation came thick and fast. Meister had to resist the urge to back away as the people advanced on him. He gathered his wits and raised his hands as if to calm the mob.

"But I was right that she was a witch. How I wish I was wrong. Andreas didn't believe the curse. Actually I was trying to convince him not to go out." He knew the crowd had not heard what he was saying to the farmer.

"But you angered her," shouted someone. "She hadn't done any wrong till then."

"Yes," said another, "but having angered her you tried to be merciful. There's only ever been one way to deal with a witch."

"But who knows what she was planning," said Meister. He looked towards Pfarrer for support, but the gaunt priest simply returned his panicked stare, self-preservation uppermost in his mind. "The priest will tell you, she was doing ungodly things;" he pointed to the heavens, "breaking His laws. A dead creature moved in her house."

Another angry man jabbed a finger at him. "Well you'd better go and find out how that trick works, because you might be needing it soon. We all might. And whatever she was planning, it can't have been worse than cursing all of us."

Meister wanted to swat the impertinent man like a fly, but realised he wasn't at his strongest. Instead he threw a pleading glance at Arzt and the doctor seemed to realise that there was safety in numbers, even if the number was only two. The mood was worsening, and if the people were of a mind to make someone pay, they might not stop at just one member of the Council. He stepped forward.

"Citizens of Reimersberg, what good will this do us? Our mayor tried to do what he thought was best for us and he may still have done so. We need to keep calm and think this through. Although we may have angered the witch, she was no white innocent, and has shown her capacity for evil and vengeance. Perhaps her curse will feed off our fear and if we defy it, maybe it will lose its power." Desperation had made him eloquent and he grasped the nettle. "Attacking our mayor is not the answer; he tried to show leadership when you needed it and we need it now more than ever. And look also to yourselves, for she claims to have fallen pregnant by a man of this town. All you men denied it. So that means either one of you is a liar and a fornicator, or she was carrying the spawn of the devil. Eh, priest?"

Taking confidence from a slight change of mood in the crowd, Pfarrer spoke up:

"Yes, we could not allow her to stay. And as our good mayor said, she was breaking God's laws. Let us wait and see; I'm sure this curse will lose its strength the further away from us she is."

There were a few sounds of agreement and the mayor took courage. "We have our beautiful town; we have each other. Not a bad place to be while we wait on our fates." Now Meister saw Hans Baecker and his son and remembered. "And we have other hope besides. She told us that one will come who will lift the curse. Boy, do you remember her words?"

Karl turned to the mayor and the hatred in the boy's eyes shocked Meister for a moment. When the time was right, on a dark night, he would deal with this insolent lad; finish what he started.

"They're written on my heart," said Karl.

His insolent stare tried the mayor's patience. "Well then, write them on paper, lest you forget them. We, the Elders, will sit together and work out exactly what they mean." He turned to the crowd, which he seemed to have pacified for the moment. "And the rest of you should continue, like any other day."

"Except, of course, it would be sensible to remain within the walls," shouted a man.

Okay, pacified, but not yet won over, thought Meister.

"What about the sheep," asked Michael Bauer. "Won't the flock need to graze – and the cows?" Bauer forced down a smile. He owned the sheep, but knew he would soon own the cows too, since a widow and child could not hope to run that herd.

Meister thought quickly; he wasn't mayor for nothing. "Let us hope – if that is the correct word - that she has cursed *us*, the people of Reimersberg, and not our livestock. How much rope do we have in the town?

Mr Seil, the rope-maker, spoke up. "Enough to kit out several ships. We have not yet sent our tithes to the King."

Back then, the people were expected to give a tenth of their income, or produce, to support the Church. As head of the Church, the King of the Bohemian Palatinate, to which Reimersberg belonged, had decided he would accept this income graciously on behalf of the Church, much to the annoyance of Pfarrer, who would have enjoyed a much wealthier lifestyle if it had all come to him. That frustration was part of the reason for the down-turned creases at the corners of his pinched mouth as he wandered amongst the human flock in his increasingly threadbare cassock. People feared his dark, stalking figure; indeed behind his back he was called the Priest of Darkness.

Meister addressed the crowd. "Tithes. Hah! I think our need is greater than the King's. And let's be honest; if he wants his tithes he'll have to come and get them himself."

It was a calculated risk, joking about the fact that they could not leave their walled town, but it worked, because one or two people laughed at the expense of the King. Meister felt he was a bit safer for the moment.

****

The beast wandered alone through the gates, a rope attached around its neck. When it didn't disappear, a huge cheer went up from the people of Reimersberg, to which the cow responded with a look over its shoulder and a blank gaze from a face that knew nothing much: certainly not the importance of its refusal to vanish.

"Bring it back," said the mayor. "How many cows are there in the herd, Mistress Hof, if you will forgive me for asking such a mundane question at this difficult time for you?" Meister was ever the vote-catcher, even under stress.

"One hundred and five," she said, still dabbing at her eyes and in shock. "Too many to tend. Oh what shall I do?"

A certain Michael Bauer had the answer, which he was holding back for a more appropriate moment.

"Saddle-makers of this town," said Meister, his authority growing by the minute, "I order you to make one hundred and five leather collars. We will loop the rope through them and let the herd out to wander. Rope enough we have. Mister Bauer, your flock can just wander out. I know how well trained your dogs are - they respond to you like puppets on strings – and they will drive the sheep back in each night. Our livestock will continue to graze. We will survive."

With this triumph achieved, the townsfolk went about their business. Only one or two looked longingly at the world beyond the gates – for the time being. That included Meister, who for a fleeting moment had wondered whether his essence would survive inside a cow. It was not an existence he could have borne for long, and of course the temptation would have been to cross over to the first stranger who wandered near. That would have been the test; as his spirit moved, would it survive the curse? He wasn't ready to find out yet.

****

"Why did you not speak up for her, father, after what she did for you and me?"

Hans Baecker put down his soup spoon; the broth tasted like wormwood and so did his words. "I was scared."

"She saved my life. Why should you be scared to speak on her behalf?"

"There were other reasons."

"What were they, father?"

"Always questions with you it is," said Hans impatiently.

"What do you expect?"

Hans gave a faint nod of acknowledgement. He thought long and hard about saying nothing, but all they had was each other, so it was best to start this new phase of their lives together with the truth. After all, they might have a long, long time ahead, so it would be best to be friends. "Let's just say that I was a coward and that only in recent times have I learnt the true nature of some of the people in the town of my birth." The boy continued to look at him, but said nothing. "People who would have cast me out if they'd believed that I…that I was the father of a witch's child."

Karl's eyes widened and his soup spoon, which had been hovering above the bowl for some time was lowered very gently to the table. But there was recognition in those wide eyes. "Your evening walks; the visits to the Kriegerstrasse." Hans was astonished. He boy was only…wait a minute; he was *sixteen!* How had the years crept up? He tried to look confused and in denial, but his son gave him an old-fashioned look quite out of place on his fresh features. "Oh father, I have seen the cows and the bulls in the fields. I don't think children are found under bushes." He reached across the table and put his hand on his father's. The gesture sent tears rolling down Hans Baecker's cheeks. "Were you lonely, father, after mother died?"

Hans could only nod, but after they had sat in silence for perhaps a minute his voice returned. "I still am. And Ilsa was lonely too…just lonely. I think I only helped for a while. Till she found you."

They sat and finished their soup like two men together.

CHAPTER 7

Atinker came to town a few days later; the first visitor since the curse; a reminder that the world outside did indeed move on with no knowledge of Reimersberg's plight. Kesselflicker – no-one knew whether that was his first, last, or even his real name – was a regular visitor, travelling up and down the Hexental over the course of a few months, selling his wares from each town to the buyers in the others. As he drove his horse and covered wagon through the gates he called to a man who leaned against a nearby wall smoking a clay pipe

"Hey, Marcus, what's the meaning of the ropes on the livestock? Found yourselves some new pets?"

Marcus laughed. He held a piece of meat on some bread in his other hand and he waved it in the direction of the tinker.

"As long as they still turn into one of these at the end of the day, I don't care." Marcus hadn't left the town since the day he was born; neither had his parents, nor his grandparents. The fact that one of his eyes moved in a different direction to the other as he spoke bore testimony to that. He almost welcomed the curse, as he needed no excuse to stay exactly where he was now, and there were a few like him. This narrow-mindedness was part of the reason he hadn't considered yet how many cows would be needed to keep him in beef for eternity.

Knowing it was the best answer he would get for the moment, the tinker rode on into the main square, stopped in his usual place and took the cover off his cart, which he had turned into a type of mobile stall, with shelves, hooks and drawers, filled with pots, pans, knives, pieces of cloth, cheap jewellery and all manner of items with varying degrees of usefulness.

Today he was particularly excited, having come by a collection of musical boxes, decorated with exquisite carved scenes of beautiful towns of the region, including Reimersberg itself. He doubted many of the townsfolk, if any, had seen or heard of a musical box; as it hadn't been invented here. The people of the region were not known for travelling far beyond the place of their birth. Indeed the tinker himself was viewed with that mixture of fascination and caution reserved for the exotic or wild, with his battered hat, his pony-tail and his bright waistcoat. Children approached his mysterious wagon as they would a dark cave in which twinkling lights shone. There was always the delicious anxiety; the chance that it might swallow them up, taking them from everything they knew to a world of horrible wonders, where they might end up as wooden puppets.

The Half-Torn Page

The tinker felt something in the air today. The town seemed different, even allowing for the time that had passed since his last visit. It had started with the sight of an entire herd of cows tethered by a rope to the battlements. Yet it was in the people and their reaction with the space around them that his Romany blood sensed it. They were both friendly and suspicious as usual, but if he'd had to put his old, gnarled gypsy finger on it, he'd have called the feeling *desperation*. It was even there in the way they examined the pots and pans, handling them with deference, as if they were works of art.

Then his eyes narrowed. Perhaps there was a plot to put him off his guard while others stole his goods.

"Hey, Kesselflicker" - one of them was holding up one of the musical boxes - "what's this?"

Ah, his first chance for a sale, and he had a larger audience than usual. He came over and took the box from the man.

"I'll show you." He turned the key five or six times, not all the way; he didn't want to overload the spring. Then he opened the lid.

Nothing.

"Not very practical, having to have to turn a key so many times just to open a little box," said the man, unimpressed.

"No, no, it's…wait a minute." Kesselflicker picked up another one. He turned the key all the way till it stopped. Perhaps it needed to be wound fully. He opened the lid, to be greeted again by silence. Damn! He tried another, then another, but always with the same result.

"Well they're very pretty," said a woman, taking pity on him, "but I don't want a box where I have to turn the key so many times to get at my trinkets."

He carried on winding and opening mute boxes, and said with frustration, but also contempt for these people who didn't seem to understand: "They're supposed to play music."

"Of course they are," said another voice. "Boxes are known for playing music." A few people laughed.

He turned on the man. "That's why they're called musical boxes."

"Well the musicians must be having a beer at the moment."

The laughter grew, as did Kesselflicker's anger.

"You tinkers," said somebody, "always trying to charge us too much for nothing."

Kesselflicker looked around at the fifty or so grinning faces. "Bah, you people!" With that he dropped the canopy over his wagon, mounted up and whistled to the horses, flicking the reins so that the beasts turned and headed back towards the town gate.

His real annoyance was with himself for having allowed the merchant to sell him these dud goods. He'd been outdone by his own trick; bringing the second rate goods from the back of the stall. That must have been it.

Behind him the laughter grew. Even Marcus stopped chomping on his food and stood grinning - though he didn't appear to understand why - as the tinker drove on past.

And then; the strangest thing. As Kesselflicker passed through the town gate, a sound started in the back of the wagon; delicate notes of a piece of music from a faraway land; the same song playing in simultaneous disarray from fifteen musical boxes. Kesselflicker realised he'd ridden away in anger without bothering to close them. He stopped, turned around, and noticed that the mocking laughter in the market place had ceased as abruptly as the music had started. Now it was his turn. At first, in his determination to have his moment, the mystery of it passed him by.

"See...see...eh?" He nodded triumphantly, leapt down, went round to the cart and reached in to pull out one of the boxes, which he held up for the townsfolk to see. "Who's laughing now?"

Well clearly it wasn't them, but again their reaction was strange. So they'd been proved wrong; there was no reason for such desolate faces. He felt almost sorry for them. Perhaps there was a sale to be had here after all. The delicate song was sure to cheer them up. He wandered back into town, holding the box out to show them, since it appeared they weren't going to come to him. But as he came back through the gates the music stopped again. It must have played through; that was it. He closed it, wound it again, but opened the lid to the sound of silence once more. As he wandered back to the cart to get another box, the one in his hand started to play, so he turned again, till he began to resemble one of the figures from the town clock. It was too much for Kesselflicker, who stood in confusion, which turned to dread as he realised, suddenly, that his earlier unease had been justified; something was wrong with this town. It was time to be away from there, and he didn't think he'd be coming back. He looked at the people; as they stared back at him, he thought he'd never seen such an unhappy group. It sent shivers down his spine. He said the first thing that came to mind: "This is a cursed place."

"We know," said a solitary, sad voice. "We'd almost managed to forget...till today."

Kesselflicker rode away. His tale, told in other towns and taken to be a tall story from a tinker, nevertheless added to the legend of the Valley of the Witches.

****

Meister leaned back in his chair and puffed out his cheeks

"Are you sure of this?" he asked.

"Yes," said Metzger, the butcher, "there are plenty of witnesses."

Meister prodded the piece of paper on the table with his finger. "In that case all the more reason to try to solve this riddle." He looked at Metzger again. "What were these…things?"

"He called them musical boxes."

"And this wasn't just some trick by the tinker."

"Why would he try to trick us into believing they didn't work if he wanted to sell them to us?" said Droger.

"If he was sent by *her* to make us believe the curse was true." The mayor paused. "But I think not, on reflection."

Meister picked up his beer and took a long draught. His quick thinking with the grazing cattle had helped him to regain a lot of his standing with the people, but now this apparent proof of the power of the witch's curse had caused the mood in the town to blacken again. It wasn't a calamity, of course, for most of them, having to live in the place you loved best in the world, but he didn't dare think of what it might mean if that was your lot for eternity. He certainly still had ambitions – needs - beyond the walls, but for the moment holding onto his standing in the community was the most important thing. He turned to Baecker. "Your boy is sure these were the words?"

"They were addressed to everybody, not just to him," said Hans defensively, "but I'm confident. He tended to hang on her every word."

"A good thing for you then, that we're rid of her. Now let's look at this." He read: *"A stranger who is no stranger."* I might have known her words would seek to deceive us while she pretends to help."

"That is, I believe, customary in a riddle." Droger's sarcasm was unmistakable.

Meister ignored him. "What can it mean?"

They sat there scratching chins and heads, and then Droger said:

"Perhaps it means someone like Kesselflicker, the tinker; someone we all know, so he's not a stranger, but doesn't come from this town, so he is."

Meister pointed towards him with an approving gesture. "When you're not being smart, you can be quite clever." Droger raised his eyebrows, but said nothing. "Good thinking."

"Yes, Kesselflicker," continued Droger in that dry tone of his, "the man we drove from our town today with our mocking laughter." The others looked at their hands or at the weathered surface of the Stammtisch. "I think we may have to review our attitude towards strangers if we want the next word to come true."

"Mmm, yes, yes," said Meister thoughtfully, "so, on to that next word; *stays and at the ending of the days.*" Well, that seems fairly clear, doesn't it? Whoever this stranger is, he stays here forever."

"Perhaps," said Michael Bauer, daring to speak up at last in his first meeting of the Elders, "but the wording is a bit odd; *the ending of the days.*" It's rather clumsy, as if it has added meaning."

"An attempt by the witch to sound ominous and significant?" suggested Meister rather weakly.

"I think she achieved that by putting an entire town under a curse," said Droger. "No, I agree with Michael. There might be some other significance here, perhaps suggesting a particular date. Otherwise I'd have expected *until the end of his days*." He shrugged. "But one thing's pretty clear; that would rule out somebody like Kesselflicker. He's never going to stay longer than the time it takes him to make a sale."

"Nor is anyone, unless we behave differently," said Metzger.

"Meaning?" asked Meister rather aggressively.

"Well, let's face it," interjected Droger, "we've always welcomed people into Reimersberg with a great sense of pride, as if they should be grateful to be here, rather than the other way round. We're happy enough to take their money, but if this riddle does mean that the person must stay for some length of time, we must do more than that; we must welcome him."

"Or her." They'd almost forgotten that Hans Baecker was there. He'd sat as if lost in his own thoughts till this point, and even this comment seemed addressed to the table-top rather than the Elders.

"Hans," said Meister, who was sitting next to him, "we understand your feelings because she helped your boy, but look what she has done to our town. She was a witch and now we're all paying the price for allowing her to stay."

Hans looked up, gazed around the table at each member in turn as he spoke: "She didn't do this to us; we did it to ourselves; brought it on ourselves. We were all so proud of our town and our traditions. The world out there seemed of less importance. Well we're reaping what we've sown. And don't forget, she has doomed us to stay *exactly as we are.* Let's see how in love we are with our own little world – with our own little selves – when a few hundred years have passed."

Meister picked up the piece of paper and waved it. "Yes, well thank you for reminding us of the blindingly obvious." *What did they know of eternity?* "Why do you think we are trying to solve this?" He sensed the chill that Baecker's words had cast over the others. "One thing's for certain; if we want people to stay here, we have to make sure it stays looking like that beautiful town our friend Hans here now seems to despise."

The others murmured their agreement and Baecker seemed to withdraw into himself again. Meister continued, after allowing himself a moment to enjoy his triumph over the baker.

"Now, this next line makes no sense at all. *"With a broken verse might lift the curse."* He shrugged, looked around and was met with blank faces. "Any ideas? Dr Arzt, you've said nothing; most unlike you."

"I'm sorry," said Arzt, "I've just been thinking."

Indeed he had, for he, out of all the Elders, had been worst hit by the curse; once he'd thought about it, he'd been shaken him to the core, especially as he alone had been mentioned in person, if not by name then by profession. The fact was – though he would never admit it to the others - during her stay in the town Ilsa Wlich had, indeed, cured many ailments that were beyond his powers to heal, but he'd refused to admit it and had hidden behind his complaints that the patients should have come to him. Now that cushion was no longer there. He'd made secret notes of the plants and herbs she used when the patients mentioned them, but now he would have to rely on people passing through the town to collect them for him. Even then, he couldn't be sure what to do with them.

But worst of all was his own vision of hell. If some sort of epidemic struck the town they would all look to him and there would be no escape, for them or for him. And if the graveyard overflowed, what would they do with the bodies? Ilsa might have doomed them never to change, but she hadn't said they wouldn't get sick. In fact she'd rather suggested they would. He'd had a dream a couple of nights before where he was throwing dead bodies over the town wall and they were falling only a short way before landing on heaps of others. Yes, of all the men in this town, his responsibility now weighed him down the most.

And of course, there was even more likelihood of a mysterious 'plague' now and an increasing body count. His mentor – his master? – had his needs and appetites. How had he allowed it to happen? A stupid question, of course. His own pride had ensnared him. Meister, or the demon he had become, had recognised the ambition in him to be more than just the town doctor. It had been easy at first. Bleeding people for their own well-being was the recommended practice; he had just kept the blood and given it to the mayor, who had his own special way of keeping it fluid.

But soon it became clear that the blood of strangers was more intoxicating and invigorating compared with the old, inbred, tired strain that flowed in the veins of the Reimersbergers. When visitors disappeared, it was assumed they had simply left – and good riddance to them. Down in the woods, where the River Regen no longer babbled, but argued and fought its way through the rocks and rapids, the bodies – always poisoned at the end lest they became visions of their maker – were never found. They wouldn't be able to *disappear* quite as easily now. Rather, they would be the subject of discussion and scrutiny. Nor would the locals feel such a need to be bled, when they knew there was a better-than-average chance they would live forever. This could mean trouble. Meister had grown somewhat bored with life as mayor of this parochial town; grown more reckless with it. Maria Baecker – he'd taken a fancy to her and seduced her carelessly; bled the boy too, just to taste young blood again, before leaving Arzt to clear up the mess. That had nearly been their undoing. In fact, on reflection, it had been the first step towards it. Was it mere chance that the Wlich woman had entered the town that day?

But for now, he could see that something better was expected of him than to say just that he was thinking.

"Well, my feelings are that, until this stranger who is not a stranger shows himself – or herself -" he looked pointedly at Baecker, "there is little point in trying to guess what they can do."

Pfarrer spoke up: "But what if this stranger is actually someone already in our town? It says a stranger who is *not* a stranger, so looked at another way that possibility cannot be excluded."

"Alright, but until we find them the question of the broken verse must remain a conundrum."

"To be honest," said Droger, "if it is a member of this town they have no choice but to stay. Maybe there's hope in that; maybe not."

Meister spoke again: "Anyway, as I said before, we must look after our town; keep its structures in place. If we all surrender to despair it will serve no-one well. The outside world does not yet know of our predicament. We are still Reimersberg; last and most beautiful stop on the Adventurer's Road. We must not disappoint. But remember;" here he gave a dark look at everyone around the table, "if our stranger comes from beyond these walls, we cannot let them go. Only by staying here can they be a stranger no longer, and reach the end of the days."

CHAPTER 8

Visitors to Reimersberg were used to being looked at. There was usually nothing malevolent in it; just that most of the townsfolk were curious about outsiders, and were strangers themselves to the world of etiquette. So, if something intrigued them, they found it natural to stare at it for a while.

But those stares had a renewed intensity in the weeks following the curse, and by his third glass of beer, young Philip Lehrling was finding it disconcerting. For him, the time it took to drink two beers should have been quite long enough for people to get used to him. His glass stopped halfway to his mouth and he turned.

"What?"

"Nothing," said the people at the next table, who had the grace to look embarrassed.

But the young man wasn't letting it rest.

"No, tell me. You've all been staring. Have I turned green? Is there a third eye growing in the middle of my forehead?" He raised a hand in mock acknowledgement. "Oh, I get it. One of you put something strange into my drink and you're waiting for it to take effect."

The drinkers looked mildly offended now, but stayed silent. Then Mr Wirt, the landlord, spoke up from behind the counter.

"Oh please, take no offence and no notice, young Master…" He paused in the typical Reimersbergisch way, waiting for the guest to give his name.

But the beer and the unwanted attention had made Lehrling obstinate and courageous. "I would give you my name, but I fear it would be examined or laughed at."

He got up, leaving his beer on the table, and headed for the door.

"Please, sir," said Wirt, "don't take things wrongly. Perhaps we're a bit naïve here. Look, why don't you have this beer on the house, by way of an apology?"

The young man stopped, frowned, and appeared to be considering the offer. He watched the fresh glass of Weizenbier – wheat beer – being poured; it was renowned through the region, and this one did look tempting, with its thick, frothy head and the condensation running down the side of the glass. So, with a *'humph'* he sat down at the bar and started to drink.

At last he felt the tension drain from his shoulders again, and Wirt seemed to notice it was safe to talk to him.

"You see, sir, it's just that we're always curious about people who come here. The Adventurer's Road is a long and sometimes dangerous way; hence the name. And there are wolves in the forest."

Lehrling looked up sharply. "A much maligned animal, the wolf. It doesn't, as a rule, attack humans." He sounded like he was trying to convince himself.

"Not groups of men, perhaps." Wirt shrugged. "But maybe it's just the ones around here. So you see, anyone brave and hardy enough to complete the Road on foot is usually worthy of a few stares."

Lehrling shivered a little, and not just because of the cold beer. "Well, perhaps I'll have to stay around for a while." Lost in his vision of snarling muzzles, he didn't notice the way everyone glanced up as he said this. "At least until I can find some other people going the same way as me."

"And what direction might that be?"

"I haven't yet decided. You see, although I've a little bit of money in my pocket, and have been travelling a while, I'm really looking for work. I finished my apprenticeship in München six months ago. But my experience of towns like this is that there's nothing to be found – unless you want to sweep the streets for a pittance."

"On the contrary," said Wirt in his most enthusiastic voice. "What skills do you have?"

"I can work with wood. My father was a carpenter."

Wirt looked around at everybody for their agreement as he spoke. "Old buildings like ours have a constant need for repair." The other drinkers nodded and murmured. "We would welcome your help. If you ask me, there's at least…" he made a big show of thinking, "…a year's work here on repairs, and there's an ongoing job preserving and maintaining."

He had Lehrling's attention. "And the wages?"

Wirt opened his arms in an expansive gesture. "Well, I guess you could name your price. Good skills always find a home. Talking of which, I have a room upstairs here that you could live in for free, as you'd be helping the town."

Lehrling could hardly believe his luck. He'd landed on his feet here. Still, he couldn't appear too eager. It would probably be worth having a good look around the town as well. After all, if he was going to be here for some time, there'd better be some pretty girls.

"I'll think about it," he said.

And soon word got around the town. It couldn't be coincidence; a stranger had come and he wanted to stay! It was a sign. He was skilled with his hands; someone who could repair things – broken things. Pfarrer even started a frenzied search in his church, to see whether any of the carved verses on memorials, tombstones or pews were damaged. Unfortunately Reimersberg had always been the sort of town that took care of such things quickly. The broken verse remained a mystery for the moment. But hopefully they had some time now for it all to become clear.

But six months later, Lehrling had become restless and, in truth, a little uncomfortable. Also, the wandering spirit in him was feeling hemmed in and finding the town claustrophobic.

For a start, though people went about their daily business like in any other town, he sensed a cloud hanging over them. It was as if nobody felt joy in anything they did. People swept streets, painted buildings, hung washing, brewed beer, but he couldn't recall anybody ever whistling while they worked, or greeting each other like long-lost friends, or joking in the street. And he couldn't be sure if he had ever seen anybody leave the town. That may have been a trick of the mind, but once he started looking for it, he realised they seemed happy to remain in their own little quaint, half-timbered world. Then there was the peculiar business of the cattle let out on ropes. They told him it was to stop them wandering off down the valley, but he'd never seen the like before, and tried to pass it off by assuming that the farmer must be a bit eccentric.

He could see trees in the forest groaning under the weight of their berries, but no-one went to pick them. In fact on one occasion he overheard a woman whispering to another about how she would have loved to go and pick some of the blackberries. The woman didn't look lame, but Lehrling wondered whether she was scared of the forest. Indeed, people had dissuaded him many times from taking walks in there by continuing to insist that the wolves of the valley were particularly daring and ferocious. Still, in the end he volunteered to go picking. At this point, the woman had contradicted herself by saying the berries were poisonous. With a shrug of the shoulders, Lehrling had taken a casual wander towards the gates. He got the impression that nearly everyone was watching him. He gave the occasional glance over his shoulder, and could almost hear the sound of many pairs of eyes turning away suddenly, as if a pebble had fallen into a lake just beyond the limit of his senses, its presence made known only by the ripples.

Once he got friendly with a girl. She seemed to like him, but it didn't last long. There was something disturbing in her behaviour towards him, as if she was uncomfortable. She lived at home with her parents, like all the other single girls, and when he suggested that they might to go on a trip one day, perhaps take a ride to another town for a change of scenery, she refused, quite simply.

He started to notice how people became friendlier than usual if he was ever heading towards the town gates. Someone would come up to him on some pretext, even put an arm around his shoulder, engage him in conversation and – now he thought about it he could see – lead him back towards the town.

All in all, he began to feel trapped, as if he was being prevented from leaving.

Then there were the odd things people would ask him, mostly about poetry for some reason. Had he ever written any? Did it interest him? Had he ever started a poem, but not completed it?

The fact was he began to have horrible thoughts. At first he put it down to that slight madness, which can infect you when living near the woods and the mountains; the awareness that everything is bigger than you and your small existence is controlled by forces way beyond your understanding or powers to resist. He started to think that he was among evil spirits masquerading as humans, hoping to capture his soul.

The final straw was when he saw, in the arms of an exhausted young woman, an infant he'd seen during his first couple of days, and realised that in six months it appeared not to have aged a day. He tried to remember whether, perhaps, he had died and this was one version of hell or purgatory; eternally his. But the sight of the infant marked the day he decided to leave.

One evening, Philip Lehrling told Wirt that he was popping out for a stroll. He had already dropped his rucksack out of his window; retrieving it, he settled it on his back, and turned to find Wirt looking at him from the door of the inn.

"Where are you off to, Philip?" Wirt tried to sound matter-of-fact, but his voice betrayed suspicion.

"As I said, I just want to get a bit of fresh air." He knew he sounded none-too-convincing.

"So why do you need your rucksack?" The landlord took a step forwards, matched by the one Philip took backwards. "Here, I'll put it back in your room for you."

"It's ok; I thought the exercise might do me good if I carry my pack for a while."

"But you've been working hard in the workshop all day. Why do you need more exercise?"

Philip looked around him as if seeking an answer, and then patted his thighs. "Ah well, you see this is to keep my legs strong."

"Ok," said Wirt, sounding as unconvinced as Philip had feared, and he turned to go back inside.

"See you later, then," said Philip with an awkward little wave before heading down the street. He turned the first corner, waited a few seconds and then peeped back around it, just in time to see Wirt hurrying off in the opposite direction.

Damn, thought Philip, *I'm sure he's heading for the gates.*

Those gates would still be open, the sun not having set yet, and the cows and sheep being allowed as long as possible to graze. Philip broke into a run, believing he had reached some sort of turning point. He was driven by the thought that, if he didn't get away that evening, he might never escape, having shown his hand. He tore through the main square, which narrowed into a short approach road just in front of the gates…

…and ground to a halt.

He wasn't sure, but he thought he saw Wirt's figure disappear into the guardhouse, and already the two town gatekeepers, both big, burly figures, were hauling in the herd in preparation for pushing the gates together. He knew there was at least one other exit he could try, though he'd never been down that lane and had been told the gate was always kept closed. Still, he would put his shoulder to it if he had to.

He headed off that way, and reached a narrow opening called Engtorgasse, meaning Alleyway of the Narrow Gate. When he got to the end of it, he saw that the name didn't lie. That gate would be barely wide enough to pass through sideways, and though the wood looked old it was sturdy. Besides, the tiny alleyway gave him no room to run at it and knock it down.

He ran back out, to find a small gathering of people drawn by the commotion. "What's wrong, my friend?" asked one man - as if they didn't know. They were all in this together. And as he raced in a panic down the maze of narrow cobbled streets, which had lost any power to charm him, his sense of direction and his breathing became more ragged. But he was resolved to escape, no matter what it took.

This was when he noticed that the people were starting to block off roads; were no longer bothering to hide their determination to stop him. He had to get out, even if it meant jumping from the walls…no, he didn't want to think of that yet; but that would be better than being caught by these wicked spirits in their freakish, unchanging world.

He found his way back to the main square, hoping they wouldn't expect him to head for the gate again. The steps up to the battlements might be his last chance, although he fought still against the awful possibility of having to jump. There were footsteps echoing down streets to either side of him as they tried to cut him off.

Then he stopped horrified. So much for his theory about sneaking back to the gates. It was as if the ghouls had read his mind, and a crowd of hundreds stood waiting for him in silence. Many more watched from windows. His blood ran cold at the sight of them, just standing there with their false smiles. Worst of all, the mayor was at the head of them.

The tall, powerful yet somehow wraith-like figure stepped forward. He'd not bothered ever to say much to Philip. Indeed he seemed always to watch him if he was around, with sidelong glances from his glinting eyes. But now he spoke, and the words were all the more scary for being friendly:

"Philip, please don't run any more. Let us explain."

Lehrling shook his head, let out a horrified whimper, turned and, seeing people arriving in the square from other streets, headed for the only street left open to him. He soon realised what a mistake that was.

The narrow way led him to a series of twisting, shadowy lanes, then on into a dark and seemingly deserted part of town. The streets were unlit; likewise the houses with their black windows. He stopped for a moment and realised that there were no footsteps following him yet. Clearly he'd run into a trap. Despair threatened to swallow him. He didn't fancy hiding in any of the creepy houses with their sad, brooding aspects. And what would be the point, since the demons had wanted him to come here?

Then, impossibly, things seemed to get worse, as a figure appeared in front of him; a boy, seemingly of a similar age to him; possibly another young, lost soul they'd banished here. But the boy was gesturing, appearing animated and very much alive as he beckoned with his arms, saying:

"Quick, come with me, before they regain their courage."

What choice did he have? Before he could even consider that question, the boy had disappeared round a corner. Philip followed. When he got to the bottom of the next street the figure had vanished, but the mop of dark hair above a pale face popped out from an even narrower alleyway. "Come *on!*" he said impatiently. "You'd better hurry if you don't want to end up with all the time in the world."

Philip didn't understand the comment, but it sounded ominous, so he ran.

Round another corner and...nothing.

Ahead he saw a strange sight; a walled up street. And then from an alleyway just beyond it an arm appeared, beckoning. Was this another trap? Somehow he didn't think so. And if he needed any extra incentive to move, it was the sound of voices and footsteps, still a little way off, but definitely on the move. He dived into the alleyway and found the boy waiting for him.

"This way," said his young guide. "Once she escaped they lost interest in their brickwork and I made a way in as the mortar hadn't settled."

"A way in?" said Philip, watching while the boy removed a cunningly concealed plug of bricks from the window- frame of an old house, which he noticed abutted the town wall. "You mean we're going to hide in there?"

The boy looked at him. "Believe me; it's safer in there than out here, certainly in your case. Besides, in there is the only other way out."

Those words were enough to get Philip crawling through the gap, and he found himself inside an old house. There was a peculiar ambience; a mixture of long neglect and recent occupation. As they wandered through to the side which he assumed opened onto the bricked-up street, he noticed that there had been a fire in the grate at some point in the recent past. But the really puzzling thing was the little collection of objects on a table; a small glass sphere standing on a metal base, a pouch like a money-bag and a book. He glanced at the cover: *The Travels,* but couldn't make out the name of the author as he hurried through.

Philip peered around in the gloom, seeing the dark, daunting street through the window.

"God, what manner of place is this?"

"Many people fear it," said the boy, "but that makes it a perfect den for me where I can be by myself, and imagine that...my mother is still here. I don't really have time to explain." They heard footsteps and raised voices. For a moment they stepped outside. There was a flickering in the air at the far end of the street, which meant that the pursuers had brought flaming torches. "Don't worry, they won't find you. But I can't wait around. After all this fuss, I'm sure my father will seek me out, if only to talk about it. Come on; help me with this."

He led the way back into the house and Philip watched in amazement as the boy revealed another exit hidden with astonishing artfulness.

"You're quite a stonemason," said Philip, looking in admiration at his rescuer.

"This is not my handiwork," said Karl, "and if you knew the story behind it, you would wonder at it all the more. But again we have no time. Come, help me with this."

They heaved together, entered the short tunnel, pulled back the second door, and then Philip was looking out on blessed freedom – the fear of wolves had long since vanished and for all he knew their existence had been invented to keep him prisoner. The boy urged him to step through. With a surge of remorse and gratitude he turned to the lad.

"Please forgive my rudeness." He held out his hand. The boy clearly wasn't used to being offered a hand to shake, but took it. "Philip Lehrling."

"I know who you are. Everyone knows who you are?"

"Why?" asked Philip, amazed. "What have I done?"

"It's what they were *hoping* you would do. And who they were *hoping* you were. I'm Karl; Karl Baecker." The voices outside seemed to be fading. "Don't worry, you're safe now. As soon as you step out no-one can follow you."

"I've noticed nobody ever leaves the town; why is that?"

"The town was cursed by a woman they thought was a witch." Karl waved a hand in the direction of the house. "They made her live here, would you believe, and when they didn't understand her they tried to wall her up, just as they'd done to a lot of sick people many years before. Is it any wonder she cursed them? But she wasn't a witch, she was a wonderful person. I hope to meet her again one day."

"Come with me." Then Philip saw the look on Karl's face and cursed his own insensitivity. "I'm sorry; you can't, can you?"

"That's the nature of the curse, I'm afraid. But she also told us of a stranger who might save us." Karl smiled. "I'm guessing, now, that's not you after all."

Philip hesitated. "Well, if you want me to stay – if you think I should…"

"No, I think you should get away. I've seen how angry some of the people of this town are. I don't know what would happen to you if you weren't able to help them. If you weren't *the one.*"

Philip shuddered. "I think you're right. Tonight I believed I was going to die."

"Look, you must go now," said Karl. "But Philip, please, don't tell anyone about this place and what happened. I think whoever is meant to save us will do so, and we must hope that they will come. I believe anyone who comes here might end up having to save themselves, but I will try my best to help them." He pointed towards the forest.

"Find yourself a tree and climb up for the night. You're safe from the townsfolk and their ghastly leader, but the wolves won't bother waiting to find out if you're a stranger. We all taste the same to them. But they fear the valley, so you can head down there again at sunrise."

Suddenly, Philip stepped forward and gave Karl an almighty hug. "I shan't forget this, Karl. And if prayers and thoughts can help anyone, mine will help you."

Then Philip Lehrling ducked through the hole in the wall. Karl watched him head towards the trees until he merged with the horizon and the falling night.

One day, thought the boy.

He closed the outer door and then pushed the stone block back into place. He noticed that his frequent visits here had left a track on the ground where the door had rolled. This he scuffed over, and then he rubbed some moss against the mortar around the door to give the impression of ancient immovability. He knew no-one came in here, but just in case the look-outs decided to patrol this part of the wall again, or the Elders re-opened the street, he was taking no chances. However, he knew the possibility of this was remote at best, so he felt the house was still the safest place for his precious objects. Every day he'd come here while the other children played, to read more of Marco Polo's fantastic story and gaze out at the valley. The glass light no longer worked, of course; he'd hoped it might have escaped the curse, since it had been given to him before, but it wasn't to be. The seeds remained in their pouch. Yet he still took pleasure in having these secret gifts. Sometimes, he could even feel the light brush of Ilsa's kiss against his cheek. It filled him with unutterable sadness – she'd been his only friend and he missed her so much – and yet happiness at the same time.

He was certainly right in assuming his gifts were safest in the derelict house, because now, no-one ever thought of daring to venture there. If the disappearance of Philip Lehrling into thin air near the Kriegerstrasse hadn't already added to the legend of that part of town, then a repeat performance a couple of months later by another apprentice who'd grown suspicious much quicker than Philip, meant that everyone now believed Ilsa Wlich had cast a worse spell on those old sad streets.

CHAPTER 9

Almost three years had passed, so by the time a young carpenter called Friedrich Zimmerman came to Reimersberg looking for work, the townsfolk were more desperate than ever. Though many of them had never left town before the curse, the knowledge that they couldn't was an almighty albatross around their necks – not that any of them would have recognised an albatross. Indeed, if one had landed in the main square, they would probably have pounced on it and kept it captive for a while, just to have something different to look at, before tiring of it and making it into an exotic pie.

Most people's well of contentment had run dry and they were finding it difficult to put on a brave front. Men struggled in the morning to make the effort to shave; many grew long beards, which only added to the image of castaways adrift from the ship of life.

"It's unfair," moaned one man to his wife, "nothing changes, but our beards grow still."

Children had their own problems to deal with. At a certain age it became difficult for them to cope with being three years older, finding that their bodies hadn't kept up with the development of their minds. Many tired of their toys and games, and longed for more challenging pastimes, such as the chance to hike in the woods or the mountains. Looking years younger than your age – usually a much-desired state - led to all manner of confusion and disappointment. And how the parents suffered too; as if dealing with children were not hard enough, having to raise a child that had knowledge beyond its physical years, but not the emotional development to go with it, was a challenge too far. Worst affected was a mother with a baby; there was no break from the sleepless nights and the cries as an undeveloped brain and vocal cords sought to process the frustration. In time, she could take it no more. Before anyone could stop her – though none were sure how hard they tried - she walked through the town gates one day, placing her fate and that of her crying baby in the arms of the universe.

Folk had everything they needed except the fresh air of freedom and the changes brought by the winds of time; changes normally taken for granted, resented, or barely noticed, until they happened no more. For most, it was hard to watch the passing of the seasons, yet be excluded from them; forgotten by Mother Nature. Of course there was frost in the town like anywhere else on a cold morning, and snow still fell on the streets; the wind still blew through open windows and the sun cast light and shade, coolness and warmth, as it did on the rest of the world. But rather than feeling any gratitude for the prospect of being able to enjoy these wonders forever, the people felt they were no longer in tune with the world.

This was only made worse by the fact that the town was starting to age and show signs of disrepair. There were so few visitors, and the townsfolk had so little lust for life, they found it hard to care or feel pride in the place any more. This meant no-one wanted to stay, so the town was caught in a vicious circle. So, paint was left to peel, moss grew on cobbled streets once kept scrupulously clean, windows weren't cleaned as regularly as before, and tiles weren't replaced on roofs. After the first winter the firewood supply had run very low, and people had been forced to tear down some of the houses, which had been earmarked by families for their offspring, to find more wood. The streets around the Kriegerstrasse escaped this fate because no-one dared to venture near. However, the twisted steeple of the church did not escape.

But perhaps worst of all was the smell that hung over the town. In its prime, Reimersberg had employed a group of men to transport waste to pits outside the town. It was a journey that could no longer be made of course, and the only solution was to burn the waste. That smell might have been just about tolerable, but there were still certain citizens who would sneak onto the battlements at night and throw the detritus of their lives over the wall at the far end of the town. They got away with it for a time, but the latest summer had been very hot and the smell of decay became particularly bad. Eventually the mayor had deemed it necessary to ban people from the battlements after sunset, though he was perhaps the worst culprit of all, sending his handful of newly-acquired bodyguards to dispose of his waste when no-one was around.

And what of that mayor? Meister still clung to his position. Partly no-one could be bothered to challenge him; also they needed someone to blame, so it might as well have been him. He still called meetings of the Elders, and they sat drinking more beer than necessary as they discussed the same old points, but to everyone attending those meetings, it felt as if they had given up hope of ever solving the riddle of Ilsa Wlich. The people saw less and less of Meister, and when they did see him, it looked as if he had been spending too much time watching the world through the bottom of a glass. As a metaphor it was more accurate than they knew.

Now there were still occasional groups of intrepid travellers, drawn by tales of Reimersberg's famed beauty. Always they left disappointed and unaware that only the fact of them being in a group had spared them the experience of Philip Lehrling, since it was assumed the fabled stranger, in keeping with many mythological characters, would be a lone traveller.

So it was part of Friedrich Zimmerman's sad fate that he did arrive alone. He was happy enough at first; indeed considered himself lucky when the most beautiful woman in town fell in love with him. But he wasn't ready for marriage, so when it seemed the whole town was trying to force it on him, he decided to sneak away.

Besides, he, too, had started to notice the way the town was coming apart at the seams. But the townsfolk were watching him like a flock of hawks, and on the night they pursued him, his thoughts were those of Philip Lehrling, and his hurrying, terrified footsteps rang like echoes of his predecessor's, when he decided that he would climb down the town walls if necessary - take his chances with fate - to escape.

So, when he found himself trapped on the battlements, with the good people of Reimersberg approaching from either side, their faces wreathed in frightening smiles, none more so than Meister, he did indeed put himself in the hands of fate. But she let him fall through her fingers as he lost his grip on the treacherous stones.

And there the body lay, close to the town gates; a horrid, broken reminder to everyone of the reality of the curse and the evil they had not only planned, but perpetrated. They feared it would also serve as a dire warning to anyone approaching the town that this was a place to avoid. The legends would grow as dark as the surrounding forest. No-one would ever come again.

Worse was to follow. One day, there was a noticeable smell from the body and people knew the wolves would come. Though they would have welcomed those beasts consuming the body, making it disappear from view, it meant they would become bolder, putting the lambs and calves in danger.

That same day, against his father's wishes and despite the mayor's ruling, Karl sneaked onto the battlements and looked down. He knew the guards would drive him away soon enough, but felt he owed it to Friedrich Zimmerman to come to pay his respects. Part of it was guilt; he'd failed to save that life. He had tried making friends with the young man, but what eighteen year old would want another lad hanging around when there were girls in town. Besides, Hans Baecker was trying to keep his son away from Zimmerman, knowing the town's plans for him.

Karl felt great sorrow for the plight of the young, broken body lying at the base of the wall, with no decent burial and no family to mourn him.

And suddenly he had an idea. Ilsa's words came to him. The seeds!

"What grows from these grows quickly, and is strong and hardy. It will take root in the unfriendliest of places. It brings life where there is none."

And hadn't she said he would know when the time was right?

Also, the town's supply of fruit had almost run out. They'd tried to turn a few patches of open land and gardens into fruit and vegetable patches, and there had been some yield. The first potato sprout to appear had been greeted by more joy than the arrival of any previous spring; the first strawberry celebrated with greater zest than a new-born child, because everyone had been holding their breath; would the planting of such things be considered something new and therefore doomed to failure?

They'd dried or preserved all they could, but it was not enough.

That night Karl sneaked from his room and returned to the Kriegerstrasse. He alone of all the people in the town had no fear of that place. Collecting the pouch of seeds, he climbed up to the empty battlements. He'd brought also a bag full of broken bricks left by the men who'd walled up the street. It was too dark to see the body of Friedrich Zimmerman, but he'd marked on the wall the point below which it lay.

As he leaned over the battlements he heard below him the sounds he had dreaded; snarling and tearing. He took the pieces of brick and hurled them down into the darkness. Now he heard more snarling, but this time mixed with yelps of surprise and pain, and he continued throwing until all he could hear was the smacking of the bricks against the ground, though the odd one hit something he didn't want to think about.

Now Karl emptied some of the seeds from the pouch into his hand and stretched his arm out over the wall.

"I ask whatever powers gave strength to Ilsa Wlich to bless these seeds."

He opened his hand. It was a still night and he prayed the seeds would fall true; that wherever they landed the earth would give them life.

The next day Karl sneaked up to the battlements again. Many people had given up looking out, or at the sorry sight below, so at first he was the only one who noted with joy the green stalks that were growing next to and around Friedrich Zimmerman's remains. But soon others noticed them too. They were the cause of much comment and excitement. Within a week the trees had grown to the height of a man; within a fortnight they were halfway up the wall! From the battlements the bones were no longer visible, and people gave thanks for this blessed mercy; indeed the roots of these miraculous trees were so thick that the remains were soon covered from view entirely. The wolves had not returned, scared away by the night of the deadly rain of stones, but also because they were seeking pastures new – or hopefully even the shepherds that tended them!

And the tree bore fruit. No-one recognised the variety, but it appeared to be an apple, and the branches were laden. As they grew closer to the top of the wall and the townsfolk thought they would soon be within reach, there was talk of a celebration.

No-one was counting their chickens – or their apples; after all, the fruit had not yet crossed the town wall, but the success with the potatoes gave people hope that the planting of seeds would not be affected by the curse. They would call the celebration The Coming of the Fruit. Pfarrer preached; it was a sign from God that they weren't forgotten; new life springing from old. And after all, hadn't it been an apple on the tree in the Garden of Eden? There were those who argued that the apple was the root of all sin and was there as a reminder of the town's wickedness. But as Pfarrer finished his sermons in the packed church with the words: "See how good triumphs over evil; see how God triumphs over Ilsa Wlich", Karl asked Ilsa secretly for her forgiveness.

Then his thoughts, as always, turned to her and he wondered what had become of her and her child.

****

Not all had gone well for Ilsa. She'd returned to the way of life she'd known - had hoped to leave behind - with only herself, her unborn child and the wolves for company. Oh, living off the land and the bounty of nature was no problem for her, but she was caught in between fearing her fellow men more than ever before, yet craving their company. As her belly grew, she knew there was no chance of seeking help; her face didn't fit in this part of the world even without the added problem of a bastard child in her stomach. So she was faced with the daunting prospect of giving birth herself; alone.

Yet even that was not the worst of it. She was weighed down by the terrible burden of the curse she had laid on Reimersberg. It was a double weight, a yoke across her shoulders; the knowledge that she had condemned so many people to a possible eternity of despair – though that was out of her hands now – and the spiritual, indeed visceral scars that came from having used her body as a vessel – a channel – for powers nearly beyond her control. It had drained her, and she believed her full strength would never return. Now the child sapped it even more as the time for birth approached. Yet for all that, it had been necessary, to trap the primeval spirit that now lived in Meister; keep it from gathering strength and roaming free again.

Which in turn made her think of Karl and question why she had left him potentially at the mercy of that vampire. It seemed he was her only chance. She had to trust him, and did so without questioning. Something in her blood told her that one day he would solve the riddle, and that the time would be right. The universe upon which she had called would protect him and not allow the curse to break until it was ready. He was stronger than anyone knew; possibly stronger than her in his own way. Still she didn't tell him about the vampire; he would have been young, brave and foolish enough to try to kill the evil spirit and that would have been his undoing. He didn't possess her knowledge, or her oneness with the earth; that was something to which you were born. But he was so bright. Truly he was her light in the darkness.

She put her hand on her stomach. Perhaps there was another light. She couldn't control fate, but she had done what she could to help things along.

The birth was extraordinary; like feeding the roots of time. The earth had smiled on her and the delivery, though painful, was quick; the child - a girl – healthy. She'd chosen to lie down by a river, and she washed the child clean in the purest of water. She didn't indulge in giving it a name; not with the plans she had.

For a time she stayed by that stream, letting the baby's earliest memories be those of babbling water, birdsong and the warmth of a fire built from wood that had fallen and not been cut from its mother tree. There was an irony in that; more than one. Then at night the wolves came and shared the warmth of the fire while continuing to guard her.

After a few weeks she gathered her things and set off to put her plan into action, though it made her heart ache to contemplate it.

It was the first civilised homestead heading east from Reimersberg. There'd been two other farms, but on one the animals appeared mistreated and on the other she'd seen the father beat the boy at least twice. This couple, however, she had observed for at least a week, sometimes from a distance, other times closer than they knew. That was the hardest part; looking in on warmth and happiness and not being able to share in it. They appeared to be in love, spoke gently to each other, but were strong and tireless as they worked the land. Their animals, even the dogs, appeared fit and well. Best of all - from her point of view – she knew the woman would never bear children. It was in her aura. The woman knew it too, but coped well with it, and her husband loved her despite it, which was unusual in those times.

One dawn, just before the couple rose to milk their cows, a hooded figure approached across the misty farmland, so quietly that even the dogs slept on. The figure placed a sleeping infant in a basket by the door to the farmhouse. She checked that the little brass vial was tied securely around the baby's neck. As she did so she saw tears fall upon her hand, but made sure that none landed on the child.

"May the fates guide your blood," she whispered, then turned and disappeared back into the mist.

CHAPTER 10

Most of the people of Reimersberg were overjoyed at their stroke of good fortune. Some said the fruit would surely not survive its journey over the town walls, but others argued that the cattle grazed and still the grass that they had eaten outside turned to milk. One bright spark even suggested stuffing the apples inside the cattle, but no-one could quite imagine how. However, to general celebration one apple started to overhang, touched the wall and did survive, and those outside were then caught in huge nets that the people pushed out on poles. The trees grew so tall that they started to dwarf the walls.

Many agreed that perhaps Friedrich Zimmerman was the stranger who was now no stranger. Certainly it looked as if these trees would be staying for a long time, though people chose not to question whether the stranger was supposed to stay inside the town. They were determined to enjoy the moment. Still no-one understood the broken verse, but whatever it meant, it seemed there was at least a chance the curse might lift one day. Perhaps Zimmerman himself was, in some obscure way, the verse that had broken as he'd fallen. Everyone grasped at slender lifelines.

Yet, as always when fortune allows the door of the future to creak open a touch, some grow impatient to burst on through. Late one afternoon, after a couple of strong beers, Stefan Schmied, one of the town blacksmiths, was talking expansively – in other words he was drunk – with some of his friends.

"The tree seems safe," he said, hooking his thumbs for emphasis into his thick, black belt. "Here's a chance to see if the curse can be beaten."

What he was really saying of course, like most drunken men, was that here was an opportunity to impress the girls with some hare-brained act of bravado. Egged on by the other bucks, he strode, or rather weaved his way across the town, followed by an increasingly large crowd, and up the steps towards the battlements and the overhanging branches. They followed him up. He clambered onto a sturdy bough and then shuffled his way along it. Soon he was clear of the wall and he removed his cap, waving it as he said:

"Hail Stefan Schmied; the first man to leave Reimersberg for years – alive, anyway."

His friends cheered. "Be careful, Stefan," cried Margarethe, a town beauty. That was music to his ears, so he decided to carry on in the direction of the trunk. As he looked down, the height sobered him up a bit, but he was feeling heroic. Could he be the man who had the guts to show that the curse had ended? People watched with hands held to mouths or eyes, as Schmied lurched his way down the tree, branch by branch, till at last he set foot on one of the roots.

People cheered, many still drunk on the marvellous cider that had come from those apples. Stefan spread his arms to accept the applause. As he did so, his foot slipped between two roots and touched the ground, and Stefan Schmied was there no more.

Many wept that day, more for themselves than for brave, foolish Stefan, and the arguments raged.

"The Friedrich Trees have not been here for a year; not even half of one. He tried too soon. Let us not give up hope."

"I gave that up years ago. I'll settle for no hope and more cider, and just drink myself into oblivion."

"What will be will be."

Whilst those citizens in the inn that night were just learning the meaning of patience, Meister was a past master of the art of waiting. He had been a survivor in the face of hatred since time began, always coming back stronger. Yet even he, as he felt power slipping from him, found it hard not to rage against the fading of the light. Despite his words at that first council meeting, he had failed to take care of his town; his fool's kingdom. He heard the rumours; they said he spent more time than ever in the big wine cellar beneath the town hall – all the work of a previous life, of course, when Meister's alter ego had controlled Reimersberg.

They didn't know about his other 'wine cellar'.

The more he sensed that people were no longer looking to him for leadership, the more determined he became to show them. Forgetting for a moment that he was a vampire, his drive was no longer just about slaking the thirst of centuries; he was their mayor and they had better not forget it. The final straw was when they all started to worship the big tree, even deciding to have a special day to celebrate...the wine had flown up his nostrils and made him splutter as he laughed in derision...celebrate the arrival of some apples! He was of a mind to have the overhanging branches lopped off; except there was something about the tree he mistrusted. Normally a creature of the shadows, he couldn't bring himself to stand in its shade, and the whisper of the breeze in its leaves sounded like the taunts of angels.

Still, he would show them all. He still had a few allies and between them, they'd solve the riddle and rescue the town. And then? Well, then he'd remember who'd shown him the proper respect.

Down in the oubliettes beneath the town jail was *his* wine cellar. Three men - there would be others; symbols of his desperation; his need to hang on to power at all costs; the madness of being a vampire. For a vampire's life was spent in thrall to its appetites and in fear of discovery. He needed to find the stranger, because someone with the power to end the curse was a terrible enemy. Find him, take his body for his own. Meister would die, but the man who lifted the curse and freed the town would be a thousand times more powerful than him. And at liberty once again.

The three men were unfortunate lone travellers, snatched from their beds while most of the town slept. *By order of the Mayor* – it had felt good to give that instruction. Apart from Meister, only Dr Arzt and Mr Wachter, the town jailer, knew of the existence of these men. Pfarrer would not have approved; misguided though he was, he was still a man of God.

Meister had addressed each of his terrified 'guests' when they were first brought to the jail, just before they were thrown down into their windowless dungeons.

"The rules of this game are quite simple. No amount of shouting will do any good; you will not be heard, so you might as well accept things and save your breath. If you don't, you will annoy Mr Wachter here, and that, believe me, is not a good idea." Now he held up a piece of paper, with the final words of Ilsa Wlich written on it. "On this is a riddle. You have a year in which to solve it. If, after a year, you have not solved the riddle, or if, before that year is over, the curse on this town has lifted, you will be released."

They were lied to. They and many others in the dark days that followed, who were dropped into the oubliette along with the piece of paper. The only truth was that they had a year. After that their blood was too tired and they were discarded like rotten fruit, by whichever means Meister's henchmen could find.

None came close, in their terror, to solving the riddle.

PART TWO

The Earth slumbered in the dusk, heading towards the deep sleep of night; not the best time for a boy to be standing alone in the cooling air and contemplating facing his fears. As he looked towards the distant mountains, which were almost, but not quite lost to the gloomy horizon, he knew he would have to travel several days' journey to the east, where his nights would be truly lonely. There was nowhere to stop to rest his head along that road – *if* he went. At that moment it didn't seem such an inviting prospect.

But he knew deep in his stomach that he had no choice, now that this mystery had revealed itself to him and adventure beckoned. Something old had stirred in his young blood. He realised the farm could no longer be his life.

But still, why did his first proper adventure have to involve such a challenge; heading deep into the black heart of the Hexental? He'd known grown men who'd turned white as they'd spoken to his parents about their journeys through that place. There were wolves, though of course they were everywhere. They'd even been known to sneak onto the farm and steal lambs. Wolves you could cope with. Other stories had come to his ears; twisted, doubtless, by time and superstitious imaginations, but still, you couldn't smell bread unless someone was baking. People had disappeared. And not just people; an entire town had vanished, so they said; a town cursed by a witch. Some folk said that when the wind blew down from the mountains, on certain nights you could still hear the voices of the lost; and if the forest was being buffeted by a storm, faint lights might show between the dancing branches. They said that, if you were lucky, the lights were all you saw in the trees. But he'd heard bedtime stories about figures wandering through the forest; only wandering; forever wandering.

It was enough to make a boy want to stay at home and till the soil – but not a boy like him; and not after that evening's amazing discovery.

****

But what events had shaped the history and reputation of the Valley of the Witches, and that of Reimersberg in particular, in the years since Ilsa Wlich had left it doomed. How had a town that had been one of the jewels of the Bohemian Palatinate become part of a scary legend? Why had its existence been forgotten by some people, and feared or denied by others?

Well, of course, myths and legends usually contain at least grains of truth, and those grains would normally be carried in the pockets of people who have lived at least part of the legend, or known someone who did. For sixty years, no citizen of Reimersberg had left the town and lived to tell the tale. So the seeds were carried away by visitors, and since there hadn't been many of them – and they were not really sure what they'd been through, or what they'd seen - their stories became half-truths at best, and therefore only half-believed.

But the most remarkable thing of all was that the truth was stranger than the fiction.

So here's what really happened.

CHAPTER 11

First there was the Tithes Inspector, who was called one day into the office of the King's Minister for Taxes.

"His Majesty has been spending rather a lot of money of late," said the Minister. "It is time to claim a little of what we are owed by his subjects, to help pay for his...um...expenses." The Tithes Inspector nodded obediently. "There are several Royal towns that need reminding; although the payment of tithes is voluntary, it should also be considered one's loyal duty to the Royal Family, and non-payment is very much frowned upon. Punishments can include the removal of royal privileges."

The Inspector looked down the list. There were a couple of surprising names on the list. "I thought Reimersberg was the very model of a proper Bavarian town," he said.

"Humph." The Minister snorted and pointed to the list. "If you ask me, many of those places are a bit full of themselves; led by pompous mayors who give themselves more airs and graces than the King. Take some men and find out why these towns haven't paid."

The Inspector's mouth opened in shock. "But Reimersberg is..."

"...a long journey." The Minister smiled to himself. Some of his inspectors got a bit too comfortable; their bottoms became too big in their seats. "Well you'd better get started then."

"And anyway, I thought we sent Secretary Taschenratte to find out what was going on in some of these towns."

"We did. Unfortunately, Secretary Taschenratte didn't come back. It was about six months ago now. Which leads me to two possible, unfortunate conclusions; you can take your pick. Either something happened to him along the Adventurer's Road, which is why I suggest you take several men with you," – the Inspector looked up sharply – "or he collected the tithes and decided to run away with the money. Remember, it would be nearly five years' worth – a good booty."

The Inspector tried to hide his dismay, nodded and turned to leave the room. But the Minister had one more joke up his sleeve. "Oh my good Inspector," - the other man turned again - "Do watch out for the wolves; of both kinds. I think the ones in the forest will be more trustworthy. After all, they won't have five years' worth of tithes to give up.

The Half-Torn Page

****

Despite the odd things he saw as he approached along the valley, the Inspector was pleased to reach Reimersberg. The Adventurer's Road was a far cry from the comforts of the capital city, and your willingness to believe superstitious tales grew, the further along it you travelled. The thick forests played tricks with your mind, as did the looming mountains. You shivered in the cool shadows of those towering peaks even though the skies above were azure blue. And the Inspector might have been forgiven for thinking that his mind had been badly affected, because he could have sworn that a herd of cows appeared to be tethered to the town battlements, and a stand of huge trees, bigger than and quite unlike any he'd seen before, was growing alongside the high walls and overhanging them. It was only when he got closer that he was convinced he hadn't contracted forest fever.

He called his party to a halt and said: "It is my plan to stay here tonight." There were sighs of relief all round; everyone was tired from that day's long ride. "But I warn you all, be on your guard. Although payment of tithes is voluntary, loyal citizens would pay them anyway." He indicated the town. "This lot haven't come to the capital with theirs for five years. Keep your eyes open and your wits about you. My first impression is that something's not right here."

That impression was supported by the fact that no-one stepped out through the town gates to greet them, as was traditional and courteous, even though they rode under the King's banner. For all these peasants knew, the Inspector might be the King himself. Not that he could blame people for failing to come out to greet that old fool; he stayed cooped up in his palace indulging his appetites; had done for decades. It was unlikely he had ever visited these more remote reaches of his kingdom, or cared about them.

But still the Inspector's arrival had a huge impact in the town. Everyone stopped what they were doing and stared as the royal party rode through the gates. As the Inspector surveyed the scene he turned to his assistant and said:

"It's as I expected, yet not so. Is it me, or was I right in my feeling about there being something strange here?"

The assistant nodded deferentially. "It has changed, sir, since my family brought me here as a little boy. If it had looked like this back then I would have been scared. Then it was like a pilgrimage, and the town was gleaming and beautiful. Now it seems to have fallen into disrepair."

"Exactly; good word. And I'll give you another good word: disrespect. The look-outs must have seen us. Where's the damned mayor?" The Inspector sat up in his saddle and tried to look imposing. He pointed to a man in a grubby apron, who was standing staring along with everyone else, and said: "You! Fetch the mayor. We're here on the King's business."

As the man scuttled off, the Inspector turned once more to his assistant and said softly: "I'm not happy with the way they've formed a circle around us. Pass the word quietly down the line; the guards must make sure that their swords are ready." Then he took another look around the town square. "I smell the influence of a small town mayor with big city ideas. These people bear the look of city folk; tired, but threatening." His nose twitched. "And that's not all I smell."

"Well you can judge the mayor for yourself, sir," said the assistant, "for here he comes."

"No robes," said the Inspector. "Again, disrespectful."

The mayor worked his way through the crowd of people, none of whom looked him in the eye, and stood before the mounted party, making the slightest token bow of greeting.

"Welcome to Reimersberg, sir. Mayor Meister at your service. How may I be of assistance?"

"We're here on the King's business," repeated the Inspector. "This town has paid no tithes in five years and I am here to find out why."

Meister looked both defiant and shifty. "It was my impression, good sir, that tithes were voluntary."

The Inspector shifted in his saddle. "Indeed they are. As I said, I am here to find out why none have been paid. Just because something is not enforced doesn't mean you shouldn't do it."

Meister gave a charmless smile. "We haven't paid them for the very reason I have given."

The Inspector didn't like the way the people seemed to be taking in every detail of his horse and its fittings. Suddenly he felt very far from civilisation. He looked around to see that the circle of townsfolk had closed in ever so slightly and now seemed also to be eyeing-up the rest of the party. It might have been pure curiosity, but the Inspector saw only threat. He decided to give the mayor one more chance before making a dignified escape.

"I can understand you would not want to make the long journey to the capital to pay the tithes in person. But we can collect them now; maybe just one year's worth; the rest to be paid at a later date."

Meister swept his hand in a circle, but swayed slightly, giving the impression that he might have been a little drunk. "I'm afraid, sir, we have hit on hard times and have nothing to give."

The Inspector's face hardened. "In that case I have no alternative, but to revoke royal privileges from this town."

There was a murmur from the gathered people, and the Inspector saw a look close to misery settle on some of the faces. Could it have been that he had just pushed proud but desperate people further down a slippery slope?

"Meaning what, sir?" The mayor remained challenging and off-hand, as if he was performing for the crowd, an impression that was strengthened as he looked around for support. "The King has not visited us in years; certainly not in my lifetime. So he will not come and visit us in future; so what?"

"It goes beyond that," said the Inspector, shocked by this open display of disloyalty, even though he could understand it. "The forests are royal property. One of your existing privileges is that you are allowed to hunt there; but no longer."

He was amazed to find the mayor unmoved and increasingly surly. "You will find, sir, that being unable to hunt in the forest is of no consequence to us."

The Inspector stiffened and anger flashed in his eyes. "Then there is nothing further to be said." He turned to his party. "Gentlemen, we shall not, after all, be staying here the night." There wasn't a single protest from the royal party.

But suddenly another man stepped forward; tall, with thick silver hair, and a keen intelligence in his eyes and expression. He bowed courteously. "Sir, please forgive what may appear to be our rudeness. My name is Droger; I am the town apothecary and a member of the Council of Elders." The Inspector saw how the man's eyes flashed with anger as he glanced sidelong at the mayor, who stood by in disdain. "You are welcome in Reimersberg, and would be extended every courtesy should you decide to stay."

The Inspector nodded his acknowledgement. "Thank you, good apothecary, but to me there seems little point in staying. Enough of the King's money has already been withheld. I would not pour any more of it into the coffers of this insolent man." Here he pointed at the mayor, who looked both startled to be insulted so openly and yet unable to summon the energy to care. The Inspector addressed his next comments directly at him. "Know, sir, that tithe payments are only voluntary for towns with royal privilege, which you no longer have. For your disloyalty to the crown and your insolence, full payment is demanded within the next month."

"You'll have to come and get it then," said the mayor. He sounded almost petulant. It wouldn't have surprised the Inspector if he'd stuck out his tongue.

"I beg your pardon!"

"You see, we're cursed."

"This town is cursed in its mayor; that much is obvious."

Meister shrugged his shoulders. "You can believe it or not. We are cursed. None of us may leave this town."

"The Inspector turned to his assistant. "Well, I've heard of some excuses for not paying, but that's the best yet."

"He speaks the truth," said Droger, "if not with enough respect."

"Of course he does." The Inspector's curt reply could not have sounded more sarcastic. With that he signalled for his party to turn and leave the town. "I expected better from the apothecary," he muttered to his assistant. "But you can see; it's a town full of in-breeds. And what is that smell?"

"Yes," said the assistant. "It hangs like a pestilence over the place."

They rode on.

"Well, I doubt we shall see any monies from them," said the Inspector. "But frankly, I'm not coming out here again. Let's see whether they do pay; if not, I'll send some soldiers to collect."

****

As it was, none of the Inspector's party returned to the capital. Indeed, he was looking in the wrong direction for danger.

Soldiers were paid worse in those days than they are now, and by the time the Inspector had visited the other ten towns on the list, the amount of money and goods gathered was enough to establish a small principality, never mind tempt a man to mutiny. And the final town on the list lay very close to the border of the Palatinate. Just a few minutes' walk, even for a man weighed down by heavy bags full of money, and you were out of the reach of the laws and the justice of one country and free to start again in another.

So it was that the Inspector and his assistant woke one morning to find all of the tithes gone, along with the soldiers and the horses.

Now tax collectors are not very popular, particularly when they've just taken one tenth of your hard-earned money, so the two men were unable to purchase a horse anywhere and had to set off on foot to the next town. They didn't get there. We have to assume that tax collectors are not very popular with wolves either.

And although their disappearance had no connection with the town of Reimersberg, as time moved on and twisted the facts it added them to the legend of the Hexental.

****

There were other visitors to Reimersberg during the following years, but not many. The Minister for Taxes now considered the Hexental too dangerous a place to send anyone; and besides, it wasn't worth the expense. What he gained in goods and monies from the town would be outweighed by the cost of losing men and horses, and the inconvenience to him of having to replace his dishonest inspectors. As he didn't want to draw attention to his failure to bring in the money, he simply had the name of Reimersberg erased from the official records.

A few more lone adventurers arrived. The people of the town had learned from the sad incident with Friedrich Zimmerman and no longer tried to prevent these visitors from leaving. Yet so wrapped up were the folk of Reimersberg in their day-to-day battle with fate, that they never questioned a particular fact; none of them ever actually saw these lone travellers leave.

And thus it was that tales of wolves, witches and cursed towns combined to keep most people away from the valley, or were held responsible for the mysterious disappearances of those who were brave enough to venture there.

One lucky person who did survive a trip to the Hexental, though not in one piece, arrived with an invention, which he claimed was a new type of small gun; it could fire six shots before needing to be reloaded. When he tried to demonstrate, the gunpowder, being nothing new at that time, worked perfectly, but the mechanism jammed and the gun exploded in his hands. His shocked reaction was so amusing to the townsfolk that it took them a while to notice that he'd lost a finger off each hand. The inventor decided it was a punishment from God for him trying to sell this instrument of death. He said he had seen the light, and the townsfolk, deciding he was too much of an idiot to be the mythical stranger, didn't try to stop him as he went on his way into the valley to preach. His invention didn't see the light of day for at least another hundred years.

The Hexental's reputation as a place of superstition and danger grew. Even the peddlers and tinkers of the region visited less and less. But for the mountebanks - those sellers of quack potions - there were surprisingly rich pickings in Reimersberg and a few would chance a visit if there was good money to be made. Their stories provided entertainment and a lift for people in need of hearing a different voice or a tall tale. And people, remembering the words of the Ilsa's curse - knowing that new medicines would not help them if an epidemic hit the town - stocked up on the old, traditional ones for sale here. If there was even half a chance that some old wives' remedy might work, they were prepared to take a bottle of it. After all, what harm could it do? As Droger watched this happening one day, he thought it might all come down to one thing; buying something from an outsider quite possibly just felt good, like doing something normal again; being part of the world.

Which might also have been the reason why, one day, he found himself looking through the bottles for sale, although he had a valid reason for doing so; his supplies of medicines were running low, even though he tried to ration them. As he moved through the small crowd, which had gathered to hear the mountebank's patter, he bumped into Karl, whom he hadn't seen for a few days. Or was it months? Time had taken on a different dimension, now that it meant nothing. It was always strange talking to the boy, for the very reason that he wasn't really a boy any more. His body and his voice were still those of a sixteen year old, in memory he was in his twenties, but even so, his brain had not developed enough for him to become a man. Droger felt for him; it must have been hard to bear in so many ways.

They talked for a few minutes as they looked at the various potions and packets of unfamiliar powders for sale. Karl recognised certain items as having been on the shelves in Ilsa's house. One powder in particular caught his attention.

"She said this could cure certain types of madness," said the boy.

"What is it?" Droger picked it up, read the label, and then looked shocked. "Powdered mandrake root! But…"

"Yes, she told me the legend that, if it screams when you pull it from the ground, it drives you mad. She said it was just a story put about by people like her to stop folk from pulling up a valuable medicine."

They wandered on, and now it became clear to Droger that their bumping into each other had been no accident; that Karl had actually been seeking him out.

"Mr Droger, have you seen the belt Mr Wachter is wearing?"

Droger looked across at the jailer, who was haggling with a man over the price of a hat, and saw a very ornate belt around his middle, certainly not one he could have bought in Reimersberg, or even in the other towns locally. He was sure he would have noticed it before. But perhaps a mountebank had sold it to him. Droger told Karl to stay where he was and made his way over to Wachter.

"Nice belt you have there."

"What? Oh…yes, er…" Even through the blue-black stubble on his face, Wachter's cheeks reddened.

"I saw one just like that, many years ago, in Augsburg."

"Yes…I…" He gave an embarrassed laugh. "I bought this there…a long time ago."

That was all Droger needed to hear for the moment. He'd known Wachter a long time and he was definitely one of those Reimerbergers who'd never left the town in his life.

That night, Droger made his secretive way to the jail. It was at the far end of town, near the Engtorgasse, where Philip Lehrling had tried to escape through the narrow gate. In fact the gate had been made narrow for two reasons; to stop invaders breaking into the town and to make it harder for escaped criminals to break out. Droger was accompanied by Karl. He'd tried to stop the boy from coming, but Karl had insisted. Droger could understand that; life in Reimersberg couldn't have been much fun for him; it was tedious enough for an adult and Elder. Besides, Droger had a growing respect for this young man, who, out of everybody in the town seemed to have coped best with their plight. Indeed he never saw him moping around.

Droger had never had children; he had always known Hans Baecker was a good, honest man, but also a weak one, and not for the first time he found himself wondering how a father could be unaware that his son wasn't asleep in his bed this night. Hans had nearly lost Karl once; surely that should have made him all the more precious. Perhaps that was being unfair. There was no mother to keep the boy in check, and Karl seemed a bright child, probably more than capable of deceiving his father. And of course he'd spent time in the company of Ilsa Wlich. She might have taught him the art of disappearing!

Then again, perhaps Hans had simply started to succumb to the despair of what faced them all. His bakery was struggling, reliant on the limited crop of wheat grown in the town, or on purchases from occasional passing merchants. Soon his bakery would close down – forever – and Hans Baecker would have nothing to do but contemplate the past and the future; a man with no present.

The jail itself was possibly, in its own way, a more intimidating building than anything the Kriegerstrasse had to offer. Squat and ugly, tucked away out of sight from most of the town, its old, cruel stones had witnessed many bad deeds in times when punishments were supposed to fit the crime, and people confessed to anything with the right persuasion. But in recent years it had stood mainly empty. They might have been a bit narrow-minded, but the citizens of Reimersberg had mostly been good, ordinary folk, with the exception of one or two characters from their darker history.

Droger told Karl to stand out of sight, but where he could see what was happening. As he entered the jail he saw that his luck was in, because so was Wachter; obviously he had taken the night shift - as he was the only jailer this was usually a sign that he had argued with his wife! Also, hanging on a hook behind the door he noticed a flamboyant hat, which Wachter had had the good sense not to wear in public – unlike his belt - as it was clearly not from their part of the world.

Wachter greeted his old acquaintance, but not without suspicion.

"Hey, Droger," the jailer didn't rise from his chair, just lifted a big meaty hand in acknowledgement, "to what do I owe the pleasure of your visit? I haven't locked up any of your family as far as I remember." He laughed and waved the paw-like hand towards the row of empty cells.

Droger sat himself down, trying to sound companionable. "Ah, well, you see, when I saw you this afternoon I realised we haven't had a chat for a while. The way things have gone in this town, I think we're all guilty of forgetting…" here he produced a bottle from his jacket pocket, "…some of life's important pleasures."

"Apple brandy!" said Wachter, pulling himself upright in his seat. But then his brows narrowed. "I shouldn't; I'm not supposed to drink on duty."

Now Droger gestured towards the empty cells. "What duty?"

"If Meister came by…"

Droger leaned forward. "Look; firstly, our good mayor hasn't shown his face much of late. Secondly, if he were here he'd probably drink the whole bottle. You and I know he seems happiest guarding his wine cellar these days, and trying to reduce the amount there is to steal! Thirdly, even if someone was in the cells and escaped, they wouldn't get very far if they were a citizen of this town, would they?" He watched Wachter's face very closely as he said this last part and thought the man's eyes became increasingly shifty. "Lastly, who's going to tell him?" He looked around theatrically. "You, me or the prisoners? Why are you so scared of him anyway? You're not a little girl"

The last words did it. Droger despised the crass analogy, but he knew it would get to a big thug like Wachter. Though there was still hesitation in the other man's eyes, Droger opened the bottle and wafted it close to the jailer's nose.

Wachter grinned. "Ah, what the hell?" He took the brandy and had a big nip, smacked his lips and gave a satisfied sigh, accompanied by a wheezing cough as the moonshine caught in his throat. Holding up the bottle he asked Droger: "Is this from the Friedrich Trees? It's powerful stuff."

"Yes, it is. The secret is in the way…" With a thump, Wachter slumped forward on the table and fell into a deep, instant sleep. "…you add the sleeping draught," Droger finished his sentence with a grin, removing the bottle from Wachter's hand.

But now his face grew serious. He thought he had enough time, but he was worried what he would find.

He gestured through the window for Karl to join him.

As a fine, upstanding citizen, Droger wasn't familiar with the layout of the jail. He took a ring of keys from a hook behind Wachter's desk. "Come with me," he said to Karl.

"What are we looking for?"

"Any sort of hidden door or trapdoor. In fact, on second thoughts you look here, and I'll try the cells."

He let himself through into the corridor that ran in front of five empty cells. He examined the walls at the back of each one, but found nothing. Treading heavily on the floor, he listened for hollow steps that might indicate a trapdoor, but they all sounded solid. He knew there had to be other chambers where, in the darker shadows of the past, unfortunate prisoners had been tortured out of earshot of the street.

Back in the main room Wachter was still snoring loudly. The beauty was, he wouldn't remember what had happened prior to him falling asleep; the potion having been cunningly mixed, creating memory loss for the last half hour or so before it was taken.

"Here!" cried Karl, who then put his hands to his mouth in apology for having shouted.

There was a rug, more like a blanket, under a small wooden cabinet in the corner behind Wachter's table. They shoved the cabinet to one side, lifted the rug and saw a large flagstone with a sunken iron ring in the middle of it. Droger heaved the flagstone out of its groove, but it was heavy and slipped from his fingers, crashing back down again.

Droger and Karl froze. It was a sound that might have woken the devil.

Wachter stirred, licked his lips, mumbled something, and then continued his journey in dreamland.

Droger took better care now, with Karl's help, and soon he was staring down into a dark space, from which came a musty smell, a scurrying, as if there were rats, and a trickling sound.

"Where's the water coming from?" asked Karl.

"That'll be some tiny leak of water from the River Regen. This tunnel has been carved into the rock."

Droger took another lantern from a hook on the wall, lit it and held it over the opening. Now he could see a set of rough-hewn steps. Karl was about to climb down them, but he held him back. The boy had seen plenty in his short life, but who knew what grisly sight might be waiting down in that dark place?

He saw that Karl was looking at him in expectation and realised he must have slipped into a bit of a dream, as if he'd taken some of his own sleeping draught.

"Karl, I need you to stay here and be my look-out. Lock the door and make sure no-one comes in. Warn me if it looks like Wachter is going to wake up. We don't want to end up locked away down there, which is what he'll do if he catches us."

"Ok." Karl threw an anxious glance at the slumbering giant.

Taking his courage in both hands, or at least in the one that wasn't shaking the lantern, Droger went down into the pit.

Like the cave of a hibernating bear, it was full of latent menace and not quite silent. To calm his own nerves – to break that not-quite-silence – he said: "Hello?"

There was a muffled response; more than one. Droger could sense both fear and hope in those muted voices. Their owners must have heard the dreaded sound of the trapdoor being lifted, the awful, slow tread of feet on the steps, but this was not their usual tormentor coming to...

He cut short that train of thought.

It was a rough-hewn tunnel and he could see there were no doors along the sides, so he looked down. Then he sprang backwards as he saw movement and realised that somebody's fingertips were poking through some grating in the floor. He saw an iron ring like the one upstairs and five more at intervals along the floor, along with more grating.

"Who are you?" he said with a tremor – a mixture of dread and anger – in his voice.

"If you're asking that question," came a reply, "then you've probably guessed. According to my wall I don't think a year has passed, so I'm guessing you're not that bloated pig the mayor, or that animal he calls the jailer." There was defiance in that voice; a fighter.

"What are you doing here?" As soon as he asked it, Droger knew it was a stupid question.

"Setting up a market stall," was the sarcastic reply. "JUST GET US OUT OF HERE!"

From above Droger heard mumbling. Perhaps he'd got the mix of the sleeping potion wrong and Wachter was starting to wake up. There was really no time to lose, if he didn't want to end up down here himself.

"Karl, are you ok?" he called. The boy looked down into the dungeon and Droger saw the horror of the tunnel reflected in his face. "Well?"

"Yes, but do hurry." The boy didn't move.

"Go back and keep watch. If you must, tie Wachter's hands."

Droger turned his attention back to the first cell, from where the responses were coming. "Can you reach the door?"

"No, I left my fingertips up there on the way down."

"But obviously not your sense of humour," said Droger. Again he knew he'd asked a ridiculous question; wasn't thinking straight in the darkness. He liked this man. Whoever he was, he hadn't given in to despair like some. "Okay, okay, I may be stupid, but at least I'm here. But any more of your sarcasm and I might be tempted to leave you there." He was grinning despite his words and the circumstances. Then he heard more mumbling from above. "Right, on the count of three, push."

On *three* the trapdoor didn't budge. Droger ran the lantern along the edge of the flagstone. There was no bolt, but what he did find, to his amazement, was a keyhole. All was quiet upstairs at that moment, but that didn't stop his nervous fingers fumbling clumsily with the keys, dropping them, and then needing three attempts before he found the right one. The lock clicked and luckily, the door proved lighter than it looked. A face appeared in the opening; surprisingly bright eyes, full of intelligence, buried like treasure under long hair and a matted beard. Despite everything, Droger was still shocked by the gaunt appearance.

111

Then suddenly it occurred to Droger that he had even less time than he'd thought. Not only did he have to get these prisoners out of the oubliettes, but out of the town as well. Whatever the reason for their imprisonment – and he guessed they were more than just candidates for the role of the mythical stranger – it was almost certainly a secret known only to Wachter and Meister. The prisoners couldn't exactly wander around amongst the townsfolk without causing a huge commotion and that would lead them right back into the welcoming arms of the jail, because Wachter wouldn't rest till he had them again. Woe betide the man who let down Meister.

"How many more of you are there?" he asked. Two voices replied. "Poke your fingers through the grating so I know where you are."

Once they were all released, Droger realised that the most courageous of the three was the one who looked like he'd been held the longest. They hurried as best they could on weak legs. He gave all of them a helping hand up into the main part of the jailhouse, and then climbed out himself, to find the first prisoner had drawn a knife from Wachter's belt and was looking at the jailer, his face filled with hatred. Droger placed a gentle hand on the man's shoulder

"My friend," said the apothecary, "I was about to say I could imagine how you feel, but of course I cannot. Nor do I want to; that way lies madness. But your best revenge will be to get out of here and leave him to face the consequences. If you kill him it can only lead to one thing. Besides…" Droger made the slightest of gestures with his head to remind the man of the presence of Karl.

The man hefted the knife and said: "This blow would not be struck for me. Two other souls occupied the cells either side of me. I heard their pain each time they were bled, just as they heard mine, and knew when their year was up by the sound of silence and the dragging of their dead weight. It would have been my fate too in another few weeks." He closed his eyes tight; whether to keep the memories at bay or prevent them infecting the air, Droger couldn't tell. "He drove the knife point-first into the table next to Wachter's head. "But you're right. And who knows if the hell, which would be mine for murdering him, wouldn't be just like that oubliette, but forever, where I would long for some demon like him to come and end my misery."

Droger squeezed the man's shoulder. "Come…what is your name?"

"Joachim." The other man put out his hand and Droger shook it. "Thank you."

"There is time for thanks when you are beyond our walls. Help me put the flagstone and cabinet back, and then I've got to get you out of the town. And that could be easier said than done. Whatever happens I will need your help, for the gates will be locked and the bolts are heavy."

It was eleven o'clock as they sneaked their way across the main square towards the town gates, but the streets were silent. The famous Reimersberg Uhr no longer chimed the hour; the people had given up winding it because it mocked them with the passing of the hours.

Then Droger stopped and smacked his hand against his forehead.

"Oh what a fool I am!" The others looked at him puzzled. "There's another way out; much simpler if we still have time."

He was thinking, of course, of the Engtorgasse, with its tiny gateway. The key was with the others in the jail. He gestured anxiously. "Come on; we may still make it."

They ran, stumbling, keeping to the deepest shadows even though the lanes were empty; slipping on moss as they went.

"So what was wrong with the main gate?" asked Joachim as they went.

"For a start, it's guarded."

"What was your plan?"

"The same as with the jailer; a friendly, late-night drink with two men feeling lonely on the night-shift, including a swig of sleeping potion. But even then, we'd have had to move two enormously heavy bolts and pull back two huge oak gates, which don't shift without a lot of effort and noise."

"And the gateway we're heading for?"

"Tiny – more like a door really – unmanned; almost forgotten about."

"Shouldn't we have headed there first?"

Droger looked over his shoulder at him, but didn't stop running. "Like I said, it's almost forgotten about. So, instead of giving me a hard time, tell me; how did you come to be locked up"

One of the other men found his voice at last. "We were caught in the night; snatched from our beds at the inn; told we would be locked up for a year and given some impossible riddle to solve. I'll never forget its words; I had to memorise them before the stub of candle went out – they never brought me another. It makes no sense. I will see those words forever when darkness falls."

Droger nodded. "My friend, it makes perfect sense – eh, Karl? – if you live in a cursed town run by a madman."

Their luck held; Wachter was still asleep and the key to the narrow gate was easy to find, firstly because of its size, and also because of the cobwebs that has grown around both the key and the hook on which it hung.

It wasn't far to the Engtorgasse. Despite everything they'd been through in their hellholes, Droger and Karl couldn't help but envy the men as they squeezed through the gate to freedom. Joachim gave a salute of thanks.

"What do you mean, this town is cursed?"

Droger smiled. "It's ironic;" he said. "I have all the time in the world, but no time to tell you now. Let's just say you were safe the moment you stepped through that gate. None of us may leave this tainted place." Then Droger looked at the night beyond the men's shoulders and said: "Having said you are safe, I would nevertheless recommend you make your way round the walls and sleep well above ground in the huge trees you'll find."

"Why?"

"There may not be much meat on you, but the wolves would still fancy a bite. Hide yourselves well. There is plenty of cover. And be gone before the sun rises."

"I thought you said we were safe from pursuit."

"And so you are, but not from gunshot. Go before the guards on the battlements can see you."

The two of them returned to the jail. Leaving Karl outside, Droger sneaked past Wachter to return the key. Even as he did so, the big jailer stirred. They'd returned not a moment too soon; Wachter was on the verge of waking up.

They hid across the street in the darkness and watched though the window as Wachter sat up and stretched, like a bear coming out of its winter's sleep, a puzzled frown on his dark-jowled features, as if he couldn't quite believe he'd nodded off. He yawned, looked around him, and Droger saw his gaze settle on something.

Droger and Karl both noticed it at the same time, turned to each other and said: "The key."

The key to the Engtorgasse was still swinging lightly to and fro on its hook; doubtless the broken strands of dusty cobweb would also be dancing in the slightest movement of the air. The jailer stood up abruptly and peered at the key; took it in a mighty paw and examined it. Then he stooped; they could see him peering at something in the corner of the room. Now the cabinet flew back and the flagstone was lifted as if it was made of cork. Wachter turned, ran to the door of the jail, threw it open and looked out into the street. Droger and Karl ducked back into the cover of the shadows and watched as Wachter looked up and down in desperation. Even from their hiding place, the two companions could see the fear in his eyes. Then he went back inside and disappeared into the dungeon.

"If he has any sense," said Droger, "he won't raise an alarm. I imagine he's the only man who visited those poor wretches."

"What about the mayor?" asked Karl.

Droger didn't answer; couldn't. There was too much he didn't understand and he regretted not having had the time to ask the men more questions. Instead, he put a hand on the boy's shoulder. "Wachter still has some time to make up a story. It would have to be a good one." He laughed.

"Something beyond his ability," said Karl. It sounded strange coming from one so young in appearance.

"People can think of all sorts of things when they're desperate; find all sorts of ways of clinging to hope. Like believing a poor dead man can turn into a forest that brings fruit and wood to a town in need of food and fire." He felt Karl's shoulder tense beneath his hand." Don't worry; I don't know what you did, and I don't think the townsfolk would mind, but for as long as Meister is the mayor and needs a reason to blame someone for something, your secret is safe with me. But back to Wachter; we should get out of here; I only said he wouldn't raise an alarm *if* he has any sense."

From the comfort of his bed half an hour later, Droger heard running feet and the shouts of the town nightwatchmen; and in them he heard confirmation of Wachter's lack of intelligence.

"That'll teach you to steal clothes from dead men," he whispered. Next to him his wife stirred, but she too was fast asleep, helped by a tiny, harmless dose of sleeping potion. Droger hadn't wanted even those nearest to him to know that he'd been out that night.

He drifted in and out of sleep, vexed by the problem of how to remove Meister from the position of mayor. There could be no doubt, given Wachter's stupidity, that Meister was responsible for the men being held in those awful cells. The big question, which burned a hole into the night, was - why?

CHAPTER 12

If the Inspector of Tithes had been an unwelcome visitor to the town, he was the Prodigal Son compared with the cholera epidemic that came wielding its scythe. It was probably the result of unclean water, and was the worst sickness to hit Reimersberg since the plague years. The days immediately following Ilsa's curse were dark, but now the people found themselves plunged into blackest night.

Some accepted their fate, even seeing this as an escape from the eternity of frustration to which they had been sentenced by Ilsa Wlich. Others fought, but were too weak to overcome the illness.

The numbers were also swelled by a few who grew sick without the symptoms of the disease. It was as if anaemia struck them, brought by a shadow that left them confused and forgetful while their spirits were low and they never seemed to recover. Arzt seemed unable to help; none of the medicines he brought made any difference and death followed with such inevitability, it was as if he wielded the scythe himself rather than a remedy.

Karl watched his father sink into despair, yet he wasn't sick. Having lost Maria not so many years before, and being a melancholy man by nature, for whom the glass was often half-empty rather than half-full, he assumed that fate was going to take his son.

But instead, fate took a hand, and guided Karl to find a cure for the sickness.

One day he was looking at one of the magnificent Friedrich Trees, remembering again Ilsa's words about them giving life, when the colour of the bark stirred something in his memory. He remembered the strange flakes that Ilsa had tipped out of the pouch into which she had put the tree seeds. They looked the same colour and texture as the bark. And since Ilsa never kept anything that didn't have a use – and nothing is dead as long as hope is still alive – he pulled a few pieces of bark from the tree. Then, with no firm idea of what he was doing or why, he boiled it in water.

****

"What's this?" asked Droger, looking at the bottle of reddish-brown fluid.

"I don't know," said Karl. "Well, I know it's water that's had bark from a Friedrich Tree boiled in it, but I don't know why I did that, other than I can almost hear Ilsa screaming at me to do it. She'd probably have called it a tea."

"I see." Droger raised one eyebrow. "Are you telling me I should give this to the families of the sick when Dr Arzt sends them to me?"

"No, I'm saying you should give it to them whether he sends them or not. Well, it's worth a try, isn't it? Nothing else is working."

Droger couldn't argue with that logic.

Nor did he want to when, a couple of days later some of the people who took the drink were showing signs of improvement. And suddenly hope was very much alive again, leaving Droger to shake his head at just how much influence this boy Karl had had on his life. Yet before, he'd been just the baker's son; a little hidden miracle living in their midst waiting to happen.

And even while Karl's muddy-looking water was helping to fight the cholera, he was about to play an even bigger part in shaping the futures of both Droger and Reimersberg.

It started with a chance encounter that grew in significance the longer he thought about it.

Meister had decided to make a rare foray through the town's main square. The people's indifference to him had become more marked and likewise his contempt for them. He passed a trestle table, manned by two healthy citizens, which Droger had set up for dispensing the tea from the Friedrich Trees, or Tea Tree as it became known. Karl was sitting on the steps by the Reimersberg Uhr and watched the mayor's disdainful progress.

One of the citizens, remembering his station, gave a deferential nod to Meister and offered him a cup of the tea. Karl observed how the latter took the cup, before hurling it to the ground as if he had been offered hemlock. As the liquid splashed on the cobbled square, the mayor wiped some droplets from his clothing in frantic disgust, turned and headed back to his house, watched in amazement by everyone there.

For Karl, who had made it his habit to observe life, in the hope that one day he could write a journal like Marco Polo, something stirred; a memory. He looked up at the sky, and the faint swaying of the topmost branches of the Friedrich Trees caught the corner of his vision. Now he remembered the way Meister had never shared in the joy those trees brought, nor taken a glass of the cider on the days of celebration. Once he'd spied the mayor looking up at the trees with a peculiar look on his face; part contempt, but now he thought about it, part disquiet.

There was nothing more than that at the moment. But when you are stuck in an unchanging world, a conundrum is something to treasure.

****

The boy was by his secret door that opened onto the outside world; strange how that part of town had turned out to be one of the safest places during all the troubles. He'd played his usual trick that night, leaving his pillows under his blanket so that it looked as if he was asleep if his father looked in - which he did less and less - and sneaked out. The sky was full of stars and the Hexental looked peaceful in their eternal light, though he knew all manner of beasts and spirits were abroad.

Then up on the town wall Karl heard two voices; rough and coarse. He didn't recognise either of them.

"This'd be a better place. No-one would look in 'ere, and it's all walled off."

"Yeah, we could dump 'em in there. No-one comes 'ere any more. They wouldn't know."

A horrible fear settled on the boy. He thought he knew what the two men were discussing. The town graveyard was already full to overflowing. It sounded like there was going to be a terrible echo of history and the Kriegerstrasse would once again house the victims of an epidemic. And to add to his woes, his sanctuary would be lost forever. He sat still in the dark, horrified by all the prospects.

But then there was another voice, and this one he recognised.

"No, you idiots." It was Dr Arzt. "If you throw them in there, the groans and then the stink will fill the whole town. Don't you get it? Lower them over the wall and they'll disappear, just like Hof and Schmied."

"Lower them?" said one of the others in disbelief. "Sounds like a lot of hard work to me. Why can't we just pitch 'em over?"

The doctor's tongue clicked with impatience. "Fools; didn't you see the body of the Zimmermann boy, or all the others who've already given up hope and thrown themselves over the side." It went quiet. When Arzt spoke again it was obvious he'd been lost in thought for a moment. "Quite fascinating, in a way. Life and death must be separated by the smallest, immeasurable pieces of time. They say the victim of beheading feels only a tickle on the back of the neck from the blade, though we cannot prove it. And here, death must come just before the body has time to realise it has finished its journey. This is why we must be sure our…" he cleared his throat, "…um, patients are still alive, so that they disappear."

Karl's blood ran cold. It wasn't the dead they were planning to dump, but the sick. Obviously they'd decided they couldn't throw the dead; since they were no longer living citizens of Reimersberg they would lie there for all to see. He squeezed his eyes shut; it was too horrible to contemplate. He'd known for some time now that Arzt was a useless doctor, but not that he was evil.

One of the rogues spoke again. "Won't the relatives wonder where they've gone?"

"We'll tell them we've buried them," replied Arzt.

"But everyone knows the graveyard's full."

"I think the relatives are too busy trying to stay alive themselves to worry too much. Besides, they trust me. I'm a doctor."

"Can't we burn 'em?" said the other man.

"While they're still alive?"

"Oh yeah. What about when they're dead?"

"That's not really the problem we're looking at here, is it? I've a better question - why don't you try thinking occasionally?" The ruffian fell silent; he was probably trying to find an answer to the last question. Arzt continued: "The smell would fill the town for weeks. And a pile of burning corpses in the middle of the main square isn't exactly going to raise the spirits, is it? Can't you see, this is the quickest and cleanest way? Besides, it's Meister's orders and he's still the mayor."

"Just about," said the other man.

"What do you mean?"

"Well, we never see 'im, 'e don't give any leadership, and all we get to do is stand around and make sure 'e's not disturbed. If we do see 'im, there's a strange smell on his breath; alcohol and…something else. Could swear it's blood, if I didn't know better. Not sure, but it gives me the creeps."

"Well you'd better hope it pickles and preserves him, because he's mayor by right and as long as he is, you have a job and so do I. Anyway, you can tell by this task he's set us, he's still trying to think of ways to do what's best for the town. And finally, why do you think two thickheads like you were made Elders? Not for your bright ideas, that's for sure. "

"I've never actually killed anyone. I've beaten a few up; threatened a few at Meister's say-so."

"Well take comfort from this," said Arzt. "Technically you're not killing them; as soon as they touch the ground they disappear. We don't know what that means; probably never will."

"But…"

"Never mind 'but' – those are orders. Tomorrow we start moving all the weak and dying to the old chapel just along from here. We'll say it's to keep them away from those who are getting better. Then tomorrow night, we'll start our magic trick."

Karl heard Arzt start to walk away.

"'Ere, that was a bit of a magic trick by Droger, wasn't it, curing people like that?"

"Shut up," said the fading voice of Dr Arzt.

"It even tastes quite nice that stuff. Certainly kept us free of the sickness."

"That was the devil protecting you," said Arzt.

When his heart had stopped thundering in his ears and he knew they had gone, Karl pushed his secret door back into place and made his way out of the Kriegerstrasse. He had to see Droger *now*.

****

The apothecary's expression was grave. "Are you sure you heard right?"

"Yes, believe me."

"I do, Karl."

Droger's face looked suddenly very lined and old in the candlelight, as he gazed into the flame on the table between them. He shook his head.

"This is a monstrous act," he said, "dreamt up by a monstrous man."

"Dr Arzt?"

"No, Meister. Arzt is just his puppet."

"Can't we get rid of him as mayor? Why does he have to stay in charge?"

"Because that, ridiculous though it sounds, is the constitution of this town, and always has been. As long as the Council of Elders votes him in, he is entitled to hold that position."

"Well then, vote him out. He's planning to kill people."

Droger looked at the boy and couldn't help but smile, although it was a grim expression. Ah, the naivety of youth was still there. "The people whom he's always looked after will always look after him; that means Pfarrer and Arzt. Then there's Kerzen the candle-maker and Brauer the brewer – otherwise known as the two henchmen you heard tonight – and Michael Bauer, who will vote for him because Meister made them Elders. If he's no longer in power, they will worry that they might lose their position. Metzger is a good man, but like most here he is scared of losing his licence. Your father, I'm afraid to say, is the same. That leaves just me."

Karl looked frustrated. "How did Kerzen and Brauer become Elders?"

"When the curse first hit us we thought a strong Council would be needed, with more members to help us control the town. That was a mistake."

"But listen; I could convince my father to vote with you. I know he's weak, but he's a good man. Metzger's the same, so you could talk him round."

"That's true – he has no great love of Meister. But they would only vote against him if they could be sure he would lose. As things stand, that would be three of us and six of them, if you include Meister himself."

Karl frowned, but then remembered something. "Michael Bauer's brother is amongst the sick, so surely he would be angry to hear of Meister's plan."

Droger looked at Karl in admiration. "You think fast and are well informed. It's no wonder I never see you around; you must be scurrying about like a mouse gathering grains of information. Perhaps I should ask for you to be made an Elder." Then he looked down. "But what's the use? The priest, the doctor, the candle-maker and the brewer would vote with the mayor, he would have the casting vote and I would have a powerful enemy."

It seemed hopeless. All Karl could find to say – though it came from the heart – was:

"But we must stop them. It's not...it's just not right. Surely if we tell the people of the town..."

Droger shook his head. "Those who are not dead or dying are recovering and grateful to be alive. Man becomes very selfish when he is clinging to life. There are many things he will just turn his back on and hope they go away so he can live another day. Besides, we don't have time; and I think Meister will cover his tracks. He would just blame Arzt and deny everything."

"And from what you've said, Kerzen and Bauer won't talk. Besides, they would be happy for Arzt to take the blame if Meister keeps quiet about their part in the terrible plot."

They sat for some moments in a depressed silence. Then suddenly Droger's head shot up.

"Wait a minute! I've just had an idea." He leapt up and ruffled Karl's hair. "What would I do without you, dear boy?!"

Karl looked at Droger and started to grin, unsure what he'd done, but caught up in the apothecary's sudden enthusiasm. But just as suddenly, Droger turned serious, as the grim reality of what he had to do hit him."

"Tomorrow, I must call a meeting of the Elders."

"When?"

"When I'm ready."

Droger noticed that Karl's smile had faded, so added: "I didn't mean to sound abrupt. All I'm saying..."

Karl interrupted him. "It's alright. I was thinking about something else."

Droger sat again. "Tell me."

Karl was hesitant. "Well..." he drew the word out. "...you may think this is stupid..."

"Unlikely."

"It's Meister. I can't help thinking there's more to him than meets the eye."

"Go on."

"Ilsa said she saw a *dangerous being* on her first day in the town. Then there's what we found in the jail; you said you didn't think Wachter had the brains to organise that himself. Then I heard those two thugs saying Meister smelt of something like blood."

"Are you saying...? No!" Droger was amazed. The man of science didn't want to hear such things – but men of science didn't live in towns trapped by curses. What did science know? As he spoke his next words, the irony didn't escape him; that he was seeking to disprove by turning to legend. "I thought such...beings couldn't move in daylight."

"But they can! Ilsa told me tales of the east, where these spirits moved around in the day, though they didn't like it. I wondered why she was telling me such tales." He looked sad for a moment. "And I wonder now why she left me – us – in the clutches of this evil."

Droger reached across and patted his shoulder. "Perhaps she knew that only you could save the town – from this and from itself." He watched a faint smile return to the boy-man's lips. "What else do you have?"

The enthusiasm returned. "I don't believe what Arzt said; that Meister is still thinking about the good of the town in disposing of the sick and dying. It just doesn't ring true." His eyes widened. "You don't think...?"

"...that it's not just cholera victims going over the wall." Droger's face was grim.

Karl finished by explaining about the episode in the town square, concluding: "He's never shown any enthusiasm for the trees; never liked them." He paused and gave Droger a look that even that wise man couldn't fathom. "And do you know what; the trees don't like him either."

CHAPTER 13

The next day was dreary; misty. It seemed that nature was falling in with the mood that hung over the town as the sick and possibly dying – those for whom the elixir from the Friedrich Trees might have come too late – were moved by order of Arzt to the old chapel. So to add to their woes, they were now huddled together in the coldest, saddest part of town.

As a result of the mist it grew dark earlier that evening. Keen to get started, Arzt waited till the lamp-lighters had lit the crude wicks which had replaced the old lanterns, then gave the signal to his medical assistants – in other words Kerzen and Brauer – to start their gruesome task.

"First, take the very weak; those too far gone to struggle much," he said. "We're starting a bit earlier than planned, so we might be done by midnight."

"That's easy for you to say," said Kerzen, "you haven't got to carry them up the steps or lower them down the walls."

Not far from the Kriegerstrasse was a watchtower. It was no longer manned; ever since that part of town had been infected by the plague two hundred years before no-one had the nerve to stand there through the night. Now Droger and Metzger hid behind its weathered stones. Karl had wanted to come, but Droger had put his foot down. That night's deed was not for his eyes.

The steps, which the two heavies had planned to use to climb to the battlements, were a short distance from the tower. Droger and Metzger lost all track of time, so it seemed they were woken from a sleep by the heavy tread and panting breaths of someone straining under a weight. The two of them peered cautiously over the wall of the watchtower. In the dim light they saw a misshapen shadow take a final step onto the battlements and with a weary shrug drop its burden like two sacks of potatoes; except potatoes don't groan as they hit the floor. Droger could hear Metzger's jaw muscles and teeth clenching in anger.

"The filthy curs," said the butcher under his breath.

Droger put a restraining hand on his arm. "Wait till I say," he whispered. "We don't want them to escape."

There were more laboured footsteps, and another grotesque silhouette appeared, likewise dumping the two bodies slung over its shoulders with a thump and a groan of pain.

"Yup, this is the place. Here's the mark I made on the wall."

"Right, let's get it done."

It was Kerzen and Brauer all right; both the watchers recognised the coarseness of the voices.

With distaste, Kerzen wiped his hands on his shirt. "I dunno; you sure we can't catch nuthin' off these. I know we've drunk the tea, but cholera's cholera."

Brauer dismissed his partner's concerns. "Told yer; Arzt said these are not sick." He touched the side of his nose in a knowing gesture. "Meister just wants 'em out of the way. Ours is not to reason why."

Droger felt his blood run cold.

Very carefully, the two watchers climbed out of the watchtower and crept in the direction of the villains, who were now concentrating on tying a rope around an elderly lady.

"C'mon old girl," said Kerzen. In the smoky light from the streets below, neither he nor Brauer saw the two avenging angels approaching them; didn't hear their soft footfall above the weak protests of the woman, who had suddenly realised the fate planned for her and found from somewhere the strength to put up a fight.

"I thought old Arzt was going to give 'em something to put their lights out," said Brauer. He and Kerzen stepped forward as the woman shrank back against the wall in terror.

"Time to snuff out *your* lights," was all the villains heard before each registered the point of a blade between his shoulders and the coarse sack thrown over his head. They were forced to lie face down on the battlements and their hands were tied behind their backs.

On that cold, dank night, with cholera still raging in the town, those not in their sickbeds were with their loved ones watching over them. So no-one saw the four men – two prisoners and two guardians of the innocent – cross the main square. Nobody heard the big town gates being opened, or if they did it mattered less than life. People were hardened to the cries and moans of those who were suffering, so couldn't tell the difference when two hooded figures shouted for help as they were made to walk from the town to an invisible fate.

Droger shivered as the burly figure of Metzger closed the gates again. As he climbed back up to the battlements, he tried to tell himself that he had not just taken a life. Metzger couldn't have cared less, and on reflection, as Droger looked at the four sick people lying there, he thought Metzger was probably right.

Now Droger remembered something Ilsa had told him once. It had seemed a random conversation at the time, but he knew now every action she'd ever taken was part of the mosaic of universal laws that governed her life. He wasn't sure what he was looking for, but he examined the arms and necks of each of the victims. Sure enough, there were tiny cuts; the type she'd described when telling him about the vampiric practices of the ancients. He shook his head, the man of science once again dismayed to think of the knowledge he would never have.

"Ok," he said, "let's get these poor folk back to the old chapel, and then you and I will call a council meeting, Mr Metzger. And don't allow anyone to say they won't attend, not even the mayor. But do me one favour; keep hold of your anger for now. I will need your strength later. Believe me, Meister might be a much more dangerous animal that you know. Just tell him we need his immediate assistance."

Mr Metzger had always prayed for the forgiveness of any animal he slaughtered. As he stood before the door of the mayor's residence, he asked a silent pardon from all the unknown victims of treachery for not smashing down that door and killing that monster.

There had not been a council meeting for over a year and as the mayor came to the door Metzger was struck by a certain toad-like, bloated quality to him. It was as if he had eaten all the ills of the world and forgotten to spew them out.

"Good sir," he said, almost choking on the words. "Your wisdom is needed. There's an emergency council meeting and you're in the chair."

****

They'd made Wirt clear the inn of all customers – which numbered but three on that dreadful, pestilent night - and now they sat around the Stammtisch. Droger watched Meister drumming his fingers on the table, impatient, but also uncomfortable with the unexpected summons. Those who fill the world with ghosts see them everywhere.

"This is a disgrace," he said.

"You know the constitution allows any Elder to call a meeting at short notice," said Droger. "You also know," here Droger pointed to a clock, "that if any member fails to show up within ten minutes of the appointed start time, or is unavailable, then the meeting can start without them. This meeting was called for nine o'clock; it now being quarter past, and Kerzen and Bauer having not shown up, we must carry on."

"Agreed," said Metzger, Bauer and Baecker. Arzt and Pfarrer tried to look as if they both agreed and disagreed, and ended up looking as if they had strained something. Eventually they both grunted their agreement, as there was really nothing else they could say under the constitution.

"Not agreed," said Meister. Then he looked at the faces of those around him, saw determination in the eyes of some, puzzlement in others, and said "Agreed", though with much reluctance, as another droplet of his control slipped through his fingers.

Then Droger started: "As the Elder who called this meeting I will speak. A terrible deed has come to my notice, by which all of you, I'm sure, will be shocked." Meister and Arzt glanced at each other, but said nothing. "A plot has been uncovered to lower the sick bodies of living citizens of Reimersberg over the town wall, in the hope of ridding the town of the burden of caring for, or if necessary giving a proper burial to its own people."

There was a sharp intake of breath from Michael Bauer, whose brother had been taken to the old chapel that very day. A similar sound came from Pfarrer; a misguided, Puritanical, unforgiving man of God, but a man of God nonetheless.

Droger continued: "This terrible deed was organised by none other than our mayor."

"Nonsense," said Meister. His was the only voice.

"There are four witnesses, otherwise known as intended victims, to this act, and I'm sure there is at least one man in this room who, if it comes to a choice between him or the mayor rotting in a dungeon, will certainly bear witness the plot." He didn't bother looking at Arzt; there was no need. "My motion is that the mayor be removed from office and imprisoned for the attempted murder of at least four citizens."

Meister's mouth had fallen open. "But…"

"Of course, according to the constitution of this town, only a unanimous vote can remove or accuse the mayor." Droger saw a smile start to form on Meister's lips. "Are we in agreement that we should, at least, take a vote?"

"Aye," said all voices around the table, including Meister.

Droger pointed to the clock. "Now it looks to me that Kerzen and Brauer are not even going to make it in time for the vote, but are we agreed that we should still go ahead?"

"Aye."

"I wonder what is keeping them," said Metzger. He looked at the mayor and doctor by turns. "Perhaps, in trying to commit a terrible deed they slipped and fell over the battlements themselves, and have disappeared, never to return – as they intended for their victims."

Meister's brows narrowed; likewise Arzt. They could not look at each other.

"That would be unfortunate for you, Mr Meister," said Droger, "should you stay in power; and for any of your supporters, since looking around this table it seems unlikely you would win many motions in future."

Droger could almost feel a distance growing between Pfarrer, Arzt, and the mayor. He continued: "But enough of the future; on with tonight's motion." Then the apothecary paused for dramatic effect. "Oh, and one last thing; according to the constitution the mayor has a casting vote, which he can use only if the other Elders cannot reach agreement. What he cannot do is use that vote to stop a unanimous decision being reached."

With his last lifeline gone, Meister appeared to achieve the impossible and shrink.

"I put it to the Council," said Droger, "that we remove Mr Meister from office and put him in prison awaiting trial. All those in favour."

The hands of Baecker, Bauer, Metger and Droger shot into the air. Pfarrer and Arzt raised theirs more slowly, weighed down by reluctant loyalty and a lingering sense of cowardice, but lifted by a sense of the inevitable. Droger turned to the others.

"Mr Metzger, Mr Bauer, please escort Mr Meister, our former mayor, to the jail. You will find all the cells unoccupied except one. Let our friend here enjoy the good company and fine conversation of Mr Wachter, who he actually locked up after some prisoners were carelessly lost." Droger looked at Meister. "Even though I despise you, I will not do to you what you did to those poor souls you dropped into the oubliettes. In showing you that mercy, I acknowledge my part in bringing this town to its current plight."

"What's that all about – people locked in oubliettes?" asked Bauer, shocked.

"I'll tell you all the things I have hidden from you once you return," said Droger. "Until tonight I didn't know who I could trust. When you have locked up this monster, please return here and we'll vote for a new, temporary mayor."

"No need for a vote," said Bauer, "you have mine already."

"And mine," said Metzger and Baecker simultaneously.

"But not mine." The voice sounded different; otherworldly and remote. A chair scraped against the stone and Meister stood. He looked around the room at each of the Elders in turn. Metzger and Bauer, who had moved forward to take the mayor by force if necessary, stepped back in fear as the green eyes swept across them. Though it could only have been a trick of the candlelight, Meister seemed to have grown. He planted his hands on the table and leaned forward to fix Droger with a gorgonising stare.

"Gentlemen," said Droger, evincing a calmness he didn't feel, "it looks like some of my explanations might not be necessary."

"You worms!" Meister's voice seemed to have crawled through a pit of slime before emerging. Droger saw Arzt quailing. Presumably he had witnessed this before, when he first decided he had no alternative but to be the vampire's creature. "Do you really think you can usurp my position as head of this town? Did you really think I would allow your pathetic little uprising to succeed?" His head pushed forward; a snake tasting the fear. Only the forked tongue was missing, but it wouldn't have surprised anyone if it had flicked out. "I have seen them come and go; empires, nations, invaders, fools. I have slept with queens and with rats. I have outlived them all, and I will live still. When time decides that the curse will fall from this town I will be standing, even if I must scrape insects from the dust to feed this cursed body. Know this and weep. Now try to take me to your prison and see how long it can hold me."

With that he stood tall again, grabbed the end of the table and flipped it across the room as if it were made of paper, not solid oak. He grinned at their despair.

"It seems I don't know my own strength when I have fed well."

He turned his attention fully to Droger, advancing towards him with menace.

The apothecary felt the panic twisting his insides, even though he had prepared for this moment. He tried to keep the tremor from his voice as the baleful eyes sapped the strength from him, telling himself there was no shame in being scared; it was fear that made him and his fellow burghers human and for that he thanked God.

He raised his hand: "Stop and think, Meister."

Strangely, the vampire did stop. They faced each other. Droger was almost sure a slight haze surrounded Meister, as if anger burned his body – or the one he had occupied – from within.

Droger continued: "What will happen now if you follow the path you seem to have chosen? Where will you turn next? You are trapped, as are we? If you kill us all, who will solve the riddle; lift the curse? What visitor will want to stay in this empty town?"

"I will live here alone," said Meister. "Loneliness does not fill me with fear. A vampire is always solitary, even when he is in the throng of humanity."

Vampire. The word was mouthed silently in horror by Bauer, Metzger, Baecker and Pfarrer. The priest crossed himself several times.

Meister continued: "But there will be no need to kill everyone if I am you. They respect you; look up to you. How will they know that you are me?"

Now he came again and Droger could feel the heat from him. He fought the lethargy that seemed to slow the flow of blood in his veins. The green eyes held him transfixed. He was drowning; part of him still panicking, the other part accepting the end. Surely it could not end this way. He had prepared...something. He groped through the long grass that was his memory, knowing it lay hidden there.

But once again Meister had stopped, his face contorted in frustrated rage as he appeared to smell the air.

"Damn that witch! Damn her and her blood-bane!"

Droger didn't understand, but he seized the opportunity and, reaching into his coat pocket produced a wooden cross, which he held up in front of him.

Meister took one look at it and laughed, a sound worse than his previous threats.

"Your religion has no power over me. Those, too, I have seen come and go." The laughter ceased. "Very well, if I cannot drink your poisoned blood I will spill every last drop of it."

He strode forward and grasped the cross in Droger's shaking hand...

...and screamed.

Meister staggered back, holding his hand, the palm of which seemed to be steaming. Before the eyes of the Elders, the flesh broiled and already suppurated. The vampire screamed in pain and bent over, clutching the wrist of the damaged hand.

Droger was as astonished as anyone, but certain things fell into place. He came forward, feeling more confident now.

"The power of God," whispered Pfarrer, awestruck.

"Perhaps," responded Droger. "Certainly the power of the Friedrich Tree." He pointed to some sharpened staves leaning against the wall, made from the same reddish wood. "Pick up those weapons."

Metzger, Bauer and Baecker, who had been rooted to the spot through a combination of terror and fascination, grabbed the makeshift spears, and Meister looked up from his frightful hand to find them pointed at him from three sides.

Droger spoke to them. "Unless I am mistaken, it seems that the tea Karl recommended has given us immunity from vampires." He turned to Meister. "Blood-bane, eh? Poisoned blood."

Meister looked at him and almost snarled before turning his attention back to his hand. Despite everything, Droger felt some compassion. Watching this creature was like seeing a wolf limping on an injured paw. Meister was driven by primeval urges, which were part of the universe's sometimes violent laws. They could have stuck him now like a pig; ended his miserable life. Yet what would that have said about them, now that they had him in their power. Would it have brought them to his level? Actually no; it would have meant that they had sunk below that, because they had consciences, which they would be ignoring to commit such a deed.

Nevertheless, justice would be demanded, and Droger was not a god who could deny it to those whose loved ones had been taken. Like all men, he needed to blindfold his conscience. There could be no happy ending when two worlds collided.

He addressed their captive again.

"Herr Meister, believe it or not, you are safest with us. If the people find out what you are, they will kill you with fire. You cannot fight them all. My friends here will take you to the jail and that is where you will stay."

Droger looked at the other Elders. Arzt and Pfarrer had long ceased to have an opinion. He could see that the others were fighting the urge to drive their spears through this beast, but out of respect to the man who had brought them to this point they listened as he continued:

"In jail you will stay, fed and clothed of course, until the curse ends." He looked around at the grim faces of the other Elders. "You will be our dirty secret. We will not tell them the full extent of things. Gradually you will be forgotten. If that ominous day should come, and the curse lifts, I will ask the people to pass judgement. That is the fate to which you condemned Ilsa Wlich and it seems to me poetic justice. But you have my word, I will speak for mercy and propose that you be allowed to leave this town. The world will have to look to itself."

There was silence. As Meister straightened up the three spear-holders hefted their weapons threateningly. However, the former mayor of Reimersberg simply moved towards the door. As he was about to step through he paused, turned and looked at Droger, then said:

"It is a hard thing; to live forever. Let us see who comes through. You could have killed me, but it is not in a vampire's nature to thank or be grateful. My day will come. Mark well."

With the mayor's words still hanging in the air, Droger called on Pfarrer and Arzt to help him put back the Stammtisch. He looked at the damage. "Mr Wirt will be pleased," he said drily, before turning his attention to Arzt: "Honour amongst thieves, eh Doctor?"

Arzt tried to frown. "What do you mean?"

"Were you not terrified that Meister would condemn your disloyalty?"

"I don't know what…"

"Don't insult the new mayor as you have betrayed the old." Droger stood and his eyes were as dark as coal beneath the silver of his hair. Arzt cowered before him now. "I know all about your part in this terrible plot. You are his creature; a servant of his darkness and the last person he will abandon." Droger sat down again and clasped his hands on the Stammtisch in front of him. "But abandoned you will be. I mean to start the right way; to turn things around as best I can. Having faced the horror tonight, I will not be so quick to condemn a weak, vain man such as you for surrendering to its power. So, to you I offer one last chance to redeem yourself and save your soul. You will take care of the sick and dying, whom you have so conveniently gathered together in the old chapel. That will be the new hospital. And you;" he pointed at Pfarrer, who bore the look of a man at odds with everything he'd ever seen or believed "you will minister to them as a man of God should."

Pfarrer nodded, only too happy to agree. He had lost his way and seemed to welcome this chance to return to the path.

With such simplicity, the final Council meeting of the town of Reimersberg was now at an end.

So, too, in a few weeks, was the cholera. And Arzt did at least partly redeem himself; though of course, without the potion from the Friedrich Tree the remaining tatters of his reputation would have gone the way of Kerzen and Brauer; lost forever.

CHAPTER 14

S trangely enough, the visitor who might have driven the final nail into the town's coffin - or rather, buried it - was the King. Not the old one; he died after a long and inglorious reign, having ventured beyond his walls about as often as a typical citizen of Reimersberg. But when the new king discovered that his father had spent nearly all of his inheritance, he sought new ways to raise money, and the question of tithes reared its head again.

He looked down the list of towns and cities in his kingdom and decided that he would visit them all, to raise funds for a new war; one that would never take place because he had invented it. Not that his illiterate subjects, leading their remote and tiny lives, would ever know the difference, or care, as long as they didn't have to fight. The King decided he would visit all of these outposts himself. What better way to ensure people paid? Who could deny their ruler money when he stood before them in person, overpowering them with his divine bearing? Besides, he was bored with life in the capital, and this offered a good opportunity to go hunting, both for venison and women.

So it was that he came, after a long and arduous journey, to Reimersberg. Like the Tithes Inspector before him, he saw instantly that things weren't exactly normal there. Unlike the Inspector, he wasn't expecting to find the town. He summoned forward his chief advisor.

"What manner of place is this?"

The advisor looked down the list, then at a map and scratched his chin. "I am at a loss, Your Majesty. According to the official register and the latest map, the next town should be another twenty miles further on. Most peculiar."

Another voice spoke up from behind them. "If I may be so bold, Your Majesty." It was one of the generals; a stocky man with a splendid, imposing moustache and an aura of authority that put the King's in the shade.

The King signalled him forward. "What is it, General?"

"I fought in this region for many years in the Palatinate Wars, Your Majesty, and if I am not mistaken, this would be Reimersberg; jewel of the Adventurer's Road." He frowned and rubbed at his moustache. "Though mistaken I could be, because the place I remember was like a gleaming, resplendent citadel, not this sad and faded apology for a town."

The King looked grim. "I wouldn't put it past those petty thieves my father called advisers to have hidden this place on all official records, so they could feather their nests with its taxes and tithes."

Suitably angered, the King, like that Inspector before him, was deeply offended that no-one came from the town to greet him. But when a King is offended, the anger of a Tithes Inspector is but the cry of a sulking child in comparison.

He sent forward the general. "People of Reimersberg," cried the old soldier, with a voice used to issuing commands above the noise of battle, "show yourselves!"

The general could not have known the impact of those words, with their echoes of the day of the curse. Almost instantly a crowd of ashen-faced people gathered at the gate, though still none came forward. Then a man pushed through from the back; the chain of office around his neck. He bowed deeply as he saw the King's banner. "A thousand pardons, good sir. I was at the far end of the town when the look-out summoned me. You are most welcome in Reimersberg. My name is Droger; I am the mayor."

A figure resplendent in dress uniform and riding a white horse came forward.

"Why have you not come forth to greet the King's banner?" he demanded.

Droger guessed instantly that this was a member of the Royal Family and he dropped to one knee. "A thousand pardons, sire." He hesitated. "I know how strange this will sound, but there is a curse on this town and none of us may leave its walls."

The uniformed man rode right up to the gates. "Not even for a King; one who is mightily offended by this insult?"

There was a gasp from the crowd and Droger, who stayed kneeling said: "Your Majesty, please believe us. I know it sounds incredible, but it is the truth. If any of us were to step beyond the gate, we would disappear to heaven or hell knows where."

"Prove it."

Droger looked the King in the eye and each man saw the determination of the other. It was a question of who would back down first, though Droger knew the risk he was taking by this apparent insubordination. But the knowledge that he was about to die made him careless of his fate, so he continued to hold the King's gaze. Then of a sudden, the King looked away.

Droger knew it made no difference. In those moments he had seen the fate of Reimersberg in the other man's eyes.

The mayor stood and prepared to step forward.

"Halt!" said the King. "We believe you. You would not have risked looking a fool or a liar otherwise."

No, thought Droger, and you would have been proved wrong, which wouldn't have looked good in front of your men and a bunch of simple townsfolk.

Now the King looked past the gathered people into the town. "Besides, we see that there is indeed something peculiar, something weird at work in this place. We had heard that Reimersberg was beautiful. How correct that statement is; for Reimersberg *was* beautiful, but no longer." He turned to his retinue, who laughed dutifully at his wordplay. "What we see here is decay." The King lifted his head and his nostrils flared till he resembled his horse. "And that smell; there is..." he searched for the correct expression, "...wrongness in the air."

"There has been disease here, sire," said Droger. He saw the King flinch, but to his credit there were enough vestiges of royalty in his blood to prevent him retreating. Still, his eyes betrayed his meanness.

"Then you are cursed indeed, and if so, then it must be for a reason. Only God would know."

This King was a petty man; bitter from having had to wait so long to come to the throne while his father just carried on living; resentful of the less than fawning reception he had received so far in this disappointing, inbred corner of his kingdom. Where the townsfolk might have expected mercy or aid, they were pushed, instead, back down the path along which they had struggled so hard. "By our command, close up your gates; allow no innocent person to wander in and become a part of the history of your forsaken town, with its curse and its sickness." Then he looked to his left and, despite every privilege he enjoyed in his life, envied the people the beauty and strength of the Friedrich Trees. They had no place here; just as this sick town had no right to his protection. "And so that no innocent man or child may climb these trees and enter your town, we will hack them down."

The crowd gasped.

"NO!" shouted Droger, who then just about remembered this was the King. "...Your Majesty. Please."

But that presumptuous response had angered the King beyond recall. "Indeed *YES.* We will have them removed."

"Your Majesty, they bear the only fruit we have, and are our only source of firewood."

The King looked at him, revelling at last in the wielding of power. "As we said, if this town is cursed in the eyes of God it must accept its fate. It is not deserving." With that he turned to one of his advisers. "Which way now?"

The adviser pointed, and then followed this with a sweep of the arm. "Down the valley, Your Majesty. Those are impassable mountains, and only a madman would try to come through this forest, with its gorges, and its wolves."

"Very well. Leave enough men here to cut down the trees. Burn the roots, and then post guards at a day's distance in either direction along the valley. Let this town remain forgotten; wiped from the map; removed from any lists that inquisitive people like us may find. It is a blot on our kingdom."

****

As the axes of the King's men hewed at the Friedrich Trees, the misery of the townsfolk, which had begun years before with the curse of Ilsa Wlich, seemed complete. People winced at every blow, deep into their very souls, till it seemed they would carry the wounds to the end of time. Those trees had come to symbolise their determination not to succumb to despair. The irony was; before the curse, the nearby forest had always seemed threatening and dangerous, inhabited by wolves, haunted. No-one had ventured further than the fringes for berries or timber, fearing the dreaded, vengeful spirits that inhabited the trees. Yet folk had come to see the prolific, almost fecund Friedrich Trees as bringers of life and hope.

Droger stirred the people out of their despair long enough for them to gather quickly whatever fruit they could, and salvage some of the branches. But at last, as those magnificent living things toppled back from the walls to the shouts of 'TIMBER!" from below, there was an audible lament in the creaking of their limbs and the shrieks of the townsfolk. Then came a silence, which if anything, was more oppressive than the stillness, which had followed the curse.

As the King's men departed and the smoke from burning roots turned the sky black, Droger knew his leadership would be needed more than ever; his resolve tested to the full.

He called the people together in the main square. What was left of the town was gathered. He saw tearful eyes set in expectant faces, and had, for a moment, no clue what to say.

And that was when Karl came forward, pushing through the crowd as he had on the day of Ilsa's banishment. Truly, thought the apothecary, this was an astonishing boy, though of course not many sixteen year olds had the accumulated knowledge of nearly thirty years in their heads. Droger could feel it; sensed that he came now to give the mayor his support. Droger intended to make him his right-hand man – or boy. It was no wonder Ilsa had chosen Karl. Or maybe they'd chosen each other. How ironic that Karl should lose his mother on the very day Ilsa arrived in town, all those years before.

For his part, Karl planned to do more than give his support. He had another trick up his sleeve. He climbed the steps near the gate, where Droger had positioned himself to address the crowd. As Karl turned to that crowd, it struck him; despite everything, he was indeed still a child, because he had held on to hope, whereas on many faces before him he saw none. He wouldn't want the duty of leading these people; was glad Droger had taken that role; it was an adult responsibility.

The crowd watched as Karl whispered something to Droger before pushing a small object into his hand.

Droger smiled at the boy's words and looked down at the pouch resting on his palm. He knew now exactly what he had to say.

"Good townsfolk of Reimersberg, I address you for the last time." There was a murmur and a gasp from every mouth. Droger smiled and calmed the noise with a palm-down gesture. "Let me explain. A wise man once asked, quite appropriately given our circumstances today, whether a tree, falling in the middle of nowhere and heard by no-one, makes a sound. Well, in the same way, if a town has no visitors, if no-one sees it or hears its people speak, if it is wiped off the maps and the registers, does it exist? It seems we are abandoned. In many ways it is what we deserve, for we were always too proud. When someone came who brought new and different ideas – brought good things to which we were not open because we didn't understand – we abandoned her." The crowd shuffled its feet and looked down. "And if you abandon a single, good person, you abandon the whole of humanity. We allowed evil to convince us it was right. We sought to wall her up in an old, frightful part of town. Now there's an irony, because we are the ones walled up from the rest of the world. We are the ones who are marked out as different and misunderstood.

"Now all that we have"- here he swept his arm across the crowd -"is each other." He lifted his voice. "And that will be enough." Droger saw the people look up at him intently and placed his hand on Karl's shoulder. "For this boy, who has done more for all of you than you can possibly know, has given me these." He showed the pouch. "Seeds for the Friedrich Tree." Mouths opened as one. "Yes, it was Karl here who planted the original seeds, which were given to him by Ilsa Wlich. And he kept some back – wise boy – in case we should ever need them again. You will have noticed that the fruit from the trees bears no seeds. Miracles are not there for just any man to help himself.

"Let us plant these trees in the middle of our town and as they grow, they will symbolise our own rebirth." People were smiling now and chattering. "We will eat of its fruit; use its wood, not just for fires, but for rebuilding our town. We will pull together. And, my good people, just as Ilsa has proved capable of doing so much good and has shown herself to be powerful, so we must believe that in the words she left with us, there is still hope; and the stranger who is no stranger will still come. And he or she will find a town worthy of saving. That stranger will not be forced into some cell and held against their will. They will want to *stay* – the original word in the riddle. That town will not just have been rebuilt, but also renamed. Yes, my friends, we know now that we did someone a great wrong and that even as we plotted against her, she left the door of hope open. That was what I meant when I said I address the people of the Reimersberg for the last time. That town was cursed for a reason.

"I propose that, from this day, our new town be called Ilsa-stadt."

There was a chorus of approval from the people.

Karl looked to the skies and smiled, somewhat sadly. Ilsa-stadt – *Ilsa's town* – she'd have liked that.

CHAPTER 15

In the years that followed under Mayor Droger, the people of the town did indeed pull together, accepting that just as they had shaped their own past, so they could shape each day. Life was a struggle, but they knew that was their lot. Old skills were rediscovered, as they used wood from the Friedrich Trees to rebuild and repair. They kept their streets and houses clean again, grew wiser in the care of their animals and the managing of their resources. There were no years of plenty, but they got by. They learnt how to make candles, which meant that there wasn't one single reason to regret the disappearance of the thug Kerzen, and more than one person was capable of making beer, so his henchman, Brauer, wasn't missed. The tale of their treachery never got out and while many questioned their fate, few wasted time thinking about it. All the Elders remained true to their oath of secrecy. They didn't want a lynching in Ilsa-stadt.

Of course the town could never regain the beauty of its glory days. In many ways life continued along the path it had taken after the curse, except now, because of the King's guards, there were no merchants, tinkers or mountebanks to bring items of luxury or even necessity. Broken pots had to be repaired, clothes darned and re-darned, food re-heated and leftovers made into broths, candles burned to the stubs. People went to bed early to avoid wasting light – so there were advantages to the times! – but it meant that the streets remained empty at night and the town lay in silence. One night, as Droger and his wife returned from a walk along the town walls, during which the vanguard flakes of a snowstorm had drifted down, Frau Droger turned in the doorway of their house and looked out.

"Do you remember, my love," she said, "how the snowfall always twinkled in the many streetlights and in the lamps that shone from almost every window in the winter?"

She sighed and went indoors, leaving the mayor lost for words of comfort.

One thing that returned to its former glory was the town clock, the famous Reimersberg Uhr. It had been allowed to stand silent and still for some years, as the passing of time became a sore point for the town, and the chiming of the hours had begun to sound like a tolling bell marking the death of everyone's hopes. Droger decided that it should be seen rather as a sign they were alive; that the universe had not excluded them completely from its laws.

There had been talk of rebuilding the church spire, but people decided they would put their physical needs ahead of their spiritual ones. And anyway, who would be coming to look at it. Most felt God had abandoned them, and many remembered Pfarrer's part in misleading them. The old, twisted spire, which had been pulled down for firewood, suddenly seemed a very apt symbol of religion in Reimersberg. The church remained unattended except by a hardy few. If ever proof was needed that religion simply prompted people to think about death this was it; an empty church in a town where no-one died any more.

When the shadow of despair fell, as it did from time to time, Droger encouraged apple brandy, music festivals, and a bonfire in the main square – made possible by the prolific growth and plentiful branches of the Friedrich Trees. He would open a few bottles of wine from the massive collection that Meister had built up in the old days. Also, he would remind the townsfolk that someone with the powers of Ilsa Wlich would not have wasted her words, which surely meant that her riddle – her prophecy – was not an empty one. It was a sign of the great leadership of the mayor – ably supported by Karl – that people still listened to such encouragement.

****

And in this way, somehow fifty years had passed. Half a century. Some coped with this anniversary better than others – it helped if you were one of those people whose eyes had never lifted beyond the ramparts of the town wall - but everyone struggled.

They were not helped by the sneaking approach of the forest. No-one was immune to this unnerving process. It was like trying to catch yourself blinking in a mirror; you couldn't see it, but everyone knew it was happening. It felt as if nature and the universe were trying to hide the town.

In that other world beyond the walls, there was now another king on the throne, the previous one having died, unmourned, in a hunting accident when he was gored by a wild boar. The new King never bothered the people of Reimersberg. It was as if the town had disappeared along with its name.

Since many families had been carried off by the cholera before Karl found the cure, Droger had ordered the pulling down of certain empty streets, though Karl ensured that the old part around the Kriegerstrasse was left alone. The available land was used to plant vegetables and certain manageable crops. During the years that followed most of the townsfolk played some part in producing enough food to keep themselves alive. Metzger and Baecker remained the butcher and baker respectively, though they no longer ran their shops as traditional businesses. Everything ran as a collective and bartering was the currency. The craftsmen of the town found also that, by returning to the soil, literally, and mixing it with crushed bark from the Friedrich Trees, they could produce a pigment for painting and preserving the wooden structures.

140

For a time, the question remained of what to do with Meister and Wachter. The Elders could not imagine keeping them locked up for eternity; the shadow of their presence darkened the lives of the people, hanging over them as surely as a gibbet-cage in the main square.

It was now known that Wachter had held strangers in the dungeons – Droger had to justify imprisoning him – but no more than that. Eventually judgement was taken out of everyone's hands. Prison broke him and he appeared to have shrunk. Out of pity, Droger released him to work on the land. His sins seemed to weigh him down. One day he was spotted shuffling towards the town gate. As the look-outs moved to stop him, Droger, who had been summoned, shouted "No; let him go." And Mr Wachter trudged out to whatever fate awaited those who disappeared.

Meister was a different animal entirely. The Elders told the townsfolk that he had been guilty of ordering the holding of the prisoners in the dungeons, in a misguided attempt to solve the riddle and break the curse. For this abuse of his office he was to be held indefinitely. Yet Droger knew that here too, a time for judgement would have to come.

Except one day Meister announced that the town was a prison anyway, so he might as well stay in his cell. Droger suspected that cell was preferable to facing the hatred and derision of the people he had once ruled with contempt. It was also probably the safest place for him, though no-one yet knew the full extent of his crimes. He turned down an offer of conditional liberty; the condition being that he would remain under guard. The new mayor didn't trust this state of affairs one bit and watched him carefully. Who knew what a snake like him might do when no-one was looking; where his poison might do harm? Droger instructed that the cell be made comfortable, but also that the bars should have staves of wood from the Friedrich Trees bound to them. For his pains, each day the mayor was taunted by Meister, who challenged him to have the courage of his convictions and kill him.

****

But there was one person who, one day – a very special day for him - found that he could no longer just wait for time and fate to run their course.

Karl had never given up his dream of travelling; breaking free. He had devoured every word of Marco Polo - read *The Travels* so many times that he had lost count – and anything else he could find in the town library. Whereas most people had grown almost content with their lot, or at least accepted it - like prisoners no longer comprehending the existence of a world beyond their walls - he felt suddenly as if sixty-five years of dreams and knowledge and yearning was starting to destroy him.

The encroaching forest had started to cut off his view down the valley and that might have been the final straw. Sitting in that secret archway at the end of the Kriegerstrasse one night – a place he'd kept for himself, not even telling Droger of its existence – the smell of grass, earth and dew in his nostrils became almost unbearable. He would have given anything to reach through and touch one of those blades of grass for the first time. What fresh wonder it would hold now; plain old grass.

Then one night, as teardrops fell to the ground between his feet, he just knew he must act. It was what Ilsa would have done; she wouldn't have waited for something to happen. But what would she do?

And as if in answer to him, an owl hooted in the forest. Normally a harbinger of doom for the suspicious people of those times, instead it gave Karl what he needed; a fresh idea.

He had to catch a bird. And that proved easier than anticipated.

Mr Metzger had always kept pigeons. Originally they'd been for racing purposes, but unfortunately for them, when times had grown hard the residents of old Reimersberg had developed a real taste for pigeon pie. But Metzger had kept one alive – an old favourite- for sentimental reasons.

Karl went to see him.

"Is it really?" asked the butcher rhetorically. "My, how the time flies." Then Metzger pulled a face. "Hmm, that was perhaps a stupid expression under the circumstances, eh, young Karl?"

"So is *young Karl,*" said the boy. They shared a kind of grim laugh. "But yes; sixty-five years ago today Ilsa Wlich cured me. And do you know what, Mr Metzger, it's as if she's whispering in my ear: *"Do something today, Karl. Who knows what might happen?"* The butcher continued slicing away at some meat for a pie he was preparing, while Karl spoke on: "Well, time may not fly, but I need something that does."

He gave a significant look past the butcher's shoulder towards the back of the shop, where he knew Metzger's last and favourite bird, his pigeon, Taube, resided. Metzger caught that glance, but ignored it and carried on slicing the meat.

Neither of them said anything for some time, and then Metzger threw down his knife and leaned his great powerful fists on the table.

"And why do you need something that can fly, young man?" he asked with impatience and perhaps a little trepidation.

"Because I need to send a message," came the reply, likewise impatient and fearful.

"Who to?"

"I don't know."

The butcher nodded his head for emphasis as he spoke: "You want to send a message to somebody, but you don't know who. And you want to use my favourite bird…"

"Your only bird; you've made the others into pies," said Karl cheekily.

Metzger glared at him. "My favourite bird; my companion of twenty years."

"Ten," said Karl, perhaps unnecessarily.

"You want to send it on this wild goose-chase." The butcher must have seen the look on Karl's face and nipped another cheeky response in the bud, wagging a finger at him. "And don't even think of making any stupid joke. Why don't you tie your message around the neck of a sheep or a goat and send it out?"

"It would never get past the wolves."

That stopped Metzger in his tracks, even though it hadn't really been a serious suggestion. He changed tack. "This bird has never raced; never had the chance even to fly."

"I don't want him to race – except maybe against time."

"And what good would a message do? No-one can help us, except the one whom fate has decreed will come one day. And if this message falls into the wrong hands, maybe people will come and laugh at us, like a freak show."

Then Karl thought it was time to try another tactic. He shrugged his shoulders and made as if to leave of the shop. "Okay, maybe you're right. Taube probably isn't up to the task. He would just circle around and then land on one of the trees in the forest, and never move." He headed for the door.

"What do you mean, not up to the task?" blustered Metzger, swallowing the bait. "He is bred from the purest racing line. It would be like an instinct in him to fly till he's exhausted."

Karl looked over his shoulder, and Metzger realised he'd walked right into the trap. He lifted his hands helplessly. "Why now?"

"Like I said, I realised it was an anniversary of sorts; as if fate was giving me a message." Then Karl's shoulders slumped. "And because I need to do something; have some hope. Just like it says in the Bible, when they sent out the dove from the ark."

"You've read the Bible?" said Metzger, surprised.

"Only twice."

Metzger came around the table. He was a very big man and he crouched down to be on a level with Karl. "You know, I'm sure Taube probably needs to stretch his wings. And if his instincts are as good as I think they are, he'll find his way back too. But tell me, what's your plan?"

"It's one that's hanging by a little thread," admitted Karl, "but it's the only one I've got."

"Well," Metzger patted him on the shoulder, "your instincts have been good before, and we should have listened to them. You proved a lot wiser than anyone else, and a lot braver too. So who am I to deny you this hope?"

"Could you do me one more favour?" asked Karl

"Surely."

"Please keep this a secret for now."

****

So in secret it was that they met that evening on the battlements, which were no longer guarded. Metzger hadn't been up there since the evening they'd dealt with Kerzen and Brauer. This time it was a clear night, and with his mind focussed on the surrounding universe he could hear the far-off noises of wolves in the forest. He held the birdcage close to his face and said to Taube: "Whatever you do, don't be a bird-brain and land on the ground."

Now Karl produced two objects from his pocket; one was a piece of oilskin containing a message written by him, rolled up tight and tied with a thin strip of cloth; the other was a small glass sphere. Metzger's mouth opened in surprise.

"I've seen something like that before," he said, "in…"

"…Ilsa's house," interrupted Karl.

Metzger nodded at a faint memory. "False light, Pfarrer called it."

"He would. Whatever you want to call it, it hasn't worked since she left, but I'm hoping it might now."

"Why?"

"I don't know."

Metzger frowned. "There's a lot about this plan you don't know."

Karl shrugged. "Perhaps I'm hoping it might light the way. Maybe I just want to see it work again after sixty-five years."

Metzger opened the cage and removed Taube with gentle care. He placed a ring on the bird's leg especially designed to hold messages. Karl could see that it filled the butcher with pride to use it at last, and to give his old friend freedom. By a loop through the brass attachment, the glass sphere was tied to the ring as well.

Now man and boy looked at each other and then at the bird.

"Fly safely and carry our hopes with you," said Karl.

Metzger lifted the bird close to his face and as he watched him cradling it in his strong hands, Karl suddenly felt enormous guilt for taking the butcher's companion from him.

"Wiederschauen," said Metzger. *See you again.* And there were tears in his eyes. Then he turned to Karl. "Which way?"

The boy pointed towards the forest. "Ilsa set off in that direction, so I guess it's as good as any."

Metzger lifted the bird into the air. "Show your breeding, my friend," he said, and released it.

As if it was something it had done every day, the bird soared. Karl and Metzger watched in amazement as the little glass sphere started to glow. Taube headed away, rising eventually above the trees. They watched the light accompanying all their hopes into the distance, until they could see it no more.

"I see now why you gave it a light," said Metzger, still staring at the horizon.

And at that moment, Ilsa's words came back to Karl - a prophecy if ever he'd heard one – as she'd handed him the light so many years before:

"One day it will take flight, and mankind with it."

145

CHAPTER 16

Many miles to the north-east of Ilsa-stadt, Juergen Lander sat on the porch enjoying both the glow from his clay pipe and from the setting sun. The love of the pipe was something he'd inherited from his father; watching the sunset was not. Invariably he sat out here alone. His father was a practical man for whom imagination was a dangerous luxury. For him, land was something which, if looked after properly would produce a yield. You cared for it and it cared for you. That was pretty much his view on women too, which was why Juergen's mother never joined him on the porch, unless his father was away on a buying trip.

For Juergen, it was different. He couldn't imagine his father having felt, at seventeen, as he did now. When soil ran through his fingers, he felt like he was dipping them in the earth's blood. He doubted his father ever saw the mountains as anything other than great lumps of rock that affected the weather, whereas for him they were the keepers of the earth's secrets, and a place that he'd always known he would visit one day. For Hans Lander, forests were arable land wasted; to Juergen they were the dark heart of the unknown; home to spirits and wolves.

And wolves were the reason he kept a gun propped against his chair on the porch. Though those beasts didn't love the open land, occasionally the farm's livestock made a tempting target and a rogue wolf would brave the lack of cover.

It had explained much to Juergen's mind when his mother had revealed one day in secret that his grandmother was a foundling.

"Don't tell your father I told you. When he found out, he felt shame, and disappointment that he wasn't from good Bohemian farming stock. It's why he's almost buried himself in his work here; to try to prove something – who to, I don't know. Probably himself."

For Juergen – a hard worker, but always a bit of a dreamer – that information had opened countless doors of possibility. Maybe his dreams of wandering owed their origins to gypsy blood. Or perhaps his great-grandmother was a princess, who fell pregnant out of wedlock and sneaked from her castle to hide the child before her father could kill it, but was tragically attacked by wolves once she had done so.

Pipe dreams? Well, he had the pipe, why not the dreams?

But he must have been dreaming now, because he could have sworn that he saw a light emerging from the distance against the dark backdrop of the horizon.

He'd heard the tales of strange lights from a mythical lost town way over in the east, but that would be too far to see, even if the lights were otherworldly. He blinked a couple of times and peered into the deepening darkness. Now he was sure it wasn't his imagination. He waved his hand in the air in front of him, just to be sure a burning ember hadn't blown into the air from his pipe. But the light, though tiny, was growing brighter.

Juergen could see that its path was erratic, rising and falling, swaying from side to side. His heart started to pound. It might indeed be a night for myths. Was he seeing one of the fabled will-o'-the-wisps? He sat transfixed. Not once did he think of priming his gun. He wasn't one of those people who feared something just because it was new to him, and a flying light on a dreamy night in that part of the Bohemian Palatinate was definitely something new.

As the mysterious sprite drew closer, there was no doubting it; something was flying. He wandered off the porch and was preparing to walk out to try to get a better look when he realised it was heading straight towards the farmhouse. Perhaps it was attracted to the lantern, like the moths and flies he was having to wave away from his face. Nearer and nearer; and in the now very dim twilight he could make out a bird, clearly on its last...well, wings, he supposed. And with a final, exhausted fluttering and a clumsy descent, it more or less collapsed on the porch.

Juergen hurried to it. What strange and fabulous creature could it be? He got his answer; a pigeon! And then disappointment on disappointment; the light had gone. Juergen looked at the bird lying flopped on its belly, the tip of its beak resting on the wooden planks of the porch in exhaustion, its eyes wary but dull, and he felt a surge of compassion, stooped and picked it up.

"So, what's your story, my friend?" he said.

And then, to his astonishment and delight, one of the doors of possibility stood slightly ajar. He felt something attached to the bird's leg and a dim glow emanated from a little glass ball hanging down. Juergen moved the tired bird gently backwards and forwards and smiled in wonder as the light shone. What could it be in there? Some strange sort of glow-worm? He took a closer look and saw a small rolled up piece of oilskin. He untied this and, still holding the bird with care, opened the piece of skin, and then the piece of paper within.

One thing upon which his mother had insisted – the only time he'd seen her stand up to his father - was that Juergen should be literate. In fact, despite his grumbling, Hans Lander had also been educated by his own mother, and knew there were advantages, particularly when dealing with merchants at market-time in the bigger, more distant towns. So Juergen was able to read what was written there. It made goosebumps rise on his skin.

I believe that one day this message will find the person it is meant to find. If you believe that day has come, then help us, the people of the town that was Reimersberg; help us, too, to fly free; to escape our curse. And if you believe you are not the one, then care for this bird – for it will have flown far – and release it to take our cry for help to others.

Karl Baecker

Juergen Lander's hands were shaking by the time he'd finished reading. He read the message again and again, then rolled it up and put it in his pocket, noting the strange, luxurious texture of the paper.

"Right, let's have a look at you," he said to the bird, which had hardly stirred in his hands. It had no strength. "So you have travelled far."

He examined the pigeon, and that was when he noticed some damaged feathers on the wing, as if they had been partly burnt away.

"Mmm, someone took a shot at you, eh? Fancied some pigeon pie. Well, you *do* look well fed." He looked at the bird's face. "But don't worry, my little friend, I will protect you, as Karl Baecker asks. I think you've brought me something I've been waiting for."

****

"Reimersberg? Don't know it." His father didn't even glance up from the sheet on which he was working out some sort of tally. "Why do you ask?"

Juergen saw his mother cast a nervous, sidelong look at both of them before she continued darning a shirtsleeve.

"I...found this." He put the piece of paper on the table.

Hans Lander stopped what he was doing, picked it up, unrolled it, and was unable to hide the odd look in his eye as he fingered the paper. He read the words and then looked at his son. "Where?"

"Out in the field; quite by chance. It was as if I was meant to find it. Someone must have crossed our land." He wasn't going to tell his father about the bird. He liked his pies – and hated birds, though mainly crows.

Juergen looked at his mother and was almost ashamed of the surge of pity that flooded through him. Her undoubted beauty had become frayed, like a dress you could tell had once been magnificent, but had seen too much wear. Hard work and the fearful love she had for her husband had taken their toll. The lad knew that fear; had always known that one day it would drive him away; that, and his imagination. And as his mother returned his look, he saw that she knew it too.

Hans let the paper fall from his fingertips. "Looks like someone must have lost a page from their storybook; a book of fairy-tales." He pushed the piece towards Juergen again. "No, I definitely don't know Reimersberg. Did you pen the pigs properly this evening?"

"Of course," said Juergen, unable to keep the frustration from his voice.

His father just looked at him – a long, steely glare – then turned back to what he'd been doing, while saying: " *'Of course'*, he says; so sure. Which is why two nights ago I was chasing pigs around the farmland when I should have been in my bed. Eh, mother?"

She said nothing; she wasn't expected to.

Juergen turned to leave the room. But then there was a sound; a defiant one, like a lark in a graveyard.

"That old map! In the corner of the storage room. I'll show you, Juergen."

Gretchen Lander stood, while her husband watched her with a trace of anger in his eyes. But he could hardly command her to sit; she wasn't a dog.

"The boy's only curious, father" continued Gretchen. "It won't harm to look. Perhaps we'll all learn something." She gave a brave smile. "Come, my Juergen."

She picked up the mysterious piece of paper from the table, led her son through into the next room, opened an old crate standing in the corner and pulled out an ancient, folded-up piece of cloth.

"Wow!" said Juergen, "how old is that?"

"We don't know," said his mother, "but we were told it was already in the house when our family first came here, more than two hundred years ago." She unfolded it and smoothed it out on top of the box. "That name is familiar to me." And then she pointed to part of the faded cloth. "There, look! Reimersberg; it does exist then. I thought so, and yet I don't know why."

Then suddenly she turned, put her hand on her son's cheek and her eyes filled with tears as she said: "Just as you don't know why its name has burrowed immediately under your skin, and you must go to find it." They heard movement in the other room and she said in a louder voice: "I'm sure there was a map. It must be here somewhere." She lowered her voice again and looked at the map, avoiding her son's questioning stare for the moment. "It looks like the town was on the old Adventurer's Road, which no-one travels anymore." She pointed to some faint writing. "The final stop; such an important place. What could have gone wrong, that none of us talk about it? What did it say on the note?"

"It was a cry for help, saying the town was under a curse or something."

Gretchen folded the map again and thrust it into Juergen's hand. "Here, take this. You might need it."

Juergen was astonished. "So you don't mind that..."

"And if I did, would it make a difference?"

"It might." He took her hand.

"You are my son. I've known you all your life; you've only known me part of mine. I know the farm is not for you. Besides, I know you won't forget me."

"Oh mother." He threw his arms around her and felt tears burning his eyes. He would never have allowed them to show, indeed been allowed to show them, in front of his father.

And then he felt his mother stiffen. "It can't be," she said.

"What?" She released him from her embrace and stared at the piece of paper. "What is it, mother?"

She had his piece of paper in her hand still and was staring at it. "This paper; it's so unusual and yet, I'm sure I've seen it before. Not this very piece, but one like it." She glanced towards the door again. "How did you really find this?"

"It was attached to a bird that flew here and landed exhausted on the porch a few minutes ago."

"A bird?"

"Yes, I've hidden it." He didn't bother to mention the light; that would have to wait. He was beginning to sense time was of the essence.

His mother spoke loudly again so Hans could hear. "Oh, it's really difficult to read anything, this thing is so old. I can't see any sign of a name like that."

And suddenly she pulled open one of the drawers of a crude dresser and started searching for something. "Where is it, where is it?" she whispered. Then she stopped, and pulled out a small object made of brass. "This," she whispered, "was given to your father by his mother when he reached manhood. She said it should be passed down the line if he, too, had a child that came of age. Well, I don't think you're going to be waiting here till then."

She placed it in his hand and it was surprisingly heavy for such a small thing. It was a vial of some sort, with a cork stopper

"What is it?"

"According to your grandmother, no-one really knew, but it was round her neck when she was found lying in a basket by the door of the farmhouse, and it's been treated as some sort of good luck charm ever since. More importantly…" Here she reached over, took the object back, pulled out the stopper and removed the contents; another rolled up piece of paper, which Juergen saw was exactly the same type as the one he'd found. His pulse was racing. It seemed he had stepped into a hell of an adventure. A part of him was terrified by that realisation.

As his mother unrolled the other piece, he could see that it appeared to have been torn from another sheet; as if someone had taken a page and torn it diagonally in half.

"What does it say?" he asked.

"We never knew; or rather I didn't. Your father could read it, but he said it made no sense because only half of it is there. It's written in a language I don't understand. See," she said, turning it towards her son.

He peered at it. "I see what you mean about half of it missing, but the language is clear enough."

He saw his mother's hands begin to shake, and her eyes grow wider beyond the piece of paper. He took it from her.

"It must be in your foundling blood," she said, "for your grandmother said that her husband couldn't read it either. She never said whether *she* could, but I believe that was just to make me feel better; not excluded. Tell me, my son, what does it say?"

"Well, it says: *Go to the end of the Road.*" He looked excitedly at his mother. "Perhaps that's the Adventurer's Road."

"Perhaps," said Gretchen.

He squinted at the paper again. "Then the rest looks like it might be some sort of verse, but the lines get ever shorter because of the tear." He started to read:

For equinox two days to r

At seven shall the sinki

With eagle's eye the

For man, perhaps

Then sinister

Ben

"Really mother, it means nothing as it stands, but I can't imagine that it would ever mean anything."

"Perhaps it's part of a spell;"

"Or the curse of which Karl Baecker writes."

"Or a good luck incantation for a foundling child." She smiled. "I'd prefer to believe that. And therefore you must take it."

"But father will…"

"Never mind what father will. He's not likely to look for it tonight. He doesn't believe in good luck charms, just the sun and the rain in good measures to make his crops grow, and provide feed for his pigs and his cows, so that he can buy all the good luck he needs."

Juergen looked solemn. "One thing neither of us can deny, mother; I was meant to find this message. It isn't chance that causes these two rare pieces of paper to meet."

"Strange that the message is in the language of the region."

"Perhaps; perhaps not. They're not written in the same hand. And I imagine the half-torn page was written by my great-grandmother, whereas this is from someone called Karl."

"Well, you're right about one thing," said Gretchen, "father must never believe that I gave you this heirloom, or sped you on your way with the map. He must believe you have taken these things secretly."

"But mother, that means…"

"You must leave."

"Before dawn?"

"Yes."

He felt the tears again and held his mother close once more.

She put on a brave face. "Anyway, a cry for help is a thing to be answered sooner rather than later, and that bird has travelled far, so time might be running out. If you really mean to help someone you cannot wait around." She pointed at the signature. "Such a pity it's not a princess."

He ignored the joke. "Mother, if father believes I've stolen from him, I won't be able to come back."

Now she ignored him. "I'll leave a backpack hidden just inside the doorway of the cowshed tonight. It will have food, a tinder-box – you will need fire - and shot for your gun." Here she paused and gave an anxious look at the night through the window. "Though it will take longer, go around the forest and along the mountain valley. I wouldn't want you coming across wolves…or anything else."

"So you believe the stories." Then he squared his shoulders. "Well, better one day fighting wolves than a lifetime tending sheep. Mother, will you do me one last favour – for now?"

"Yes, my son."

"The bird – it was just a pigeon; it's resting in a box of straw in the barn loft. It has some grain. When it's strong again, please release it back towards the forest. I would hate to think of father turning him into a pie."

She smiled. "You take care not to turn into a pie; I will do the same for your bird. And we will see each other again, my son."

CHAPTER 17

The forests and mountains were, of course, much further away than they seemed, and though he was strong and walked fast, it was five days before he reached the tree-line that marked the edge of the Maerchen forest, as it was called.

He was exhausted. The huge open spaces across which he'd travelled had played tricks with his mind, till he'd thought he was walking on the spot and making no progress at all. Now fear drenched his shirt and his spirits as he looked at the shadowy interior, cloaked in darkness even in the midday sun. He looked north and south along the great bank of trees and realised that avoiding them, as his mother had instructed, would involve several days' extra travelling in either direction. There was nothing for it, he decided, but to plunge into the famed and feared forest.

Immediately, it was as if he'd entered an enchanted kingdom, though whether ruled by the powers of good or evil, he couldn't tell. If the open land had confused his mind, the forest was a master in the black arts of sorcery. Daylight was a rumour. His feet made no sound on the soft ground, so that it seemed his very existence was in question. Birdsong echoed in the silence, trapped beneath the canopy of leaves, but at least provided some cheer. He lost track of time and struggled with direction, thanking the Lord time and again that he had brought a compass with him to steer him back on the right path. Once he was away from the farm he had tied the little glass sphere to his pack and took comfort, from time to time, by glancing at its light. As it went out whenever he stopped, that spurred him to keep moving on. The map, though relatively crude, contained occasional useful pointers, particularly when he encountered the meandering River Regen, and he wondered at the courage and determination of whoever had drawn it.

His mind, it seemed, had an inexhaustible supply of tricks to play on him, so he couldn't shake the feeling that he was being tracked, though he caught no sight of wolf or any other creature. This lurking threat brought home to him the necessity of finding a safe place to rest for the night. The prospect of a fire didn't bring the usual feeling of security. This was an ancient, unknown place, mistrusted even by seasoned travellers. He'd heard of the Adventurer's Road; it wasn't some romantic road followed by aristocrats on a grand tour, or by idealistic lovers. There were no guides or guarantees, no way-markers to safety. Rather it was a path picked out as the best route through a land of gorges, mountains, rivers and forests, populated mainly by wolves, sometimes by bears, and possibly by witches and the spirits of those who failed to make it past those three dangers. According to legend, if you got your directions right and listened to your sixth sense, the Adventurer's Road did lead through spectacular scenery from town to picturesque town, where people seemed to have celebrated survival by building their own little piece of heaven. Perhaps they had it better, in some ways, than the folk who lived on the flatter grasslands to either side of them, where there were few communities, just occasional isolated farms. No-one came to visit *them*; in fact they rarely visited each other, and if Juergen's home was anything to go by, even family members hardly spoke to each other! It was hard scraping a living from the soil. And it was easy to imagine that things could happen in the heart of that frightening, but beautiful land on the horizon, which would only ever reach the ears of the surrounding homesteads in the form of a legend or half-truth.

It was also easy to believe that creatures inhabiting such a place might have rules of their own and be attracted to a fire rather than scared by it. So when Juergen's first big test came – his first night alone in the forest – he stopped a little earlier than he might otherwise have done, because he found a suitable tree up which he could climb and spend the night resting, if not comfortably, then safe in the knowledge that he was well above the ground.

As night fell, the forest grew cold and gloomier still. Juergen had never known this fear – though something whispered that it was about to get worse – and jumped at every noise, of which there were plenty as the nocturnal animals became active. He reached time and again for the little glass sphere, longing for the comfort of light, but each time decided it was probably wisest to stay silent, still and hidden in the dark; his best course of action was inaction, as it were.

Except he'd forgotten that some creatures don't need much light to see their prey.

He didn't think he would be able to sleep, what with the peculiar counterpoint of sound and silence, amplified by his nerves, but must have dozed at some point, because he woke with a start – or at least he thought he did. Of course, he could have been dreaming, but he looked down into the blackness that concealed the forest floor – and saw them. Eyes gleaming up at him from far below. Once again Juergen thanked the Lord, this time for his decision to climb high that night, and then asked that same God to keep him safe. He couldn't understand how those eyes gleamed, but there was no mistaking the wolfish, pale glow, and as he listened, he heard their breath; could almost see the grinning, slavering jaws.

Juergen thought immediately of his gun, but knew he would need light to handle it, and he decided that he would rather not see any more detail of the picture below him.

It was a night when the edges of each minute were blurred in the darkness. The irony wasn't lost on Juergen; the shape of his life to that point had been moulded by the rising and setting of the sun, with the demands each brings to the simple farmer. Morning, with its back-breaking chores, always came too soon. Now it seemed like it might never come. Yet he must have slept fitfully, for he woke to the first muted rays of a sunrise dispelling the night. They seemed so much brighter than the day before. Juergen looked down, and the forest floor surrounding the tree was bare of everything except leaf-mould. When he set foot on it again, he saw the tell-tale paw-prints between the leaves, sank to the ground and said a prayer of thanks.

That day he carried his gun ready. He had no doubt now of what had been tracking him the day before, and couldn't shake that same feeling. The undoubted beauty of the trees and the dappled light that fell through the criss-crossing branches was lost on Juergen, especially as a look at the map confirmed that he was going to have to spend another night there. He found himself longing to be back on the wide open spaces of the farm, where danger couldn't hide or creep up on you. From time to time his head would jerk to the side and he would sigh with shaky relief when what he'd taken to be human forms turned out to be misshapen stumps of trees; a combination of knots and bark forming tortured grimaces on their gnarled trunks – he hoped.

He stopped even earlier that evening; might indeed have been able to travel for another hour, but couldn't be sure he would find a suitable roost further on. The difficult climb to the sturdy branch he'd spotted made him feel relatively secure – confident no wolf could attempt it - and he used the twilight to eat some bread and cheese, drink some water and then secure his pack, having first tied his gun to his wrist and placed shot in his pockets. Also he kept his tinder box handy in case the primeval need for fire became too much.

This time, as night fell, he saw them coming from the surrounding forest; dark shapes that moved with fluid muscularity to sit at the base of the tree. From time to time their winking eyes glinted at him. There they sat, as if waiting for him to slip and fall. He found himself wondering why they hadn't taken him during the day.

Their presence must have hypnotised him somehow, because the howling woke him. The sound curdled his blood before freezing it, partly because in it, he sensed fear and recognition, and he peeped over the edge of the thick branch to find that, unlike the previous night, there was a hint of moonlight; at least, if it wasn't moonlight, he was at a loss to explain the weak glow. By that light he saw the wolves rise and retreat into the forest. Also he saw why, and found himself wishing they'd stayed. At least wolves were something his mind could deal with. The figure that moved into view was not.

Juergen couldn't make out much, but he saw somebody wearing a red hat move towards the base of the tree and then stop. The presence, both sad and menacing, had undoubtedly driven the pack away, and as far as Juergen was concerned, anything that could scare a pack of wolves was to be avoided. He lay along the branch, hardly daring to breathe, trying to catch the steam of his breath in his scarf; believing the thumping of his heart must have been causing the whole tree to shake. He feared that at any moment a hand would appear over the edge of the branch.

That night was even slower than the previous one. When he next dared to look, both wolves and the ghostly figure were gone. And though he knew it would be a close-run thing, Juergen was determined not to spend another night in the forest.

That was why Karl Baecker saw the horrible events unfolding the following night.

****

He'd been up there every night since they'd released Taube, believing that, if you put enough hope out into the world, it might just bring you your desires. There were no longer look-outs posted after the sheep and cows were reeled in. The world that had closed its doors on this town was not likely to open them in the night to allow through strangers. No-one had come by for fifty years.

But Karl felt he might as well be up there as anywhere. He no longer bothered to trick his father and sneak out. Hans Baecker had long ago accepted that his son was his own person. They still worked together in the bakery, but Droger valued Karl's advice and the two of them were often busy with matters relating to the town. Hans found it hard to be a father to the man-boy.

There was something that Karl, too, found difficult to accept, even though he knew the reasons behind it. His father's refusal to speak up for Ilsa on the day of her banishment had been the action of a coward, yet he understood. Reimersberg was all Hans Baecker knew. To have been cast out from the town or forever viewed with suspicion was too frightening a prospect and he'd stayed quiet. The boy knew the guilt of this had weighed his father down ever since, making him a shadow of the man he'd been. However, when it had become clear years later that Ilsa was innocent, and Droger had named the town after her, why hadn't he spoken up then? Karl guessed it was a case of a lie having gone on too long. Nevertheless, his respect for his father had diminished at that point.

Yet there was also no denying that Karl had become a boy – and ultimately a man – apart, from the moment he'd befriended Ilsa. At that point, he'd realised that he was meant for something else. When Ilsa had placed her hand on his forehead as he lay sick in the bakery all those years ago, it seemed she'd passed her wanderlust and an awareness of the infinite wonder of the universe to him. After that, he'd never been able to settle.

So here he was, night after night, sitting or pacing up and down on the battlements, gazing into the east in the hope that the coming sun would bring what he desired, looking for signs in the skies, and still lost in the beauty of the stars.

But no light from a distant star was as wondrous as the tiny, darting glow that came weaving through the trees that night. Without knowing why, Karl recognised Ilsa's glass sphere. Somewhere in the forest it zigzagged like a firefly, and he saw it wasn't attached to anything that flew. Karl's heart leapt, and then sank. Whoever this was, they were running, and someone running through the forest at night was unlikely to be doing it for fun; rather for their life. The town gates were shut; he'd never get them open on his own and there wasn't time to call the nightwatchmen.

Karl could see that the light was getting closer. And then he saw the others; behind and off to the left and right of the single darting light. He knew they were pale eyes; wolves. They were moving with an easy, deadly grace compared with their prey.

He heard a rasping sound; the breath of the quarry. From the wolves there came nothing; just the deadly silence of intent.

And now it was Karl's turn to run. He tore along the battlements, round the town in the direction of the Kriegerstrasse. If he could just get the hidden door open. Then he stopped in despair, the door was at the south-eastern end of the town. The running figure would probably head for the main town gates in the northern part of the wall. He looked back in anguish towards the trees.

Now Karl saw the cunning of the wolves; their intelligence. They were looping around to cut off the way to the main gates. But by a twist of fate this manoeuvre gave Karl his only hope, because it would drive their intended prey round to the east of the town.

Karl tore his eyes from the horrible scene and said: "Well, there'll be no hope at all if you don't move." He ran to the watchtower where Droger and Metzger had waited for Kerzen and Brauer years before, and raced down the steps. In the dim light from the wool and oil wicks, which lit the lamps in that part of town, he hurried to the alleyway next to the Kriegerstrasse, found his secret entrance into Ilsa's old house, and then pulled out the stone block – which seemed to resist his efforts more than usual – before entering the tunnel that led to the outside world.

Of course Karl couldn't step out and wave when he opened the final door, but he kept a lantern there, which he lit now with shaking hands, hoping it would act like a beacon. Then, from just inside the tunnel he was still able to witness the final act. He could hear the ragged breathing getting closer and at last the tiny light came into view about fifty yards away.

As did the wolves.

He'd never seen them before; had heard them of course; out in the forest calling to each other – a bone-chilling sound - and snarling below him in the darkness when they'd come to rip the body of Friedrich Zimmerman. And of course he'd heard all the tales; those bedtime stories from hell. But he'd never actually seen their shape, and had to admit they were quite as terrifying as he'd imagined, loping dark forms housing light eyes full of ancient malice. The way they'd toyed with this man, letting him run himself to exhaustion as they'd bounded along gracefully, allowing him to get this close to sanctuary before pouncing; it was calculated and cruel. Now the man had stopped, because so had they; encircling him. Karl held the door half open. If this poor wretch could just get through, he might be able to close it in time.

Might.

But of course, the man wouldn't know the door was here. Karl would have to say something. Though terror had closed an icy hand around his throat, he had to try.

"In here."

It was barely above a whisper, but one of the wolves turned its cold eyes and long, cruel nobility of its face in his direction.

He tried again. "Run!"

There were twenty yards to go – Karl knew the man wouldn't make it, but he tried.

The wolves didn't move.

The figure dived past Karl, yelling: "SHUT THE DOOR!"

There was no need. The great shadowy beasts watched their quarry go. Then they simply turned and went, melting into the night.

Karl closed the door and turned to the figure now doubled over in the tunnel, hands resting on knees.

"Are you alright?" he asked.

The man panted his reply: "That depends…on how you…look at it." He straightened up, and Karl was amazed to find the face of a boy of around his age blinking into the lamplight, though already, experience was etched into his features. Karl liked him immediately. He continued, his breathing getting steadier: "From a point of view…of having been chased by wolves since dusk…then no; as someone who…has just escaped being eaten alive…then yes."

Suddenly Karl realised that he was staring at the first new face he'd seen in years He extended his hand: "Karl Baecker."

Now it was the turn of the other boy to stare. "Karl Baecker?" He shook the proffered hand, but his own shook. "Juergen Lander. Then this must be Reimersberg, you must be under a curse and this," here he pointed to the little glass sphere, "must be yours." He untied it and handed it over. Even though they stood in a dark tunnel he looked around before continuing. "So it's all true."

****

It was a strange sight; the two boys breaking bread, each with a little glass of apple brandy. Karl could almost feel Ilsa's presence in that old house. He'd lit a fire – it was always safe to do so at this hour in that isolated and forgotten part of town.

"So what do you think happened there?" asked Karl, jerking his thumb towards the outside world. "I mean the fact that the wolves didn't attack you."

"I don't know," said Juergen. "Having spent two horrible nights in the forest, I didn't want another one, so as dusk approached I decided to take a chance and run for it. I knew it couldn't be much further. And that's when I saw *them* running alongside me in the trees. They could have brought me down at any time. My gun was across my back; I'd never have been able to use it. It was almost as if they were...I don't know...accompanying me."

Karl frowned. "You're right. I assumed they were cutting you off from the main gate, but now it seems like they were guiding you to this secret door." He looked into the distance. "I've heard strange things about the forest, but that would be the strangest. Still, how else do you explain it? They had you circled at the end, but they just let you go." Then he smiled. "But if there's one thing more difficult to believe, it's that you got my message."

Juergen reached into his pocket, produced the rolled-up piece of oilskin and put it on the table between them. "I'm sure there's a lot to talk about. And we have my bread and cheese and your very fine brandy. So why don't we start at the beginning?"

"It is indeed a long story," said Karl.

The Reimersberg Uhr, which had been restarted under the stewardship of Mayor Droger to bring some normality to the town, struck one o'clock more or less at the point where Karl finished his tale. Juergen sat back on his creaking chair and puffed out his cheeks.

"Wow!" he said, "and I thought I'd had a bad few days."

"Yes," said Karl. "Now you know what you've walked into." He took a sip of brandy; an adult in a youth's body, or so it seemed to Juergen. "Let me hear exactly how that's happened. Why are you here?"

"You mean apart from the fact that your message got to me, which makes me believe I'm the one it was meant for? And the fact that I'm a boy of seventeen, who dreamt of breaking away from the loneliness and drudgery of life on a farm, and found a mysterious cry for help dropping into his hands attached to a bird carrying a magic light?" He smiled. "Well, there's also this?"

He reached inside his shirt and produced the brass heirloom he'd tied around his neck. Opening it, he pulled out the half-torn page, which he unfolded.

"It's the same paper!" said Karl in awe.

"Yes, my mother recognised that."

"Ilsa gave me a few sheets of it once. She said it was very good quality paper from somewhere in the east." He looked at the fragment Juergen was holding. "What is that?"

"I don't know. It looks like it's been torn from something. Half of it's missing."

"May I see it?"

"Of course." Juergen handed it over.

"It's from Ilsa!" Karl's face almost shone and the candlelight made the tears of happiness in his eyes glisten. It was like receiving a letter from her just seeing this piece of paper, and as he started to read his voice was full of awe. "*'Go to the end of the Road. For equinox two days to...'*" Then he noticed that Juergen's mouth was open in amazement. "What?"

"You can read it too!" said Juergen excitedly.

"What do you mean?"

"My mother couldn't. She said it's in a language she doesn't understand; says perhaps only those, like my father and I, with the foundling blood, can read it."

"Foundling?"

"My grandmother was left outside the door of the farmhouse where I live today. This vial was round her neck, with that piece of paper in it."

Karl's eyes opened wide. "How many years ago would that be?"

Juergen frowned as he looked up and calculated. "Say…sixty something."

"Sixty-five perhaps?"

"Yes, could be?"

"My God! Your grandmother might have been Ilsa's child."

"Then that means…" Juergen pointed at Karl and started to laugh. "If your father was also my great-grandfather, we're…"

Both boys furrowed their brows as they tried to work it out.

"…related," said Karl, and they burst out laughing together. "I must be your great-great-uncle or something."

They both found the thought of that very amusing. When they'd finished laughing Juergen said:

"But our blood must be the same, otherwise how do you explain your being able to read the words on the torn page."

"I don't know. Ilsa once said I was special. Perhaps when she healed me, she gave me some of her knowledge." He paused as a thought struck him. "And now I think about it, she left me a book, which I've always been able to read, but which I'm sure isn't in any language I could have learnt here." He frowned. "I can't think of any other explanation. I mean, there's been no fresh blood in Reimersberg for centuries before the curse. And certainly no-one in this town had her red hair or such green eyes."

"Is that what she looked like?" said Juergen. "My grandmother, God rest her soul, had green eyes, but not red hair."

There was a pause; both of them lost for a moment in thoughts of loved ones they would never see again.

Suddenly, Karl slapped the table. "Of course! That proves it beyond all doubt. You are the one this town has been waiting for."

"What do you mean?"

"You're the stranger who is no stranger. If you're related to me, you're not a stranger, even though no-one here knows you."

"You're right," agreed Juergen. The sense that he was about to fulfil his destiny felt overwhelming. "What was the rest of that riddle again?"

"'The *stranger who is no stranger stays, and at the ending of the days...* '- still not sure what exactly that means, but we can think about it - '*With a...broken...verse...* ' Karl's words slowed as he saw fate materialise in front of him. It had been staring at him – at both of them – for the last few minutes, and he felt suddenly giddy, as if he had looked upon some fabled creature. He picked up the torn piece of paper from the table and held it almost in reverence. "This is it, Juergen; the broken verse. The thing that might lift the curse from our town."

Juergen looked at it. "What do we do with it? Should I speak the words perhaps, and see if everything goes back to how it was?" Karl was deep in thought. He was remembering something from many years ago. "Karl?"

He blinked, and then said to Juergen: "No. We have to find the other half."

CHAPTER 18

"It's going to be like looking for a needle in a haystack," said Juergen, as his eyes continued to scour the wall of the tunnel - more in hope than expectation - for any sign of a hidden recess,

"So was finding me, or me finding you, but we managed it," said Karl.

"Yes, but I had the advantages of knowing your name and the name of the town. Plus I had the help of a map. Anyway, it doesn't look like she left it in here." They left the tunnel, convinced they had looked everywhere they could.

As they returned to the room where they'd been sitting, the enormity of the task struck Karl. The paper could be hidden under the floor, in a crack in the wall – after all, an entire door was hidden there! – or it might not be in Reimersberg at all. That was a sobering thought. Yet already his moment of inspiration on sending out the message had borne the most amazing fruit and he wouldn't stop now. Something was nagging at him. This process seemed too haphazard; not very Ilsa-like. Even if things were in the hands of the fates, she'd always believed in helping them along. She would have left some clue; and where better to leave it than in the piece of paper they had.

"Juergen, I think we, too, have a map; it's just that, unlike yours, we don't know where the finishing point is."

"Unfortunately, we do," said Juergen. He wandered over to the table, picked up the half-torn page, sitting down with a weary thump while he read it. "'*Go to the end of the Road.*' And that's what I did. Reimersberg is at the end of the Adventurer's Road."

Karl joined him at the table. "You see, that could be read differently. After all, this half of the page is meant to be read together with another one. It might be telling both of us to go to the end of a road."

"Yes, but look; this is the only complete sentence on here. Doesn't it make sense that it's a message to the person who finds this?"

"Mmm, you're probably right."

The boys flattened out the piece of paper and sat next to each other staring at it, as if they could will an answer into rising from it like vapour.

Juergen was getting frustrated. "Why couldn't she have just written this out in full, in nice, simple words?"

"We were obviously meant to work on it together," said Karl. "Or she might have known how impatient you'd be." He winked when Juergen looked at him.

Juergen smiled back. "I guess I have only been here a few hours."

"You should try sixty-five years," said Karl, "and still being sixteen. You'll learn patience."

Still staring at the piece of paper, Juergen said: "Are you sure this is from Ilsa? After all, if my grandmother was a foundling, then her mother might be a gypsy from some mysterious, far-off country, where they also used this type of paper." He looked up as if seeking that place. "You know, I used to always dream that my family history would turn out to be something exotic; hoping there would be some clue for me as to where my great-grandmother came from, so I could travel the world seeking her." He tapped the paper with his finger. "Perhaps this is that clue."

Karl shook his head. "Well perhaps, if we ever solve this, we can go together to find her, because this is definitely from Ilsa, and I'd love to see her again. I recognise the way she's written *Road*. It's…"

"What is it?" asked Juergen, looking at Karl's face.

"I'm such a fool," whispered the younger boy. Like so many things in life, now that he'd found the answer it was obvious. He looked around him, found where he'd left his copy of *The Travels* and grabbed it.

Juergen looked at the cover. "Marco Polo – great name," he joked.

But Karl wasn't laughing. He opened the ancient book in a state of absolute tension, looking strangely like an old scholar who'd suddenly solved a conundrum. He pointed to some writing on the inside cover.

"Look!" he said. "See how's she's written *Road* here, even to the capital R." He looked up towards the heavens. "Oh Ilsa, you are so clever." He read out what she'd written:

'Karl, may the end of this Road be the beginning of your journey.'

"Okay, I see the connection," said Juergen. "What road is she talking about?"

"The Silk Road, which Marco Polo travelled and then described in this book. It took him thousands of miles, far into the east."

"Well that's no good," said Juergen, "we can't even get you past the town wall here."

"I don't think that's what she means."

Karl flipped the book over and opened the back cover; felt around its edges. It seemed thicker than the front. Now, as if scales had fallen from is eyes, he could see she'd stuck another piece of paper over it. He probed with his fingernails, picking until he found an edge, which he peeled back, before looking excitedly at Juergen and saying:

"It was a double-edged clue; she meant for you to get to the end of your road and she also meant the end of this book."

As the piece of paper came away, it revealed another half-torn page. Karl slid it out and turned it over to reveal the writing there.

Two hearts hammered as one as the boys put the pieces together and then cheered.

****

An hour later cheering had given way to frowning again as they stared in frustration at the words in front of them. Karl read them out once more, as if constant repetition would erode them and expose the meaning:

For equinox two days to run

At seven shall the sinking sun

With eagle's eye the path reveal

For man perhaps three hundred heel

Then sinister the goodly path

Beneath the point of godly wrath

He shook his head. "I haven't a clue."

Juergen leaned his head wearily on his arm. "Well, we have a clue all right, but no answer."

In the distance the Reimersberg Uhr struck four. The August sunrise had started to dilute the darkness beyond the window.

"As much as I hate to admit defeat," said Karl, "I think in this case many heads might be better than just our two. I think we'll have to take this to the Council of Elders."

"What, that bunch of weasels you described? I'd rather seek help from the wolves."

"It's okay; Droger's the mayor now, and the rest aren't a bad bunch. The rotten eggs have gone; thrown off the council; Meister's in jail, Dr Arzt keeps himself to himself, and Pfarrer the priest seems to spend his days praying for forgiveness for his sins. But Droger's the main one I want to talk to. He's an intelligent man. Besides, I think we ought to go to him before the people wake. You have no idea what an effect your presence will have." Karl looked reflective for a moment. "Some people just about escaped with their lives when they were mistaken for the stranger. Others weren't as lucky. It would be good to get you across the town now."

"But you won't be able to hide me from the townsfolk forever," said Juergen.

"Hopefully I won't need to, if we can solve this riddle."

"Hmm." Juergen sounded doubtful. "Perhaps that's what she meant by 'the ending of the days'. Our Ilsa knew it was going to take that long just to work it out. But look," here Juergen put his hands on Karl's shoulders, "if that's how long I have to stay, then that's the way it is. We're family; and even if we weren't, I'd stay for as long as it takes to get you out of this place."

For once in his life Karl really didn't know what to say, and even if he had, it wouldn't have found a way out round the lump in his throat.

****

Droger found himself staring at Juergen, just as Karl had a few hours before. He'd already pinched himself a couple of times since being woken out of a sleep by the knocking at the door.

"I told you," said Karl with a smile to the other boy. "Better get used to this behaviour. When you haven't seen another human being in donkey's years it's hard not to stare. And when there's a chance that person could release you from a curse of sixty-five years...well."

"My apologies," said Droger, recovering slowly from his shock. "Yes, perhaps we'd better not tell anybody about this till..." – he waved his hand at the pieces of paper on the table – "until we solve it."

"*If* we solve it," corrected Juergen. "It's not exactly helpful. As I said before, why did she have to make it so difficult? It was hard enough to find the two pieces, never mind having to work out this hocus-pocus."

"What does it say?" asked Droger, looking at the writing.

The boys had forgotten that only they could read it, so Karl read out the words again, while Droger fetched a quill and wrote them down in the common tongue on another piece of paper. When he'd finished, they sat and stared at them; pieces of a puzzle that taunted them; defied them; refusing to link together. It was hard to believe those thin strips of parchment contained the power either to release the citizens of Ilsa-stadt, or hold them prisoners forever. Droger, Karl and Juergen were like three subjects, held in thrall by a little slip of a girl who happened to be queen; who held the power over life and death.

Karl, despite his love for Queen Ilsa, felt the frustration. She seemed to care for him, so why had she left his fate in the fickle hands of chance. *Why?* The word nagged at him, but despite the confusion, the knowledge that there had to be an answer gave him hope. And as he thought of the curse lifting, he recalled for perhaps the ten thousandth time the day it was laid on them. Suddenly, as the three companions sat there saying nothing, he thought he understood.

"She had no choice," he whispered, causing the others to look at him with blank faces.

"Great!" said Juergen, "Now he's started to talk in riddles."

"Mr Droger, you remember the day of the curse?" said Karl, ignoring the comment.

"No, it had quite slipped my mind," said Droger dryly, his own impatience starting to show.

Karl ignored his sarcasm too. "When Ilsa said she couldn't undo what she had done, she spoke of the laws of her universe; how they did not allow her to leave us without some hope. I bet, likewise, she couldn't give us the answers because she wasn't allowed to. She had to shroud the ways in the mist of a riddle. It's against the laws of nature; of..." he shrugged, "...I don't know...magic. She disturbed those laws in order to do what she did and now the universe would not be very happy with her if she asked for that work to be undone. She might have seemed powerful and strong calling on the elements, but that's all she did; she *called* on them. They cannot be controlled and there must have been a chance they wouldn't have answered."

Droger nodded, once again surprised by Karl's wisdom, though he shouldn't have been. "You mean it would have been a bit like waking a sleeping bear to cause a disturbance – you might succeed the first time, but if you prod it again a second time you might get eaten."

"So we get to go and prod it, do we?" asked Juergen rhetorically. "This should be interesting. But still, she could have made the clues a bit easier."

"No," Karl insisted, "really, we have to work it out for ourselves. She's not just hiding things from us; she's hiding them from the cosmos, so that whatever, or whoever controls these matters doesn't punish her for her disobedience."

"Well, what's done is done," said Droger. "Now let's see if we *can* work it out. Okay, let's think logically about this. *For equinox two days to run.* Do you know what an equinox is?"

Karl shook his head solemnly, but Juergen spoke up.

"As a good farming boy I do at least know when it is – or rather, when *they* are. Important dates in the farmer's calendar, those are."

"They happen twice a year and mark the beginning of spring and autumn," said Droger. "And I think we're talking about the autumnal equinox here."

"Why?" asked both boys.

"This line - *For equinox two days to run* – would then mean 20th September - two days before the autumnal equinox." He looked at Karl. "Does that date ring any other bells with you?"

Suddenly the boy's face registered amazement. "That was the day before the cursing of the town."

"The day our lives as we know them began – or ended, depending on your point of view."

Droger looked solemnly at them. "I think we now know by what date we have to solve this – as far as this year's concerned anyway."

Karl calculated on his fingers. "That's three weeks from today."

"So, on 20th September we have to do what is described here."

"And what is described here?" asked Juergen, frustrated.

"Well, part of the message in the next lines seems simple enough in its own way," said Karl. "*At seven shall the sinking sun…a path reveal.* At seven o'clock in the evening on that day, the sun will reveal a path to us. But what an eagle's eye has to do with it I don't know."

There was another silence, broken by the click of Droger's fingers. "I think I might know. Come, it's still early enough; the streets will be empty. There's something I want to show you."

****

The original, small town of Reimersberg was now the forgotten quarter that contained the Kriegerstrasse; a thinly populated area of dark houses and narrow lanes, which had gradually emptied as first the town expanded over the centuries, and then the plague came a-visiting. A few families had stayed in their old homes, though of course none had remained in the Kriegerstrasse itself, or in the surrounding streets. There were a number of squares in this old part of town, much smaller than the main square or the clock square, with dark alleyways leading off them. When the cholera had harvested a good portion of the population in the years after the curse, almost all the remaining inhabitants of these sad streets had decided to move to the newer part of town, to live closer to the other townsfolk and create more of a community; to leave behind all the bad memories; to feel less alone.

One of these squares was called the Adlerplatz – the Eagle Square. Droger took the two boys there, having first lent Juergen a hat and scarf to disguise him in case they encountered any early risers.

"Say nothing and try to look like you belong," he said. "You're tall enough to be mistaken for an adult."

The morning was still fresh. Later the day might become stuffy with the humid air trapped in the valley, but for now there was the glint of dew on stones and webs, and the sky had not lost its azure shade to the haze of heat.

They met no-one as they crossed the town and entered the cave-like coolness of the Adlerplatz. Karl spoke:

"Despite the years I've spent in this town, I can't remember ever being here before. Does that make me as narrow-minded as the people who've never left the town?"

Droger put his hand on the boy's shoulder. "The very fact of you asking that question proves you are not."

The reason for the square's name became immediately apparent, for there was a fountain in the middle of it, the top of which was a carved eagle; the symbol of Reimersberg.

"Look," said Droger, leading them up to it, "its eyes are made of gold." He turned and peered through a gap between two buildings. "And there, you can just see a part of the battlements of the town wall. That lies to the west. I wouldn't be surprised if the evening sun shines through at certain times. Yes, yes, that must be it. Karl, can you remember; on the evening before Meister..." he paused, "...no, on the evening before *all* the men of Reimersberg condemned Ilsa by our silence, was it sunny? There seems to be a dark cloud hanging over my memories of that day. I do remember it had rained, becoming misty in the evening."

"Yes, I can remember," said Karl, "she asked me to come to her. It would have been, well, sometime in the evening; and I remember as I crossed the town the sun broke through, brightening the day right at the end. I remember because it seemed to reflect how I felt whenever I visited her."

Droger closed his eyes and then nodded. "I can just picture it. While we went around the town gathering men for a meeting in the main square, Ilsa must have come here, for some reason we don't fully understand yet. Perhaps she hid something." He pointed to the battlements. "And I think, when the sun shone through that gap, it might well have filled this square. Perhaps it reflected off the golden eye of the eagle, pointing to whichever of these many lanes she then took. All of this she would have done in a hurry, knowing bad things were about to start happening." He paused. "This is pure guesswork, of course."

"Are there no other eagles in the town?"

"There were four, facing the cardinal points of the compass; the stone eagle on the town hall faces east and there were two wooden ones, which were taken long ago for firewood, before we had the Friedrich Trees;" he thought for a moment, "and their eyes were just carved into the wood, so none would catch the rays of the setting sun like this one, especially as it faces west. And remember, Ilsa wouldn't have gone into the main part of Reimersberg, because we might have spotted her. Here, we're not far from the Kriegerstrasse; she could have moved around without being seen."

"I wonder why she didn't just run, if she knew her life was in danger," said Karl in solemn reflection, the blackness of that dreadful time reflecting once again in his features.

Droger bent to look Karl in the face. "Because she cared about you – and she knew you weren't ready to leave, even though you thought you were. She had to leave you the book, so that there was at least a chance for you to solve the riddle one day." Droger stood again and looked thoughtful. "But I do take your point. There must have been some other reason she delayed."

Droger had meant by this that Ilsa must have been hiding some clue, but as soon as he saw the sadness in Karl's face and the tears the boy fought back, he regretted his words. Given the way they'd treated her it had been no surprise Ilsa cursed the town; how angry and hurt she must have been; despite everything, she was only human after all. But given how very fond of Karl she was, Droger always found it strange that she'd allowed him to be imprisoned too. He'd had his own questions about it. Had Ilsa feared that Karl might grow to betray her like his father? Droger was no fool. Though Karl had never told him anything, he'd suspected something had happened between Hans Baecker and Ilsa long before her words on that fateful morning had confirmed his suspicions. After all, who else in Reimersberg could have been the father? Except the devil, of course, which so many had chosen to believe.

But no; Ilsa could have moulded Karl into something better than his father. Perhaps, seeing that Hans Baecker was weak, she'd known he would need his son by his side. One thing was certain; Karl must have fought to hold onto his love for Ilsa, with these very questions and doubts burning in his mind every day since she'd left. He needed to hold onto something positive instead. How Droger wanted to give him that now.

"I know!" It was Juergen

"What do you know?" said Droger.

"She left Karl here because he would be the one to save the town. Only he was wise enough to find a way. He was her knight; her dragon slayer."

Droger felt deep gratitude towards Juergen as he saw Karl's back straighten with pride. He looked at the newcomer, who looked right back and winked at the apothecary. Strange how there was so much wisdom in the world amongst the young, while the old and the Elders had been such miserable failures in this whole affair. Truly the universe stood on its head sometimes.

"Quite so," said Droger. But it was time to move on. "Now to go back to the riddle, it looks like we'll have to wait till the 20th September to know the answer."

"Um, one problem there," said Juergen. "What if, on the 20th September, the sun isn't shining?"

They looked at each other, nobody knowing how to answer the question; each of them fearing there was no answer.

"And worse," said Karl, "what if the sun does shine, but still we can't solve the riddle?"

"Well," said Droger, "we'll just have to wait and see. But after all, waiting is our speciality."

He took a final look up at the eagle, the symbol of once-proud Reimersberg, and then led the boys away.

But then he stopped. "On the other hand, perhaps we don't have to wait."

CHAPTER 19

Droger knew that Mr Sternseher would be awake. The stars and the night sky were his obsession and he would have been up all night watching through the telescope he'd bought on his pilgrimage to Poland, where he'd visited the birthplace of Copernicus the astronomer. He'd chosen to stay in the old part of town because there were no lights to disturb his view of the skies. He was the only one living in his street now; a lane of ramshackle houses still lying in shadow that morning, despite the blue sky above.

Sternseher's eccentricity had always seen him branded an outsider in Reimersberg. Not that he'd have noticed, with his mind and his eyes forever wandering the heavens. If he'd been a woman he might have been burnt as a witch; instead people came to him, on occasion, for horoscopes, though even that contact had stopped after the curse, when everyone in Reimersberg knew precisely what the future held for them. Now he was just thought of as odd; the title given to anyone who'd ever ventured beyond the Hexental. Some people had even wondered whether *he* might be the stranger who was no stranger; well, they argued, he lived amongst them, yet nobody really knew him – and he was certainly strange! Others wondered whether he even knew there was a curse on the town, or had noticed that he'd not grown any older. And they might have been right. After all, time is relative when you compare the length of a human life with that of a star.

It's possible that Sternseher was the only person in the town who would have noticed nothing odd about Juergen being there that morning, or about the question Droger had just asked.

"Of course, of course I could tell you exactly where the sun would be at that time on 20th September," he said, as if the question was insulting in its simplicity. Sternseher didn't stop pacing around the darkened room on the top floor to which he'd led them, and he looked continuously at charts and the pages of open books strewn about the place. "That's an easy one, with the sun crossing the celestial equator." He looked at them with tired, rheumy eyes quite out of place in his young, pale face, which peered from beneath a dishevelled mop of blonde hair. "Why do you want to know, Mr...um...Mr...um...?" He looked back at a book he was holding.

"Well, it might help us to lift the curse."

Sternseher stopped what he was doing for a moment, like a man who'd just remembered he'd left a pot of food burning. "Oh." But then he picked up another book and was away again in the world of Sternseher. Despite the importance of his mission, Droger had to smile – it was exactly the reaction he'd expected, which was why he'd not bothered wasting breath on a more detailed explanation.

Now Sternseher looked at his guests again. "You can ask me more difficult ones, you know. Do you…" here he took a closer look at the three of them in turn, as if registering them for the first time, "…um, gentlemen have an interest in the stars?"

"A particular one," said Droger. "The sun."

The astronomer's index finger pointed at Droger from a shabby fingerless glove: "That you believe the sun to be a star makes you wiser than most people in this town. I'm sure most of them think Copernicus is a type of metal." He went into a snorting, self-indulgent little laugh at his own joke, while the two boys glanced at each other and tried not to snigger. "Well, what is the nature of your interest?"

"I see you have mirrors here."

"They help me expand my picture of the heavens. It's something I'm working on for telling the time and measuring the position of the stars. Thought I might call it a sextant. You see, in order to use the moon in my calculations I need to be able to measure angles of up to one hundred and twenty degrees and by means of these mirrors I can do that by splitting a circle into six segments and…" He looked at their blank faces and frowned. "What was the question again?"

Droger smiled. "I hadn't asked it yet – but would you be able to throw the sun's light by means of these mirrors to imitate a particular time of a particular day at a particular place?"

"Of course." Sternseher didn't even look up from the page he'd started scrutinising when he answered.

Droger waved his arm across the various documents. "So would your charts and books here enable you to recreate the sunlight of seven o'clock on the evening of 20th September 1695?"

The astronomer looked up now and there was a light in them as if they were indeed already reflecting that sun. "Well, I'd have some calculations to make – pretty complex ones, allowing for leap years and the minute variations of the earth's orbit – and then…"

"Could you do it?"

Sternseher smiled. "Yes, of course!"

"In that case, please do so as a matter of urgency." He took hold of Sternseher's hand. "A pleasure to meet you. We'll see ourselves out and leave you to get on with your work."

The astronomer rubbed his hands together. "My work, yes. I shall need my compass. And where did I put the old chart of..."

They left him mumbling to himself.

"Well," said Droger as they stepped out of Sternseher's tumbledown house into the early morning air, "I think we can safely leave celestial calculations in the hands of our friend up there." He pulled the piece of paper with the riddle out of his pocket. "We still have to work out what the rest means. Now: *'For man, perhaps three hundred heel.'*"

There was a stone water-trough a short distance from Sternseher's front door and they perched on the edge.

"*'Then sinister the goodly path',*" read Droger. "That's a riddle within a riddle. I suppose people who have magic powers are worried their spells or incantations could fall into the hands of those who might misuse them, so they disguise their meaning in this way."

"If you ask me," said Juergen, "I think it just makes them feel all witch-like and powerful, talking in riddles and rhymes. You might be right about them hiding their spells, but only so they can feel more important."

Juergen was weary and slightly irritable, having not slept since the night before last, and not very well for the two nights before that in the forest. That, combined with what had seemed to be a race for his life against wolves, followed by hours trying to find a way through the obscure language of some white witch, meant his head was spinning now. He cupped his hands in the water, meaning to throw a handful over his head to revive him, but he withdrew his hands quickly. "Ooh!" He shivered. "That's colder than a farm-girl's bed when the corn is high."

"Yes," said Droger, "The summers here can get very hot - the mountains seem to trap the heat - but that water in there always seems to stay very cold. I remember as a young lad – even longer ago than it should be – after racing around the lanes we used to come here and cool our heels and perhaps..." He stopped speaking and a smile of recognition lit his face. "'Cool our heels'! I wonder if that's what Ilsa means; perhaps by 'heel' she means a step. For a man it's three hundred steps along this path! I thought it sounded unusually vague for her – *'perhaps three hundred heel'* – but as she's a woman she'd only be able to guess at the stride of a man."

"Why wouldn't she just say it's four hundred steps, or whatever, for a woman?" said Karl.

"It's like I said, it sounds more important the more confusing it is?" said Juergen. Karl gave a tut of irritation. He didn't like hearing Ilsa spoken of that way, even though he couldn't argue with the logic.

"No, I don't think so," said Droger. "I know Ilsa was a strong person, but women like her are few and far between. I think she believed it would take a man to get to this town; along the Adventurer's Road; past the wolves."

"Then that makes me a man," said Juergen happily.

"And still the youngest here," said Karl, a little sulkily; some aspects of his personality remained as boyish as his face, despite his seventy-six years.

"Anyway, well done," said Droger, clapping Juergen on the back.

The boy looked surprised. "A pleasure."

At that moment the door of Sternseher's house flew open and the man himself came hurrying out, waving a piece of paper.

"I've done it!" he shouted. He looked at their staring faces. "I know, I know; I'm sorry it took so long, especially as you said it was urgent."

"What delayed you?" asked Droger jokily, with a glance at the two co-conspirators.

"Well, you see, a comet came very close to the earth in 1722, and that might have affected the angle of rotation…"

"My good Mr Sternseher," Droger raised his hands, "you've convinced me. Now, what is that other thing you're carrying?"

"This?" Sternseher lifted it in front of him, as if he'd forgotten all about it. "Well, you mentioned mirrors, and if a man is asking about the exact position of the sun at a certain time of evening many years ago, I assume that, for whatever reason, he wants to do an experiment."

Droger gave him a broad smile. "Mr Sternseher, where would we be without you?"

"So I'm going to put this up on the battlements." He indicated the piece of equipment, which was a long wooden pole with two mirrors at the end placed slightly apart. The mirrors were parallel to each other and could be moved independently on hinges. "Please don't let anyone disturb it once it's in place."

He reached into his pocket and produced a small, odd-shaped case which he opened to reveal a tiny sundial; then he looked up at the sky. It seemed a cloudless day was ahead, with snow glinting in the early sun from the very tips of the jagged fangs that were the mountains.

"I think by seven o'clock this morning the sun will be in the perfect position," said Sternseher. "Where, good sir, do you wish it to shine?"

"The Adlerplatz."

He frowned and repeated the name a couple more times. "I'm not sure I know where that is."

"About two minutes from here," said Karl in amazement. "Mr Sternseher, surely you know…"

"Our good Mr Sternseher is much too busy with the important matters going on in our universe, Karl, than to be bothered with such things as the location of the Adlerplatz." Droger looked at Karl, who flushed, perhaps realising that it was not his place to become irritable with the man who might just be their saviour. "What time is it?"

"Just before six," said Sternseher after another glance at the sundial.

"Well, if you would be kind enough to accompany us to the Adlerplatz, we'll then leave you to go and set up your, um, equipment."

Juergen looked at the two little mirrors. "How can two such small objects imitate the light of the sun?"

"Ah," said Sternseher, "you'd be surprised how far a reflection of light will travel. Have you never wandered half a mile across a field, wondering what glints so brightly in the distance, only to find some tiny, discarded piece of glass catching the sunlight?"

"Um, no," said Juergen.

"Me neither, but I'm told it's very beautiful." He turned to the mayor. "Mr…Mr…"

"Droger."

"May I ask, humbly, the nature of your experiment?"

Droger hesitated. "I need to prove to these two budding scientists here the very phenomenon you have just described; the distance light can travel. And how far it can travel even when it is reflected again. So for that purpose, I would be very grateful if you could direct the beam onto the head of the eagle that I'm about to show you. Come, follow me."

Sternseher rubbed his hands together again. "Most exciting."

So off they headed towards the Adlerplatz, this strange assortment; the mayor, the farmer's boy, the lad of eighty-one and the muddle-headed, but undoubtedly brilliant astronomer.

As they left Sternseher's narrow street and entered another small square, they realised that their little group was about to grow much larger.

"Ah," said Droger as he looked at the crowd of, perhaps, four hundred people standing in eerie silence, the first of whom had been alerted by voices crossing the town a little earlier. He whispered to Juergen: "I think the chances of hiding you and solving our riddle in peace are fairly slim. It is time to tell the people.

****

Their stillness was unnerving; positively frightening for Juergen as he stared at a sea of faces where every wide eye seemed focussed on him; he felt almost as if he was being led out for execution. For both Droger and Karl it brought back bad memories, as large gatherings of subdued people always did in that town. The early light also reminded them of the morning of the curse, being full of hidden resonances. Perhaps deep down it was the same for the assembled townsfolk.

"Oh my," said Sternseher, "what's going on?"

Droger gestured for his companions to stop. "I think the day of reckoning is here. I don't want any more lies. This is a different town now, and we're all in this together."

Now Droger addressed the crowd: "Good people of Ilsa-stadt…"

Juergen frowned and whispered to Karl: "I thought it was called Reim…"

"Sshhh!" whispered Karl. "I'll explain later." They listened to Droger.

"Today could be a very big day in the history of our town, or rather in its future. For there arrived in our midst last night a stranger, who is yet no stranger." There

179

was a collective intake of breath, but otherwise the silence continued. "And he brought with him a piece of paper; a torn page containing part of a verse."

About three rows back in the crowd a woman fainted – the news was too much for her.

Droger continued. "A piece of paper, which was left with a foundling child sixty-five years ago. That child was the daughter of Ilsa Wlich, and the grandmother of our guest." *He hoped.*

Juergen's cheeks were growing hot. Never in his life had he been the focus of more than two pairs of eyes – human ones anyway; cows and wolves didn't count - never mind four hundred. Indeed it might have been five hundred now, for he could see at the back of the square that more people were spilling in from the surrounding lanes.

On went Droger: "The other half of that page was found hidden in a book given to Karl Baecker by Ilsa."

There were a few more gasps, but for whatever reason the crowd were maintaining a polite silence. Perhaps the reappearance of hope after so long had frightened them; or maybe it was just respect for the words of their mayor.

"The two pieces put together form a riddle. We believe we are on the way to solving this." Still silence. It was unnerving even Droger. "But I must warn you, the last step may be the most difficult. Maybe the ground will fall away from beneath our feet. May I remind you all that Ilsa said the broken verse *might* lift the curse? If we are not successful today, or tomorrow, or in a few days, or weeks, or…then that is the nature of things. But if nothing else, we have found one more friend – our only friend in the world – who has pledged to stay with us until we are free."

There was nothing more to be said, so Droger stopped. And there was a silence so intense, it might even have been possible to hear the stones of the old town warming in the sunlight.

Then a woman at the front of the crowd stepped forward. She fixed Juergen with her eyes and said: "Welcome; welcome to Ilsa-stadt."

Suddenly a huge roar went up from all the people crowded in the little square, and they cheered. Then they came forward. Juergen's hand was grasped and shaken; people pumped his arm and clapped him on the back, until finally Droger had to step in.

"Good people, we have work to do. There's a little experiment about to happen, so you must be patient with us. Good Mr Sternseher here needs help to set it up."

Immediately, several people stepped forward. "I'm sure you all know the town better than him, so please go with him and help him to find the Adlerplatz from the western-most point of the walls."

The volunteers – folk who might have ridiculed the scruffy astronomer in the past, but saw now a man of their town trying to help them – shook his hand too, then led him on his way.

Droger continued: "And for the rest of you, my thanks for welcoming Juergen Lander to our town. We will call on you when we need you. Until then, please return to your daily activities."

Droger's request was followed about as obediently as a cat being told to ignore some unattended fish on a table, and it was strange to see *die drei Raetseltraeger*, as the people called them – the Three Riddle Carriers - pacing around the Adlerplatz, while in the street that led to it the crowd remained, talking in whispers, respectful of the small party's need to concentrate.

As seven o'clock approached there was as much tension in the air as on the morning of the curse. From their position in the small square Droger and the boys waved in Sternseher's direction, and up there in the distance he returned their wave. Then he started adjusting the contraption with one hand while looking through the small telescope that he held in the other. Droger, Karl and Juergen had to look away from the astonishing brightness reflecting into the square from the mirrors. At last, with the finest of turns of a hinge, Sternseher's beam hit first the head of the eagle, and then the eye, which blazed suddenly with an almost preternatural light. Now Droger noticed, to his astonishment, that the eagle's eyes were not made of gold, but of glass, and one of them threw the beam of light out at an angle like a prism.

"Look!" shouted Karl. "Look!"

Down one of the four lanes that ran east off the Adlerplatz, the dewy, damp cobblestones were lit so that a line of them looked like blocks of gold. Droger waved his arm in triumph at Sternseher, who saluted in jubilation. Then he looked down the main street at a thousand or so open mouths. He said to the crowd:

"I know it is pointless telling you not to follow; but please keep well behind us, in case you disturb anything. We still don't know what we are supposed to find."

Now the mayor stood at the entrance to that lane, which the people had already decided, there and then, would be named *Goldstrasse* – Gold Street - whatever the outcome of this story. In he strode.

The lane became narrower still; its twists and turns soon cutting the golden stones from view. Now they walked under the eaves of houses, which overhung so far that young lovers could have kissed from opposite sides of the road without ever leaving their houses or incurring the wrath of their families.

"One hundred."

On the winding way to destiny they continued.

"Two hundred."

Droger was looking down and counting his paces with such intensity that he seemed not to notice the junction with another street on his left as he passed it by.

"Two ninety six, two ninety seven, two ninety eight, two ninety nine, THREE HUNDRED."

"Well, there's nothing here, apart from that left turn you walked past a few paces back," said Juergen. He looked around. "And it's definitely a bit creepy; it's sinister alright."

Then they both realised that Droger was saying nothing, and had retraced his steps to the left turn.

"What now, Mr Droger?" asked Karl. He got no response. "Mr Droger?"

The mayor nodded. "Very clever; our Ilsa is very clever."

"What do you mean?"

"Well, *sinister* comes from Latin meaning *left*. The left side was always associated with evil and wrong-doing in ancient times. Left-handed people were thought to be untrustworthy, and the sword was always worn under the cloak on the left-hand side. What do you see down this left turn, lads?"

They peered down a narrow, straight lane, and at the end of it, looming above the surrounding houses, was the church.

" *'Then sinister the godly path,'* " said Droger, pointing. "We go this way."

At one point Juergen looked behind him to see the part comical, part frightening sight of hundreds of people trying to squeeze down the lane.

Droger also turned to look. "Almost a symbol of Christianity;" he said, laughing, "too many people trying to pass along the same too-narrow path, with the church at the end, but no real idea what they're looking for. Even in her hour of need, I wonder if Ilsa was trying to tell us her feelings about something."

And then they broke out of the shadows and into the cool, but sunlit square in front of the church.

Karl, who was walking ahead of Droger, stopped suddenly.

"Oh no!" He'd been staring at the final line of the riddle. "I have a horrible feeling you were right, Mr Droger; the ground may just have fallen away from under our feet."

"Why now, Karl?"

"*'Beneath the point of godly wrath'.* I'm hoping I'm wrong, but the way Ilsa's mind seems to work, I wonder if that point was the spire of the church."

Droger felt his heart sink. Karl had not been wrong many times before. What else could it mean?

Juergen pointed towards the church. "You mean there was a spire on that before? Um, silly question probably, but what happened to it?"

"It was made of wood," said Droger. "When things got very bad at one time, it was torn down for firewood."

"Ah, then I think we do have a problem. But then again surely she wouldn't have hidden anything in the spire of the church."

"Why not?" said Karl. "It would have been as safe as anywhere."

"I meant how would she have got up there?" said Juergen.

"There was a ladder."

Juergen was not in the mood to be defeated. "Perhaps it wasn't hidden in the spire, but under it. It does say *beneath*. Perhaps whatever it is will be found in the church. And look; there's another part to the clue. *Godly wrath.* Are there any paintings in the church showing God as angry?"

"It's worth a try," said Droger, who for the first time felt utterly defeated, but couldn't afford to let it show.

Half an hour later they stepped outside again to find the square full of people. Droger spoke to the crowd:

"Please, good people, with so many of us here it is hard for us to think. I ask you, return to your homes."

"Then you didn't find it, whatever it was?" asked one voice.

"Not yet," said Droger, "but give us time."

"We have plenty of that," said another voice.

This was what Droger had feared – that hope would prove to be a bubble, which would disappear, once burst.

"As I say, let us think. We've come a long way in a short time."

"If sixty-five years is a short time," said someone. Heads were bowed. Murmuring like the sea, the human tide receded. Droger's heart sank as he watched them.

"Well, they certainly changed their tune," said Juergen.

"Be understanding, my young friend," said Droger. "To live permanently under a shadow for so long has been hard; both the shadow of the curse and of knowing that we offended against God's laws – *love thy neighbour*, for example."

And that was when Karl leapt up. "Under a shadow!" he shouted. Droger said nothing. He recognised that look in Karl's eye and knew it was better not to interrupt. "Yes, yes! Ilsa wouldn't have hidden anything in the church; as you said just now, she hated what religion had become – what man had done to it. She wouldn't have gone into a church."

"She might have done," said Droger. "A last insult towards Pfarrer, perhaps."

"No, look; in this riddle of hers, she's always talked of things that are likely to be around for a long time or forever; the sinking sun; the autumnal equinox; the stone eagle that is the symbol of the town and has stood for centuries; the streets in the old part of town. And yes, the church is old, but the steeple was already twisting and could have fallen or rotted if we hadn't pulled it down. She would have known that centuries might have passed before we found this riddle."

"So you don't think the *point* referred to is the steeple?"

"I do, but the clue is in the *godly wrath*. You said it yourself; we're living under a shadow of having offended God's laws. *Beneath the point of godly wrath.* Whatever we're looking for might have been buried within the shadow of the steeple." He looked around him at the cobbled square and now it felt as if that shadow had fallen across his heart. "But with the sun so low in the sky, that shadow would have been large and long. Where do we start looking?"

The others looked around at the cobbled square.

"It could be buried anywhere," said Juergen, the general dismay starting to affect even his natural optimism.

"I'll rip up the entire square if I have to," replied Karl to no-one in particular.

Droger heard the weariness in their voices. At that moment, he felt the full weight of responsibility settle on his shoulders. "Lads, lads: don't forget how far we've come already. Less than twelve hours ago, none of us would have dreamed – well, we might have dreamed, but nothing more – that we'd be standing here, having come so far." He put his hands on the boys' shoulders. "In that short time we've found the stranger who is no stranger, the broken verse and we stand but a short distance from the end of our road. Let's just think for a minute. Ilsa would want us to solve this, so she wouldn't make it even harder than it is already. As always, we need to think about what point she's making. And let's not assume, as I believe we all have, that this thing – this answer – is buried."

Fate has a way of helping those who try to help others. Suddenly, Droger slapped his forehead in exasperation. "Of course! It's not the point *she's* making, it's the other point."

"Huh?" said the two boys as they looked at each other.

"*The point of godly wrath* might be the shadow of the steeple's point. If we can find where that fell, it may mark the spot."

"Well then, you'll still need the spire. And you're never going to get that rebuilt; not in three weeks," said Juergen.

"The three weeks don't matter anymore," said Karl. "That only referred to the position of the sun on that evening and Mr Sternseher has solved that."

"We don't know that. We haven't found…" Juergen hesitated, "…whatever it was we're supposed to find. For all we know, it might be a spell, which has to be read at the equinox."

"It doesn't matter," said Droger in excitement. The boys looked at him. "All we need to know is the exact line where the shadow fell." He looked towards the lanes surrounding the church close, where the last of the stragglers were making their way, heads bowed in disappointment, towards their homes. "Call the people. Bring them back. We need them now. And wood, and ropes. Go Karl, round them up. And Juergen, run to Mr Sternseher. Tell him we are in need of his mind and his mirrors once more."

****

And so it was that, three hours later, through the combined efforts of the town carpenters, Mr Seil the rope maker and a team of the town's strongest men, a strange structure stood on top of the square tower of the church. Looking like the frame for a large tent with a long pole through the middle, it swayed slightly in the breeze. Pfarrer had protested at first about the invasion of the house of God, based, as it was, on the words of a pagan, but his was a voice lost at the very heart of a wilderness. So by ten o'clock, which Sternseher said was still a good time for reflection – a comment that drew a withering gaze from Pfarrer even though it hadn't been meant as a joke – the sun shone via a trick of mirrors past the long pole and into the square as it would have at around seven o'clock on the evening of September 20th 1695.

Droger had to shout at the gathered crowd to prevent them rushing forward. He, Karl and Juergen looked at the shadow.

"You see," said Droger, "we don't need to rebuild the whole spire. Somewhere along this line is what we seek."

"And what is that exactly?" asked Juergen

"We don't know," said Karl. "Just look."

"The sun is so low in the sky at that time of evening in September; the shadow would be fairly long," said Droger.

"Oh." Juergen stopped as if he'd just remembered something, and the other two watched while he fished in his pocket and pulled out a piece of scrappy paper. "Mr Sternseher asked me to give you this."

"And what is it?"

"Well, while the pole was being erected Mr Sternseher started looking through the church records and made these notes."

Droger took the paper from Juergen and started to smile. "What a gem we had in our midst all these years in our astronomer friend," he said. "According to this drawing, the church was thirty-five cubits high so we need to look about two hundred and eighty cubits in that direction." He pointed to the line of shadow. "Mr Sternseher apologises for the fact that he might be a cubit out." Droger started to laugh, while the boys gave puzzled smiles and the crowd just watched, their emotions too exhausted to react any more till this whole tale was done.

Droger called for one of the carpenters to fetch his measure, and then began the painstaking task of pacing out two hundred and eighty cubits – give or take one. But at last, and with the true sun shining more brightly on their endeavours in the square now, they stood where they believed the very top of the shadow of the spire might have been on a September evening sixty-five years ago.

While Droger busied himself, Juergen asked Karl a question.

"It's been vexing me since we arrived in this square; why didn't Ilsa simply give the clue about the church, rather than leading us, literally, around the houses."

"I've been thinking about that too," said Karl. "I guess we'll never know," he looked up into the distance for a moment, "unless we get the chance to see her again. The theory about being unable to give us the key might be true. It might also be that she was wandering, trying to find a suitable place to - " he paused, " – do whatever it was she did. It was a strange evening. Though I didn't know it at the time, the Elders were gathering the people together to meet in the main square. Perhaps Ilsa kept being interrupted and had to change her plans."

Droger called to them and they stood near the edge of the cobbled square.

"If we're right, and I hope we are, she might indeed have buried something," said Droger, "or left a sign."

"And if we're not right?" asked Karl.

Droger simply looked at him, then at the surrounding people, and said: "As I said; let's hope we are."

They scoured that spot with their eyes, but every stone seemed the same. They prodded with their feet, but each cobble felt firmly embedded.

"Perhaps all the people who've walked here over the years have destroyed whatever sign we seek," said Karl.

But then Droger said: "Wait a minute; we mustn't forget that the spire had twisted. That would have shortened it slightly. It was sinking. And the shadows are long at that time of day. It could make a difference of a few feet."

They moved back from the spot, looking at every inch of their way.

"Look to either side of you as well," said Droger. "A ghostly shadow of a twisted spire is no true way-marker."

Then Juergen stopped and raised his hand. "Hey! This stone – am I imagining it, or has somebody scraped some sort of symbol on it?"

They crouched down and looked.

"That's not a symbol," said Karl, "that's the letter 'I', but in the script that only you and I can read. No-one would have guessed what that meant, even if they found it."

"And am I imagining *this*," said Droger, "or is that stone loose?" He wiggled the stone and probed with his fingers, and sure enough it lifted. Before he removed it completely, Droger looked at the boys; at Karl in particular. "Do you have any idea of the strength she required to dig out this old stone; a strength borne out of desperation, I suspect? She came here even as we Elders plotted her betrayal; likely heard the raised voices in the main square, as she hid whatever we're about to find. And what a mind she must have had, to think this through so swiftly; a far sharper mind than those who worked against her." He looked with even greater intensity at Karl. "She must have loved you, even though you may not always believe it, because she tested you. Yes, she left you; made it so hard for you to find this place; but only because she knew you would prove worthy and never give up. Remember; for you, as for her, time had become a different concept. As we have said, she was bound by laws older than any living thing; she dared not break them. Still she had the intelligence to set this test, giving you, and through you the people of Reimersberg, this chance at redemption, which, unlike forgiveness, can never be given for free. Remember that love, Karl."

Now Droger removed the plug of stone, and peering into the hole found a square folded piece of oilskin. He reached in, removed it and saw the recognition in the boys' features. And as he held it up to examine it in his shaking hands, he became aware of hundreds of pairs of eyes staring at him. He lifted the oilskin square above his head and rather than rushing forward, the people almost shrank back, leaving Droger, once again, burdened by the yoke of responsibility. Failure now would probably break the townsfolk forever.

With trembling fingers he untied the strip of cloth that held the pack closed, unfolded it and found a piece of paper, likewise folded. This he opened and read in silence what was written there. It seemed no-one was breathing in the stillness of the morning. When he had finished he stood, and called out:

"Mr Bauer, Mr Metzger, please fetch Meister. The rest of you gather by the church steps."

CHAPTER 20

The years had not been kind to Meister in many ways. The town had kept him fed, watered and clothed, but that had merely fuelled the body. His hungry spirit starved and become gaunt, leaving him looking haggard. As the decades made their inexorable way, the glint in his eyes had deadened to the faded grey of the stones in an abandoned graveyard. He spoke little.

Droger pitied him to the extent that he allowed him books, but he did not trust him, even after all this time. As far as the mayor was concerned, there was something indefinable; an ember that never quite went out. There were toads, which sat motionless, waiting with infinite patience for their prey to pass within range. This was what he still saw in Meister. Despite the evident diminution in the life-force of the creature – he found it easier to think of him in this way – on the occasions he exchanged a few words with his captive he felt monstrous powers at work and always gave thanks for the wooden bars of the Friedrich Tree that stood between them.

As the door to the prison was usually left open, with the keys to the cells kept safely by the Elders, Metzger and Bauer found the toad had a visitor. Arzt was standing by the outer bars, talking softly, doubtless filling in the former mayor with what had been happening outside. The doctor stepped back. Though he appeared to be giving a servile bow to the Elders, it was the natural crook of his back, which had become misshapen over the years. Bowed by guilt said some; loneliness said others after a few brandies.

"Arzt, what are you doing here?" said Metzger. They didn't address him as 'Doctor' – hardly anyone did these days, and most people went straight to Droger if they felt unwell.

"Just checking on the welfare of a prisoner," said Arzt, backing away and giving his best ingratiating grin. The others were surprised by how pale and shaky he had become.

"Yes, well we all know what would be the best cure for him," said Bauer.

"Have you no respect for the man who once held the highest office in this town?" wheezed Meister, the sound of any conversation from him surprising them as much as the asthmatic reediness of his voice.

"The man who abused it, you mean," said Metzger. "Anyway, you're wanted in the main square. Hopefully, by the time we get back they'll have put up a gallows."

Meister's gaze darted from Azrt to the Elders and on to the window beyond them, but Arzt shook his head. "Ignore them."

Droger stood with his arms folded at the top of the church steps with Karl and Juergen behind him. Before him, yet again, was a field of expectant citizens; possibly every man, woman and child left in Ilsa-stadt. They parted in absolute silence as the former mayor was led through; in many ways it would have been preferable if they had jeered. As he watched Meister, whose legs seemed to shake, either through inactivity or fear, despite everything he couldn't help feeling some pity for this wretch once again.

Droger had another concern. What was he going to do if and when the curse lifted? He might have developed many skills in his long life, but slaying vampires was not one of them. It looked like he might have no option, but to set Meister free; banish him from the town and hope that they could guard against him ever returning. It was a prospect that filled him with equal measures of dread and guilt. But he was the mayor of Ilsa-stadt and had to think of his people. Had they not paid dearly enough for their crimes? They deserved to be free now.

Meister was hated and still feared in equal measure by everyone and, though he didn't know the vampire's history, Droger guessed this had been his lot for millennia. Even Ilsa, in her darkest hour, had been loved by someone and respected by others, though at the end they hadn't stood by her. Droger hated feeling pity; it was a treacherous emotion, often wreathed in the deceptive mist of guilt.

Now his keen eyes noticed Arzt sneaking into the square at the back of the crowd; probably hoping nobody would see him; He was Meister's only friend and bore the marks of that friendship in his crooked back and pale features, which looked even more drawn than usual now. Perhaps *friend* was putting it strongly - ally; lackey; partner-in-crime. Slave. The only other person who had never expressed remorse for what happened to Ilsa.

Ilsa; the thought of the fate that Meister had planned for her hardened Droger's resolve again.

When at last the cadaverous figure of the former mayor had wheezed its way up the steps and made a mocking bow to him, Droger unfolded the piece of paper in his hand and said to Meister in a voice loud enough to carry to the furthest corners of the square:

"You need to be here, for many reasons; amongst them, to hear this and to help lift the curse from the town. Or at least that is everyone's dearest hope."

Meister said nothing, so Droger started to read:

"People of Reimersberg, if you are hearing these words then you have done great wrong, but also lived to regret it and done penance. And one of my bloodline probably stands before you. I am sure you will treat that person better than you treated me; because by now you will have learnt two things; not only that it is wrong to close the door in the face of a stranger, but also that there is joy to be had in throwing that door wide open. And that acceptance, that tolerance, will help to set you free; as will the willingness of my family to forgive you. Tolerance and forgiveness will help to lift the curse. This is no magic spell; just the rebirth of certain qualities that make us decent as humans.

Another of which is humility. You were too proud; a town wrapped in the cosy blanket of your traditions, while the true majesty of life in the world around you - the mountains, the rivers, the forests, the sky – passed you by. They are older, more beautiful and lasting than anything you could ever build, for they were created by the forces of eternity, one of which is time itself. And if things have gone as I foresee, you will know now that no gleaming turret could ever match the magnificence of a tree bearing fruit. All the money in Bavaria cannot buy such majesty. You may still take pride in the rebirth of your town, but this time you will be looking to the future, not the past.

People of Reimersberg, I write all of this without knowing the exact nature of the fate you have planned for me, though I can guess at it. You may wonder that I can write of a curse before the deed. Yet I know, if you are hearing these words, you have refused the chance to show mercy or compassion. And as I am but a creature of passion, at one with the sun, the rain, the wind, the frost and the snow, I will have been just as unforgiving in my anger as those elemental forces can be. But I know also that, with time, my anger will have cooled. Sadly, what I do in cursing you will not be in my power to undo, but that is why I have planned, as best a person can, that someone of my bloodline will be with you today. For only by their presence, and through the purity of their blood, untainted by my anger, can the curse be lifted."

Here Karl and Juergen exchanged a knowing nod. That the riddle was written in a language, which only someone of Ilsa's blood could understand, had ensured that one of her line would be here on this day. And the torn pages of the riddle would never have been brought together without the presence of someone from the line of the foundling.

Droger read on, his voice growing stronger:

"There is only one more thing needed to lift the curse from your backs; one man must speak. He must confess his sin and clear my name. Then, and only then, will you be free again."

Droger folded the paper, put it in his pocket and turned to Meister: "Mr Meister, I think we all know who that man is. If you ever loved and respected the people of this town, speak now and let it all be done."

At first Meister's face was like a statue's – expressionless – but then the slightest of smiles formed on his lips. It was mirthless, and sent a shudder through those close enough to see it. He turned to the crowd and, making no attempt to hide the sarcasm and contempt in his voice, said:

"Good people of Reimersberg, whom I so loved and respected; once upon a time you thought highly enough of me to choose me as your mayor. Then you saw fit to throw me into jail, requiring my services and leadership no longer. You stood there, all of you, while a witch – and yes, we all agreed she was a witch – cursed this town. You cowered, snivelling, safe behind the town walls – behind me – while I stood on the battlements and faced her wrath. And then, when you ignoramuses were all in despair, I gave you leadership; showed you how to graze your cattle; a first step to survival. Finally, when I sought to keep the town clean, free from diseased, dead bodies, you ripped my chain of office from me and threw me away to rot. Know now, I have preferred to stay in my cell than be among you mindless peasants."

At the front of the crowd, three or four men, who had been growing angrier by the word, came forward. "You filthy pig!" shouted one of them.

Meister didn't move. To Droger, it seemed this was the only time in his life the former mayor showed some courage. "That's right; kill me. And then your curse will never end."

The men stopped in their tracks. There was murmuring in the crowd. Droger could see that their opinion was swaying like a reed in a river; such was their desperation to be free.

Meister continued: "But, I was always a fair man, and so here are my terms; restore me to mayor; be good obedient townsfolk for a period of time that I have yet to decide; and then I will lift the curse."

There were cries of outrage. This was dangerous. Karl and Juergen started to shrink back. The crowd had advanced, though they hadn't yet moved onto the steps of the church, and Droger wasn't sure who they would attack if they did. Desperation combined with hope was a dangerous mixture.

But Meister wasn't finished: "And whether you agree to my terms or not, you'd better all pray that I don't grow tired of living and decide to end it all with this." He reached under his jacket and, to a communal gasp, pulled from the back of his trouser-belt a wicked-looking knife.

Metzger and Bauer, who stood at the top of the steps behind Meister, exchanged a shocked, knowing look. Bauer shouted across the throng: "Arzt! You traitor!" But the doctor was nowhere to be seen now.

To emphasise his point, Meister held the knife against his wrist. "One stroke of this blade and you'll all be faced with a stark choice: whether to live like this forever or follow my example."

Now there was silence, but different from any that had fallen over the town since the curse. Indeed, in later years a saying developed in that region: *to be caught between the madman and eternity.*

But the silence was broken by a lone voice:

"Wait! Wait!"

People looked around and saw a figure pushing its way through the crowd: another man with gaunt features, tired eyes and an exhausted stoop; someone who seemed to have the cares of the world on his shoulders.

"Father!" said Karl wide-eyed.

Juergen heard him. "That's your father...my...?"

All eyes – Droger's, the boys', and the crowd's – were on Hans Baecker as he made his painful progress; all eyes except one pair.

This was Meister's chance. This was the moment for which he had waited so patiently. These fools did not know that the spirit of a vampire was like those seeds in a desert, which waited years for the rains before flowering. How many times had Arzt come with some of his blood, or the blood of rats, to keep him going? Perhaps that simpleton had hoped to be made a vampire himself, but he was worthy only to be a slave. Eternal life was not a gift vampires gave willingly, for they gave a little of their strength with it. They were not gods, for they were not killers, leaving victims short of the point of death.

It had taken all of the consummate acting skills a vampire acquires as it hides in plain view, plus a great deal of swallowed pride, to look scared at the jail, and pretend to be terrified and weak as he was led through the stinking mob. How could these imbeciles have let him out of his prison? He could not believe his luck.

And now here was Droger, distracted like everyone else, with his back to him. One stab and he would enter Droger's weakened body. Of course the apothecary was not the ideal vessel - not intrinsically evil – which was why Meister needed him weak; unable to resist the invasive spirit. Droger was loved; revered. That would do for a start. With the vampire spirit inside him, he would make a full recovery from the attack. The people would see that the cowardly Meister was dead. No-one would know, or suspect. Long live Droger the Burgermeister.

Long live the Vampire.

As for the curse – well, the vampire knew that all he had to do now was say *I confess* and it would all go away. Fight sophistry with sophistry; words with words.

He took the blade gently from his wrist, turned it towards Droger's back and prepared to stab.

The glint of steel caught Karl's eye. *Watch out!* he wanted to cry, knowing it was too late, but the words caught in his throat.

But other words reached them from the crowd just as Meister stabbed; those of Hans Baecker: "I confess." He stumbled forward, pointing at Meister. "It's not that poison toad; it's me that must speak."

Now everyone turned towards Meister, and screamed at what they saw.

Except his blade had not found its target.

As Hans Baecker had shouted *'I confess'*, a cloud had blotted out the sun. At that very moment Meister had frozen as if paralysed, his hateful stab stopping inches from Droger's back. He looked now in disbelief at his arm; tried to force it forward the last little bit - but it wouldn't move. And worse – it was changing. On the skin of his hand, wrinkles and liver spots were appearing. He stood, stuck in that final posture while everyone watched, in horrified fascination, the scene unfolding before them. Meister's flesh appeared to be boiling as sores erupted on his face, and it was sagging from his cheeks. His hair turned the colour of steel and then white, growing longer, but thinner. His eyes sunk deeper into his head, and his face creased as if it was melting.

"He's ageing," said Droger in awe. "Not just ageing; dying."

A horrible choking, gargling sound came from the throat of this mockery of a man, until at last, to everyone's relief, the figure could stand no longer and crumpled to the floor, where the clothes appeared to be lying over nothing more than a bag of bones. It seemed fate had decreed that Meister would not just die of old age, but that all his corruption would show itself.

Now Droger looked at Hans Baecker, who was standing clear of the crowd. People had shrunk away from him, though not fully understanding why.

"What did you do, Hans?" asked Droger, already guessing the answer. "What did you confess to?"

The wind had started to pick up, and as it tugged at Hans' clothing, his son could see what sixty-five years of guilt had done to his father's frame. Why hadn't he noticed it before? Now he, too, felt shame, and his heart went out to his father.

"Ilsa Wlich was carrying my child." There was a gasp from the people who could hear, though Hans' voice was being carried away now by the increasing strength of the wind. "And I have carried the burden of my cowardice ever since, like a child that cannot be born."

The wind could be heard howling through the battlements of the town, causing the makeshift steeple on the church to wail like a banshee and shake. The sky had grown darker. Suddenly a gust tore at the fragments of Meister and blew them down the steps. And that was when it struck people.

"Oh God, we're going to die – like that!" shouted one woman, pointing at the desiccated figure that had once been their mayor. There was screaming; some people ran heedless of direction, but many sank to their knees in front of the church and prayed.

And then the real wind came.

It had roamed the earth for sixty-five years, howling and angry, unable to release its burden and blow itself out. Down in that part of the world later known as the Roaring Forties, where all the storm winds of the earth gather, it had raged, venting its fury on ships and rocks. But now the call had come at last, and the force that had contained Ilsa's curse blasted across the skies, pushing clouds and strengthening storm-winds before it in its determination to answer the call and restore nature's balance.

The wind screeched through the forest and hit Ilsa-stadt, knocking people to the ground; stronger than the storm that had greeted the arrival of the curse, with all the momentum and anger it had built over sixty-five years. The townsfolk screamed, holding onto each other, or pressing their hands to their ears in desperation. Many wondered whether they were being carried off to their judgement, but no-one could open their eyes to see if they were heading up through the clouds or down into the pit. Or worse; perhaps this was how it felt to age sixty-five years in just a few seconds. Was this how it felt to die?

The tempest knew it had a final task to perform.

Unnoticed in all the commotion of Meister's destruction, the air had shimmered for a moment at the top of the church steps. The elemental energy that was the vampire's spirit moved away. Now, as the people knelt or lay in terror, it sought a new home. But the citizens of Ilsa-stadt were not the citizens of Reimersberg. No-one carried in their heart the cruelty or rottenness of spirit to be a suitable vessel. Now the wind saw this disease hesitating, hovering in its frantic search, and swooped.

Many thought the scream they heard was the wind, and perhaps it was better they did.

And then it stopped. There was a whisper, and the wind had gone, even more suddenly than it had arrived.

For a moment no-one dared to open their eyes. When they plucked up the courage at last, it was to see the odd leaf fluttering to earth, but otherwise nothing; no damaged buildings or shattered roof tiles; no smashed windows; no doors hanging on one hinge. Even the makeshift spire of the church still stood. No-one noticed that Meister's remains were no longer there, nor that those of Arzt had gone too – not that anyone had seen him die in the dark corner to which he'd fled.

Slowly, looking around them in utter bewilderment, the people got to their feet in the sunlight of a September morning. Many doubted what they had just experienced, but then there was just the memory of doubting. All was strangely quiet.

There was one sound now - so soft that no-one who heard it would even know they had - as all the people of the town blinked as one.

It was as if they had woken from a sleep.

There was one person for whom the whole episode was different. Juergen had picked himself up along with everyone else. He might have noticed the slight shimmer that passed through the air for part of a second, though he wouldn't have known it happened at the moment the townsfolk blinked. But straight afterwards he saw Karl looking at him and frowning.

"I'm sorry, what were you saying?" asked Karl.

"Nothing," said Juergen puzzled. "Are you alright, Karl?"

The use of the name evidently threw the boy. "Yes. Sorry, do I know you?"

"Yes, it's me, Juergen."

Karl frowned again, and then shook his head.

And now a deep sadness filled Juergen, yet at the same time such happiness for the people, as he saw that it might be over. Unfortunately some good things would end too, such as this new friendship. And he guessed his adventure was over, too. Now they, the townsfolk, would all have each other again, and he would once more be alone. He wondered, with a hint of youthful self-pity, whether they would even remember that he had been 'the stranger'.

Karl was saying something to him. "You'll have to forgive me, but my father's calling me." Juergen looked over to see a dark-haired, well-built man beckoning to Karl from the middle of the square.

"Come on, young man, we've got a lot of baking to do before the Autumn Festival tomorrow. You can talk to your cousin later."

That threw Juergen. Karl's lack of recognition must have been a momentary thing.

"Okay, coming, father."

There was something very youthful in the way Karl skipped down the steps and ran towards Hans Baecker, who put an arm around his shoulder. It made Juergen smile, despite his sadness. Then Karl turned and waved, as did Hans, and Juergen knew he had a family here after all.

"Good morning," said the voice from behind him. He turned to see Droger standing there. "It's always nice to see a new face in Ilsa-stadt. Have you come far?"

Ilsa-stadt. So there was a new beginning for these people, not a return to the time before the curse.

As much as the unfamiliarity in Droger's eyes caused a pain in his heart, Juergen felt warmth spread through him. He answered: "I've travelled about five days. I have family here."

"Five days, eh? You must be built of strong stuff to have made it to the end of the Adventurer's Road. And if you have family here, I'm guessing you're Juergen, Hans Baecker's great-nephew. Well, you're welcome in Ilsa-stadt. I hope we'll see you around in the coming days – or are you just passing through?"

Juergen smiled. "Oh, I'll be here for a few days. Then I'm heading back home to prepare for a long trip. I don't know if you've heard of Marco Polo."

"As a matter of fact I have. Young Karl was telling me all about him. A fine boy, that. Well, I have to go, but I hope to see you tomorrow at the Autumn Festival. We have a special event planned tomorrow. The town astronomer, Mr Sternseher, is going to give a talk introducing us all to the wonders of the night sky."

Juergen wandered through Ilsa-stadt, trying to absorb all that had happened. It seemed the town had been given back its lost years, but lost them nonetheless. He assumed the clock of history had not been turned back, otherwise that would mean he hadn't yet been born! The thought almost gave him a headache. What this meant for the town, he couldn't begin to understand, but he was just happy that no-one else seemed to have suffered the fate of Meister.

He'd been worried that the lifting of the curse might see people returning to the ways, which had led to all their problems, but from the snippets of conversation he overheard as he went, it seemed he needn't worry:

A woman talking to her weary-looking husband: "No, we've got to get this painted. How are we ever going to attract visitors if we offer this sort of accommodation?"

Two women in a street: "I do hope the tinkers come back. I don't know why they've given up calling. I blame the wolves. We need to do something about keeping an armed escort ready to make it safer for travellers. Perhaps Mayor Droger could raise that at the next town hall meeting."

A tall, imposing- looking priest; stern, but with a zealous smile: "Hello, young man, beautiful day to admire God's works, isn't it? You're not from here are you? Hope you enjoy your stay with us and thank you for coming. I'll see you at the harvest thanksgiving service later?" He goes without waiting for a response.

Juergen wanted to check one last thing. He made his way towards the town gates. As he approached, he saw Michael Bauer herding his cows towards the pasture beyond them. Juergen watched as the farmer stepped beyond the walls and then turned left towards the richer grass.

With a smile, the stranger who was no stranger moved to the gates and stood surveying the sunlit scene.

And then froze.

The figure was standing just inside the edge of the trees; the same one he'd seen flitting across the forest floor as he'd hidden terrified, three nights before. The interplay of light and shade made its cloak shimmer – except he could see now that it wasn't a cloak, but a coat. And what he'd taken to be a red hat was, in fact, hair.

The figure waved to him, beckoning.

For a moment, that gesture filled him with an overwhelming melancholy. How brave she had been, knowing that the lifting of the curse would erase all memory of her. Now Karl, who clearly she had loved dearly, might never know of her existence or that she had saved his life. But then he smiled. In him, Juergen Lander, with his thirst for adventure and knowledge, the circle could be completed. The torn page could be made whole again.

There was no fear in the thought of following the figure; following her. Because it had to be her. Anyone capable of imposing themselves on history in this way would live on. He could feel her strength from here; powerful enough to send wolves to guard and guide him in the night. Juergen recognised now that his travels would never have ended till he'd found her; indeed they would not have begun. He sensed her restlessness, even at this distance and thought he understood why she needed to be away. Would she return here one day, to the town named after her, and would a man and a boy who once loved her be still be alive and learn to love her again?

There was time for one last surprise. In one of those tricks of memory, an image came to him, revealed from beneath the dust of forgetfulness by a sudden gust. It was of a traveller who had come to the farm from time to time selling an assortment of dried flowers and spices from a basket. Sometimes years would pass between visits. His father had viewed her with suspicion - *"Damned gypsy,"* he would mutter, - but his mother had always taken care to buy a little something. And was Juergen imagining it now, or had he, as a little boy, once spied a strand of red hair that slipped from beneath that traveller's hood? He shook his head; that was really pushing things too far.

Wasn't it?

He turned, took a last look at the town, and stepped forward to meet her.